Broken Kings

SAN DIEGO MAFIA KINGS BOOK 3

SABLE PHILLIPS

© Sable Syndicate Pty. Ltd. Copyright 2020 - All rights reserved.

It is not legal to reproduce, duplicate, or transmit any part of this document in either electronic means or in printed format. Recording of this publication is strictly prohibited and any storage of this document is not allowed unless with written permission from the publisher except for the use of brief quotations in a book review.

This book is a work of fiction. Any resemblance to persons, living or dead, or places, events or locations is purely coincidental.

1

MYLES

My dad used to say the best mob bosses are the ones most people don't know. Their names are powerful when used the right way, but the average person has never heard them before. They're the kind of men who pull strings so skillfully no one even notices the shift, the kind who can change your mind and make you think it was your idea. Even the people closest to them don't understand exactly how much influence they have on their surroundings, not really. But there's one thing so unpredictable even the best boss can't control it.

And it's fucking airline schedules.

With another frustrated groan, I glanced under the edge of my sunglasses to check my watch. 4:30. Whitney's plane was now two and a half hours late. Nobody notified me of any delay on them taking off, so what the hell was holding them up? My step-mom watched sympathetically while I paced around baggage claim. "Are you nervous?"

"What? No. I'm just irritated." Why would I be nervous about seeing my own thirteen-year-old niece? Just because it had been over two years since I'd last seen her? Because her dad, my oldest brother, was so incredibly hesitant to send her over? No, I didn't care about any of that. "Royce is gonna get pissed off and think I lost her already or something."

"I don't know why you always assume he thinks the absolute worst of you," Rena said, frowning.

"I don't have to assume. He's made it pretty clear." I'd be lying if I said this visit with Whitney wasn't intended to spite him just a little. She was going through a rebellious phase, and even though we all knew he was against it, she'd still convinced her dad to let her come back to San Diego for the summer. In UK school terms, that was barely a month and a half, but it was something.

"You two might have had your differences, but he's still your brother. He doesn't hate you." Even though I knew she was just trying to help, I wasn't really in the mood for another "family is family" lecture. If anything, Royce was the one who needed to hear it.

Luckily, before she could really get going, she was interrupted by a PA announcement that informed us Whitney's flight had finally arrived and would be disembarking soon. "Finally," I muttered, keeping up my pacing. While we waited another half hour and people finally started coming down the escalator, I realized that maybe I was a little nervous after all. I would say I hardly recognized Whits when I saw her, but she was kind of hard to miss.

For one, she seemed to be the only thirteen-year-old traveling unsupervised. Her head was covered with little braids, black interspersed with purple and gray. Most of the pink in her wardrobe had been replaced with black, but there was still a splash of it on her t-shirt and shoes. The backpack slung over her shoulder was plastered with the Michael Kors logo, and even though she'd adopted this new punky aesthetic, I was still willing to bet a couple hundred bucks had gone into that outfit. Was her dad's *financial* work paying him that well? Or was he still using our family's dirty money?

"Whitney!" Rena hopped up from her seat and held her arms out for a hug. With a tight smile, Whitney accepted the gesture, but she was obviously less than enthused.

"Hi, Nana," she said, tossing her head to flip her braids over her shoulder. "Hi, Uncle Myles."

"Hey, Whits. You look like shit," I said with a grin. Rena hissed my name, shocked and horrified, but Whitney was fighting a smile.

"You would too if you were on a plane for eleven hours, you pillock." She tried to kick my shins, but I stepped out of her short-legged reach. "It's after midnight in London right now. I've been up all day!"

"Oh my God, you sound so old right now," I told her plainly, and she stuck her tongue out at me. "Come on, grandma, let's go get your bags. You can have a nap when we get back to the house."

"Tosser," she muttered under her breath as she walked past me toward the baggage carousels. It had been a few years since she'd done this, but it seemed like she remembered the place pretty well.

"You shouldn't say things like that to her," Rena said, following along at my side. "She's barely even a teenager."

"Did she seem like she was upset? You know she doesn't like being babied."

"It's not appropriate! And even if she thinks it's funny, you could be hurting her self-esteem."

I had to physically force myself not to roll my eyes. As if Whitney had ever had a problem with her self-esteem. She was the most confident kid I'd ever met, even more than I was at her age. And she could handle a *bad word* here and there. Still, I didn't feel like arguing with Rena about it.

"All right, all right," I said, despite knowing I would do the same thing again later. "I'll try to watch what I say."

I won't.

After we'd picked up Whitney's luggage, we headed back to the garage where my adviser, Nathan, was waiting with the limo. "Whits, did you ever meet Nate?" I asked, nudging her shoulder as we came to meet him.

"No. I've been gone for forever, remember?"

"Well, he's my right-hand guy; if you can't find me, bother him." Pushing my shades back to rest on top of my head, I added to Nathan, "This is my precious niece, Whitney, and she's very fragile, so we're not going to let anything happen to her." Whitney made a gagging noise and shoved my arm, but the look I gave Nathan said this wasn't actually a joke. I was *not* going to allow anything to happen to her while she was staying with me, partly because I didn't want to prove Royce right, but mostly because she was pretty much the only good thing about our family. Other than me.

Nate gave me a curt nod of understanding. "Right. It's nice to meet you, miss."

"Yup," she muttered, not looking at him. Disregarding the snub, he handed me a set of car keys.

"The Aventador's on the next level up," he explained.

"What?" Rena looked to me with yet another frown. "You're not riding with us?"

"Whits has been in a limo before," I said, spinning the keys around my finger. "But the Aventador's *new*, which makes it more fun. Right?" I glanced down at Whitney, who looked at Rena briefly before answering.

"I can ride with Uncle Myles. We'll still meet you at the house."

"Exactly." Already pushing her in the direction of the elevator, I tossed the bag I'd been holding over to Nate. His eyes narrowed behind his glasses as he caught it. "Take care of that, would you?" Lamborghinis aren't known for their trunk space.

"Not really my job, but okay."

"Your job's whatever the hell I tell you to do," I reminded him without looking back. Once we got into the elevator, Whits looked up at me.

"What happened to the Huracán?"

"Eh, it was getting old. Besides, this one's red." My brothers had criticized me plenty of times for being too "flashy," but what could I say? I wasn't one of those bosses who wanted to go unnoticed, and I made sure it showed however I could. When Whitney saw the car—the only one on this level, somehow—she let out an appreciative "ooh!" She got in, and the bucket seat practically swallowed her, leaving her plenty of room to stretch out. At this rate, she wouldn't end up any taller than her mom.

"Is this one faster than the Huracán too?" she asked with a mischievous smirk, and one I returned conspiratorially.

"Y'know, I'm not really sure. Maybe we should find out." But there were better places to do that than in the middle of town. When we got away from the airport, instead of turning toward the house, I headed north looking for a stretch of road where I could really open up the engine. In the meantime, I asked Whitney, "So, what's up? Any particular reason you wanted to get away from home?"

Her smile faded, and she sat back in her seat, crossing her arms. "How do you know I didn't just come to visit?"

"Well, you're here by yourself. If you'd wanted to, you could've convinced your parents to come," I reasoned. "Hell, you probably could've convinced Roger and Jill to come too.

But you didn't. So that tells me you wanted to be away from them." She let out this big dramatic sigh and stared out the window for a few seconds.

"My parents want me to be a baby forever," she said finally. "Deanna teaches Year Five and she still treats me like I'm ten years old. Mum's not any better; she never gets mad at me. Like I can't do anything wrong, no matter how hard I try." Silence for a second.

"And what about your dad?" I prompted. Knowing Royce, he was probably a category of his own.

"I don't know. I don't know what he's thinking. It's like he forgot who I am or he's not okay with it all of a sudden," she muttered, sounding more lost than angry. "I got one little nick"—she held out her hand to show me a pretty noticeable scar on her palm—"and he took away my new balisong, the one you sent for my birthday. Even my practice one! And he knows I'm good enough to be in higher level judo classes, my senseis say so all the time, but he still won't let me move up!"

"I mean...that sounds like he doesn't want you to get hurt," I pointed out. Far be it from me to defend my brother's overprotective parenting, but it didn't sound like he was being crazy about it.

"No, it's like he thinks I'll *die* if I get hurt," Whitney insisted. "Like what you said earlier. I'm 'fragile.'"

"Come on, Whits, I was joking—"

"But he means it! He thinks I'm weak. I hate that."

I could definitely relate to that sentiment. And how was she supposed to learn how to do anything if she wasn't allowed to try it out. "Hey," I said as I shifted into fifth gear and stepped on the gas. "You've got, what, six weeks here?"

"Yeah."

"Okay. So for that time...fuck your dad's rules." I couldn't help smirking as I said it, watching the needle on my speedometer pass the 90 mph mark. "I've got a whole collection of knives you can practice with. I'll teach you some new tricks. I bet we could even get you back in your old dojo here for a month or so. Your dad's, like, five thousand miles away. What's he gonna do about it?"

When I stole a look at her, she was looking between me, the speedometer, and the road, eyes wide, a smile spreading across her face. Wasn't that a better way for her to be? Not pissed off and sulking and thinking about her dad telling her she couldn't do shit? I still planned to keep her safe, don't get me wrong, but if Royce thought there was *anything* she couldn't do, she needed the opportunity to prove that that was bullshit.

After we got bored of doubling the speed limit—where was the challenge if no one was racing you?—we headed back to the house. Whitney's bags were still sitting by the door, and Gregorio was on the couch focused on his tablet. When we got in, he looked up for a second and asked, "You two get lost?"

"Nah. Just took a detour."

"Mom was waiting for a while," he informed me, and I tried to brush off the little pang of guilt from that thought. We did say we were going to meet her there.

"I mean, Whits is gonna be here a few weeks," I said as she was gathering up her stuff and heading off to her usual room upstairs. "I'm sure they'll get to spend some time together."

"It's not a big deal. I think she's just been looking forward to having another girl in the house," Gregorio laughed without smiling, eyes back on his tablet. I wanted to believe that, but I couldn't help feeling like things had sort of changed between me and Rena since Dad's death.

More specifically, since I killed him. It wasn't like he didn't deserve it. We all knew what a piece of shit he was, constantly putting everyone down, killing and threatening his own family members when they defied him—I couldn't believe anyone really missed him. But the fact that I had been the one to do it was apparently a problem for some people, and not just my step-mom.

"Myles." Nathan came into the living room from the hall that led to my office, all business as usual, hands folded behind his back. "We should talk."

"Yeah." I crossed the living room, headed to my office, and Gregorio got up to follow me. I didn't miss the "no one invited you" look Nathan shot him, but he didn't argue out loud. Things between me and Gregorio had always been a little weird, maybe because we were a lot alike. After Dad's death, there were a good three months where he just wouldn't talk to me. He was still in the phase of idolizing our dad, thinking that whatever he did, there must've been a good reason. But since I'd started involving him more in the business and spent more time working with him, it seemed like he was coming around.

"So?" I said as I sat down behind my desk, finally able to resume my favorite fidget of flipping a butterfly knife in one hand. Keeping my hands occupied made it easier to focus, somehow. Gregorio took one of the chairs across from my desk, and we both looked to Nate. "Talk to me."

"We finally got a response from Don Capelli today. He's agreed to meet with us to discuss the Moretti family's future with the Council."

"That makes all four family heads, right? About damn time," I muttered. We had been trying to call a meeting with the rest of the West US Council, the most influential families from California to Texas, for months. Not long after

Dad's death, they had started slowly but surely drawing away from us, and I didn't have to guess why.

They didn't care what our dad had done to us. They didn't care that he forced my hand or that letting him live would've, *without a doubt,* meant he would just take advantage of us again later. All they saw was a son who had killed his father, and in a business that values family above literally all else, that was unforgivable. For the past three years, I'd repeated over and over that I would never betray my own and that Dad turned on us first, but it didn't change anything. A lot of the other families—even small fry who had no right to make the call—had decided I was untrustworthy, not fit to lead. And maybe I had trouble listening to shit like that without retaliating.

It was only last year that the Council stopped working with us altogether. I was trying to take my dad's place, and we were only just making any progress. It wouldn't have surprised me if they were discussing it amongst themselves before the official meeting ever happened. But being part of the Council was a huge part of our family's business, and losing that would mean bad news on every front. So I had to play their game for now.

"I figure you've already set everything up?" I asked Nate, knowing how much better he was at diplomacy than me. He nodded.

"They want to meet at the Lucianos' villa this weekend."

"Well then." I flipped my knife closed again. "Looks like we're heading to L.A."

2

SOFIA

While I was very patiently waiting to get off the plane, courteously trying to make life easier for the flight attendants, I was nearly knocked to the ground by a little girl shoving her way through the aisles, even climbing over the seats to get out ahead of everyone else. She looked every bit like the hellion her actions suggested—her hair a mess of colorful braids, her clothes dark and artfully ripped here and there. She threw me a sideways glance and a brief "sorry" as she pushed past, but she didn't seem otherwise concerned with her own rudeness.

What a brat. And no one even tried to stop her or tell her off! That was a definite disadvantage of traveling outside California; no one knew who I was well enough to give me the respect I deserved. The man from across the aisle checked on me, the same way he'd been checking on me throughout the entire flight, offering his hand to help me right myself. But I ignored him and straightened up on my own, tossing my hair back over my shoulder to reclaim my dignity. I was so beyond ready to be back at home, away from creepy men and impetuous teenagers.

I didn't know the San Diego airport as well as I knew LAX, but there were no available flights from London to L.A. with first class seats left, so my brother had agreed to pick me up in San Diego instead. Once I managed to get out of the crowd, I found him waiting around baggage claim like he'd said he would be. Flanked with a couple of bodyguards, black hair perfectly arranged, he looked exactly the same as when he'd seen me off for work a year ago—and *so* much like our dad.

"Danny!" I squealed, hurrying down the escalator as fast as my heels would allow and rushing over to hug him. "I missed you so much!"

"I told you not to call me Danny in public." He mussed my hair a little, but there was no genuine irritation in his voice. "How was the flight? Weird just being a passenger for once?"

"You have no idea." Over the past few years of working as a flight attendant, I'd more or less gotten used to the role. But on this flight home for some much-needed time off, I had been with a different airline. I had to stop myself more than once from helping people store their luggage in the overhead bins when they were slowing down boarding. But then, I got used to being waited on again fairly quickly and reminded myself that as Marcell Luciano's daughter, I deserved to be pampered.

When the concept of work had first been proposed to me, I was totally against it. My father worked very hard to ensure that I didn't have to. I didn't want to waste all his efforts. But my dear sister, Gemma, had insisted that it was about time I started "making myself useful" to the family. The flight attendant job was her idea; she wanted me to play the part of a pretty but harmless *servant* while gathering information that would help the business. During the moments I wasn't pouring tiny cups of soda or giving safety demonstrations, I was listening closely to the conversations our first class and business class passengers would have after a few shots of whiskey. I would remember anything important, then write it down and send it home, hoping it was useful somehow, that there was a point to me debasing myself like this.

My sister, by the way, never had this sort of job. She was too busy chasing and drooling over Royce Moretti despite his obvious disinterest in her. But thinking about Royce was a mistake, I quickly realized, because it forced me to think about his brothers too. One of them in particular. I didn't have the patience to address that subject just yet.

"Ugh, I have jet lag from Hell," I whined, tilting my head back dramatically to push my hair out of my eyes. "Can we go?" Danny sent one of his guys to pick up my bags—which I sweetly thanked him for—then led me outside to the waiting limo.

"Welcome home, Miss Sofia." Papà's driver, Marlon, was pleased to see me as always, and I waved back at him with a smile.

"It's so nice to be back," I answered honestly. Although I usually got a few days off between trips, it still felt like I'd been working nonstop ever since I'd left. When I couldn't come home to see my family or relax in my own bed, it was hard to really get comfortable. Even though Gemma wanted me to keep working a while longer, Papà and Danny had overruled her and arranged for me to come home. I would have a *lot* of work waiting for me once the holidays rolled around, so Danny thought it was best for me to have a few months at home before then.

"Still no news about the Morettis, huh?" my brother

asked, and I blinked at him in confusion. "You were just in London, right? You would've seen if they were making some kind of move out there."

"For the last time, Royce and Roger aren't involved in *cosa nostra*"—the mafia—"anymore." After the two oldest Moretti boys had moved off to the UK, there had been all sorts of rumors about their motives. Some people even thought they were trying to spread the Morettis' influence over to England. But I had passed through London plenty of time since their move, and every aspect of their lives still seemed totally mundane. Our dad had been good friends with their father, Deron, so it almost seemed like he was *hoping* for some news about Royce and Roger carrying on his legacy away from home. No such luck. "How is Gemma dealing with Royce's new marriage, by the way?"

"That almost sounded spiteful, *sorellina*," Danny said, watching me with a knowing smirk.

"Oh, no, I'm just curious," I argued, doing my best to seem innocent and sincere. "I know how much she cares about him, after all." As if. Gemma had only ever seen Royce as a target, a goal, her means of elevating the Luciano family by marriage to the Morettis. She didn't actually have any feelings for him.

"You know her. She refuses to believe she's lost, even when the evidence is staring her in the face. Technically, there are still a few loyal Morettis left...but the way things are going for them, I'm not so sure Dad wants that partnership anymore."

I managed to hide my frown and forced myself not to ask what he meant. It didn't matter. The Morettis could choke for all I cared. Every last one of them, their current excuse for a boss included. This wasn't the first I'd heard of their business declining, considering the kind of passengers I usually spied on. Maybe if Myles weren't so stubborn and selfish, they would be better off.

Once Danny's guard came back with my luggage, we left the city and headed for L.A. My brother tried for a bit to keep asking me about work, but when he realized how exhausted I was, he mercifully let me sleep. He only woke me as we were finally pulling up to the villa, the sun setting over the house I'd grown up in.

"Ahem." As I forced myself out of the car, Danny gestured to his head with a badly-suppressed smile. "You might want to do something about that." Peering at my reflection in one of the tinted windows, I saw that I'd somehow turned my hair into a frizzy mess in my sleep. With a frustrated groan, I clawed through it and tried to make it at least somewhat presentable for when I saw my dad and sister again. I didn't need yet another critique of my appearance from Gemma.

When I opened the front door, however, I was even more relieved that I'd fixed my hair; the house was decorated for a party, filled with our family and a few of my friends. Seeing me in the doorway, several of my cousins called out to me and rushed in for hugs and kisses, welcoming me back.

"Remember to let her breathe, girls." My father's voice carried over the chatter and the music floating through the room, and I managed to extract myself from the gaggle of ladies to find him waiting with a smile. Without hesitation, I threw myself into his arms for a hug. "Welcome home, Sofina."

"Thank you, Papà." Looking up at him with a pout, I added, "You could have told me about the party. I would've worn something nicer!"

"Don't look at me. It was Nadine's idea." He nodded to the door, where my sister-in-law had come to greet Danny with a kiss. Catching my eye, she gave me a playful wink. "Besides, you look beautiful as you are. We've all been looking forward to your arrival."

"Oh yes, we were on pins and needles." Ugh. The one reunion I *wasn't* looking forward to. Drawing away from my dad, I found my sister near his side, arms crossed. She made no move to hug me or kiss my cheek, and instead, smiled coldly. "But of course, you had to make us wait an extra two hours for it."

"I couldn't control the delays on the flight, Gemma," I told her with a pleasant smile of my own. "But I'm sorry to keep you waiting. I know you were just dying to have me back in the house."

"Well, how could anyone not miss your sparkling presence?" she asked flatly. "You should catch up with all your admirers, in fact. I'm sure we'll have the opportunity to talk later." Without another word, she crossed the room, probably for another equally unpleasant conversation, and Papà sighed.

"She missed you as much as anyone. Try not to let her upset you." Looking out across the crowd, he added, "You should find Antoni. He's been asking about you all day." Antoni was my nephew, Danny's son, and if everything went to plan, our family's future don. At the moment, though, he was only seven. I would definitely have to see him before I went to bed.

Even though she was being facetious when she said it, Gemma was right: everyone *was* happy to see me. I could hardly step away from one conversation without being met immediately with another one. Nadine had done a fantastic job choosing the guest list. All my favorite cousins were there, the ones who would listen sympathetically while I complained about working and then prod me for any interesting gossip I had come across.

"*Zia* Sofi!" called a tiny, familiar voice while I was relaying one of the more scandalous recent events in hushed tones. A pair of little arms wrapped around my legs, and I looked down to see Antoni clinging to me with a grin on his face. "I missed you!"

"Oh, I missed you too, my little man!" I knelt to grab him up in a tight hug, excusing myself from my previous conversation. He clutched a toy airplane in one hand, so I asked, "Is this a new part of your collection?"

"Yeah! I wanted to show you." Leading me to sit on the stairs with him, he handed the solid metal model over to me. I looked it over carefully while he told me all its specifications and details. He had been collecting models of commercial airliners for a year or two, part of his long-standing love for all things related to aviation. He was usually a little...quiet, not very social, but my job must have won me some favor with him; since I'd started flying myself, he had gradually opened up to me more and more over the years. Every time I came home, he had new questions and facts of his own to share. Taking the model from my hands, he indicated the tiny door on one side of the plane and continued, "But you can't actually open the doors while you're in the air, because of the pressure. Maybe if *everybody* tried all at once—"

"There you are, mister." Nadine found us, hands on her hips, and Antoni smiled at her sheepishly. "Don't you give me that face. What did I say?"

"Stay with you and wait for Zia Sofi to finish talking," he mumbled, eyes on the little airplane as he fidgeted with it.

"You know it's rude to interrupt."

"It wasn't really an important conversation," I piped up, trying to defend him since I knew how strict Nadine could be sometimes. "I didn't mind the interruption."

"That's not the point. The best way to get respect is to give respect," she said, probably quoting my brother, who took the quote from our grandfather. "If you're rude and difficult, you'll have a harder time convincing others to listen to you. We've talked about this." I knew she was only trying to prepare Antoni for the responsibility he'd have in the future. That was why she worried so much about his difficulty socializing "properly." But it still seemed like such a small transgression to gripe at him over.

"I understand," Antoni said, sneaking a brief, puppy-eyed look up at her.

"Don't tell me; show me." Her eyes softened a little, and she bent down to plant a kiss in his messy black hair. "It's time for bed soon. You can talk with Zia Sofi for a few more minutes, but then you need to head upstairs, okay?"

"Okay."

With a smile in my direction, she added, "It's good to have you back. He hasn't talked this much in weeks."

Exhausted as I was, I still managed to maintain my pleasant attitude for the entirety of the party—even when talking with my sister. Once Antoni had gone to bed, Gemma cornered me and, in a much less friendly tone than before, gave me a summary of everything that had happened while I was away. Unfortunately, that included the details of how badly things were going for our former friends, the Morettis. I had to listen while she talked about what a miserable job Myles was doing of running the family, how the Council had practically stopped speaking to him, how it was a miracle he hadn't gotten himself killed yet but that luck couldn't hold out forever.

Hearing her talk about him that way made my blood boil. Even if I had my complaints about Myles, we had known him and his brothers ever since they'd moved to San Diego, and our dads had been friends even longer than that. But of course, Royce was the only one she ever cared about. Now that they weren't doing as well, now that they weren't as useful to us from a business standpoint, she seemed ready to write them off completely. So much for loyalty.

Disgusted, my good mood ruined, I excused myself from the party around 10 p.m. and headed upstairs to my room. When I got to the third floor, however, I was stopped in the hallway by a hand on my shoulder. I whirled around, ready to snap at whoever thought they had the right to touch me without permission, but the reprimand died before I could get it out as a pair of powerful arms wrapped me up and pulled me close.

"Finally. I thought you'd be down there all night." Lips pressed to my shoulder, and I had to suppress a shiver. The man holding me was one of Papà's personal bodyguards, Arturo. He and I had dated off and on for years, and the last night I'd spent at home, we were very much on. He was blond, gray-eyed—unusual in our circles—fit, and *so* tall. I should've been happy to be back in his arms.

But after all the time I'd spent thinking about Myles that evening, something about being with Arturo felt wrong.

"Sofi?" He bent down a little, trying to catch my eye. "Is something wrong? You and Gemma have an argument?"

"Hm? No, no, it's not that." I pushed away from him gently and took a step back. "I'm just really tired. I've been up for, like, sixteen hours straight, so I was headed to bed."

"Oh. Right, I didn't think about that," he muttered,

seeming embarrassed. "So I guess you don't want company, then...?" There was a very small note of hope in his voice, hope that I would invite him to come with me, even if it was just to sleep. As much as I hated to disappoint him, I disliked the idea of going to bed with him even more.

"Not tonight. Maybe once I've gotten some rest."

Maybe once I've gotten Myles Moretti out of my head.

3

MYLES

"It's not fair. I want to go too!" Whitney stomped her foot, suddenly looking a lot younger from the pout on her face.

"Not negotiable, Whits. You think your dad would ever let you see me again if I took you with me to an Official Business Meeting?" And to be honest, if there was even a chance it would be dangerous, no way was I taking her to my meeting with the Council. The way things were going lately, it seemed like that chance was pretty high. Nathan and Gregorio were already waiting in the car, but Whitney had stopped me at the door before I could join them. "Rena's really been looking forward to seeing you. So use today to hang out with her."

"And do what, embroider something?" she grumbled. "She won't want to do anything fun. I'm just going to be sitting here all day bored out of my mind."

"Can't you just do it for her sake?" That was a weak argument, especially coming from me; it wasn't like I often did things for anyone but myself. "Look, I'll make it up to you, okay? We can go to L.A. some other day while you're here, and you can pick whatever you want to do. But today, I *really* need to get going."

She gave me another melodramatic teenage sigh but stopped arguing. "Fine. Go have fun doing cool mob stuff. I'll be here knitting a jumper, I guess." As I walked past her, I flipped her braids over her head, forcing her to smile just briefly. But if she thought anything about this trip was going to be fun, she was dead wrong.

The drive to the Lucianos' place would take a little over two hours, so I'd agreed it wasn't really practical to take one of my own cars. Besides, it was better for appearances if we did things as traditionally as possible. The Council cared about shit like that. So I had plenty of time to think about what this conversation would entail and how I should handle it.

"Thoughts?" I asked, glancing at Nathan.

"No positive ones," he answered plainly. "I don't think it's an accident that they've 'fallen out of touch' with us, and I think this meeting is more about confirming that than changing anyone's mind."

I snorted. "Great. Very encouraging."

"You asked for my thoughts, not encouragement."

"What can they do to us, anyway?" Gregorio asked, leaning back in his seat and bouncing his knee impatiently. "We're the *Morettis*. Don't we have more weight than any of them?"

"In terms of individual families, maybe. But as a group? It's four to one; we wouldn't stand a chance trying to fight them." Nate explained all this as patiently as ever, but the look on his face said it was a stupid question. But then, Gregorio didn't have the education I did. As much as I hated giving Royce credit for anything, he had taught me pretty much everything there was to know about being a don. I didn't have the time, the patience, or the attention span to do all that for Gregorio, so he was learning in a more hands-on kind of way. And not knowing the potential consequences for fucking up made him reckless—even more reckless than me.

"I want to believe Marcell will stick up for me," I said, "but I don't. He was too close to my dad, and pretty much anyone who was close to my dad hates my guts these days." Not to mention what I'd done to his precious little princess Sofia. It wasn't likely she'd told him all the details about our...uh, "relationship" seemed like a strong word. Whatever had happened between us. But if he knew I'd hurt her, that was probably all he needed to hate me even more.

In the silence of the drive, I quickly realized that thinking about Sofia for even a second was a mistake. Now I wouldn't be able to get her off my mind the rest of the day. It had been nearly three years since I'd seen her last, and if I knew her, she was still pissed at me for how we left things. Despite myself, I felt my lips tug into a smirk. The girl could hold a grudge, that was for sure. She had always been a little spiteful, a little spoiled, a little bit of a brat. I liked that about her. She had guts, and she didn't take shit from anyone—including me. It made her way more fun to fight with than just about anyone else I knew.

Maybe five years ago, she'd started working as a flight attendant, eavesdropping and gathering information for her dad to use or sell. She would be gone for weeks, even months at a time, so I hardly ever saw her anymore. But then, while we were in London for Roger and Jill's wedding, she had just finished up a trip and was staying in town for a few days. We ran into each other at a pub. I'd be lying if I said I wasn't happy to see her. It had been forever, and the two of us had a lot in common. So we talked for a while. We drank for a while. Then we somehow wound up in my hotel room, all over each other, finally addressing the ten years' worth of sexual tension between us.

I was supposed to fly home the next day. I didn't. I worked from my hotel room, wandered around town, did whatever to pass the time, and then that night I met Sofia again. This time we skipped the bar and went straight to my room. Judging by the way she pounced on me when we got there, I figured she'd spent all day thinking about it just like I had. She was still just as smug and demanding as usual while we were in bed, which was so refreshing compared to most of the women I'd been with, women who knew who I was and assumed I'd like them better if they were doormats. Sofia had no qualms about fighting with me, and the conflict made her a hundred times more interesting. And the shit she could do with that mouth when she *wasn't* using it to argue with me?

Remembering where I was, I shifted in my seat and swallowed hard, trying to take my mind off Sofia's lips, her tongue, her throat—*shit*—so I didn't end up popping a boner just from the memory. Three years and she still did this to me without even being there. Which was the reason I'd broken it off.

Maybe a week after our first night together, after we'd finished another round, Sofia took a step out of character and pressed herself close up against my side. Usually, when we were done, she insisted on taking a shower immediately, and even when she slept next to me, she kept to her side of the bed. So this was...different. Unexpected.

"So did you decide to stay here permanently too?" she asked without looking me in the face.

"Pff, no. Definitely not. I'm just..." I stopped myself as I realized what I was about to say and how it would sound. *I'm enjoying being with you.* Yikes.

"So that means you'll be going back to San Diego soon."

"Uh, yeah. Soon. Why do you ask?" The way she was positioned, it seemed natural to put my arm around her. But I didn't.

"I don't have another trip to work at the moment," she explained, "and I'm sure my dad and my brother would like to see me. You said you came here on your family's jet, but you don't really need all that space to yourself. So I was thinking it would be efficient for me to go back with you."

The weird thing is that I considered it. I actually gave myself a second to think about what she was proposing, like it was at all a good idea, like her dad hadn't already decided that he hated me for killing my old man (not that I didn't have cause). Like he would be thrilled to know I'd shared an eleven-hour flight with his beloved youngest child. Like I would be able to look him in the eye and say that "nothing happened" between us after a week of spending more time in bed than out. Instead of dismissing the idea right away, I let myself think about all that.

When I didn't answer for a minute, Sofia let out an irritated sigh. "Or not. It was just an idea." She drew away from me and headed to the bathroom for her shower without another word. I was still completely in my head about the whole thing. Why didn't I laugh at her and tell her it was a stupid idea? Why didn't I say she couldn't afford me or tell her she'd have to do something pretty mind-blowing to pay her way?

Why the hell was I taking this so seriously?

I checked out of my hotel room the next day and flew home, too freaked out by my own weird, uncharacteristic behavior to stick around and let her mess with my head any more. I had a business to run. I had my family to look out for. I didn't need her making me doubt myself. And she didn't try to contact me after I left, so it must not have bothered her too much. It was just sex, right? Neither of us really had any right to be "bothered" about how it ended.

"Myles?" I jumped at the sound of Nathan's voice, and he narrowed his eyes at me. "We're going to be at the Lucianos' villa in just a few minutes. You look a lot less mentally present than I'd prefer."

"I'm here, all right?" I growled, shoving my hair back and trying to get a grip on myself. Thinking about Sofia was *definitely* a mistake.

...

"I shouldn't have to tell you this, but I'm going to anyway," Nathan said to Gregorio as we were heading up the walkway to the main house. "Myles and I need to do all the talking. Don't speak unless you're spoken to. No, don't speak even if someone addresses you."

"Are you serious?"

"Listen to him," I added without looking back. "He knows what he's talking about. Just pay attention and use this as a learning experience." Gregorio scoffed but didn't argue. When we got to the front door, Marcell's chief of staff met us with a falsely pleasant smile.

"Don Moretti, we've been expecting you. The Council is assembled in the conference room. Please follow me." Walking through the halls, I felt like Marcell must have done some remodeling since the last time I'd been there. Everything looked cleaner, more modern, not hyper-traditional like it was before.

"Myles?"

Shit. The sound of Sofia's voice made me go rigid and stop in my tracks. I should've known she would be home, just to make this more difficult for me. I glanced over my shoulder to see her coming down the stairs, straight black hair pulled to one side, makeup flawless as usual, curves wrapped in a tight dress. How was it she looked even better than the last time I'd seen her? For a split-second, I saw shock on her face, but she quickly arranged her features into something cool and distant.

"Hey," I said lamely, trying hard to stop my eyes wandering.

She crossed her arms as she came to stand in front of me on one hip, staring up at me like I owed her some kind of explanation. "What are you doing here?"

"Business." I forced myself to meet her searching hazel eyes as if that was a better option than looking at the rest of her.

"Sir?" The chief of staff had stopped and was now watching me expectantly. As far as anyone knew, I had no reason to talk to Sofia any more than a polite greeting.

"We can talk later," I told her, turning away.

"Oh, don't worry about that," she said, her voice dripping with false sweetness. "I'm sure you're a very busy man. I won't take up any more of your time." As much as I wanted to respond to that, she turned on her heel and left, not giving me the opportunity. Which was a relief, frankly. Nathan cleared his throat, and we continued on to the conference room.

There was a long table inside, with the other four family heads and their advisers or underbosses seated on one side, making this feel a lot more like a trial than a meeting. We went through all the mandatory introductions, but my eyes stayed shifting between the other bosses in the room.

Marcell Luciano, the force that moved half of L.A.'s business. Dominic Capelli, who ran both Seattle and Spokane. Luisa Maldone, a severe matron who had taken over her family's business in Denver after her husband's death ten years ago. And Vincent Carlyle, the youngest on their side of the table but still ten years my senior, who managed his family's Texas-wide business from Dallas.

Nathan, Gregorio, and I took our seats, and Nate launched into a polished spiel about, first, how much we respected the Council and how grateful we were to have them there. Then he brought up the business issues we'd had since the others had started withdrawing their support. And of course, because we couldn't ignore the elephant in the room, he mentioned the fact that this decline in our business had started not long after my dad's death.

"Young man," Luisa said, looking at me, not at Nathan. "For how long have you been overseeing your family?"

"About four and a half years, ma'am," I answered. She smiled tightly.

"And prior to your father's disappearance, for how long did he train you for this position?"

"He...didn't," I was forced to admit, refusing to let the fact shake me. "He focused most of his attention on training my oldest brother, who abdicated the throne, let's say." Vincent chuckled at that. "But I *was* trained by my brother, Royce. I know some of you"—I glanced in Marcell's direction—"already know how valuable a resource that is."

God, I hated having to stand on ceremony like this. Why couldn't we just have the conversation without worrying about exactly how it looked or who might get offended by me choosing the wrong word? Bluntness was so much easier to deal with.

"But that isn't really the point," Dominic said, folding his hands on the table in front of him and fixing me with a hard stare. "Even leaving aside your leadership abilities and qualifications, or lack thereof, I'm much more concerned about your loyalty."

"Could you elaborate?" Nathan managed to be polite even when I was already getting pissed off.

"Deron Moretti was a valued member of this Council, a great don, and a true friend," Marcell said, just giving me more reason to think they had all discussed this before I arrived. "We were concerned for the Morettis when he disappeared, but we did our best to support you as his replacement." His frown hardened. "When the news arrived that he had been found and rather than bringing him back, you chose to kill him? That was very difficult to accept."

Nate opened his mouth to answer, but I beat him to it. "Even knowing what he did to me and my brothers? That he was threatening our lives and our loved ones? None of that matters?"

"As his sons, you should have respected his judgment enough that he didn't *need* to resort to manipulation of that sort," Dominic agreed. "But he did what was necessary to get you back under control. That is what a boss does, Myles."

I bit down hard on my temper and the retort I wanted to shoot back. These people would only see me as irrational and childish if I got visibly angry. "He was threatening my family," I ground out. "You want to talk about loyalty? You want to talk about 'doing what's necessary'? *He* turned on *us*. And because he was my father, I should've just accepted that?"

"Because he was your father, because he was your elder, because he was your superior—yes, you should have accepted his decisions," Dominic said. "You've proven that you can't be trusted to know when you're wrong. Under your leadership, the Moretti name is more a liability than an asset."

"Are you kidding me?" I demanded, fists clenching as I sat forward in my chair. "I have been the only thing holding this fucking family together for the past four years."

"Calm down," Nathan said quietly, and I pretended not to hear him.

"Holding together, perhaps, but not thriving as you did under your father's direction." Luisa wasn't even looking at me by this point, examining her fingernails instead, seeming bored. "As I understand it, your brother Royce would have been a suitable replacement for him. It's no secret that you aren't."

"If you do want to be part of the Council, I suggest you seek other leadership," Dominic said, leaning against one of his chair's arms. When I realized he was addressing Nathan and not me, white-hot fury shot through me again. "Or transferring your contracts to a family better-suited to handle them." He gestured to himself and the others on their side of the table.

"Are you really trying to blackmail me into paying you to be part of the Council my family helped found?" I demanded.

"You do have other options," Vincent said, finally speaking up and seeming a little uncomfortable in this conversation. "You can always carry on your business outside of the Council's authority. Your family still has power of its own."

"But for how long, I wonder?" Dominic was still staring me down. All four of them were looking at me like I was in over my head, like I was incompetent. It was the same way my fucking father used to look at me every goddamn day.

"Fuck this," I muttered, shoving to my feet. "Keep your fucking Council blessing. I'm not changing shit for you." Starting toward the door, I snapped over my shoulder at Nathan and Gregorio, "We're leaving." They at least had the decency to listen and not embarrass me any further.

...

"I'm not sure how much worse that could've gone," Nate muttered once we were back on the road.

"No one died," Gregorio pointed out.

Nathan sighed and shook his head. "The bar is low."

"What the fuck what I supposed to say to them?" I asked. "You heard the way they were talking to me. They weren't interested in working with me. They think I'm the cause of all our problems right now. You want to go back and beg their forgiveness? Tell them you'll get rid of me if it means you get back on their good side?"

"Myles, you know we wouldn't do that."

"Don't say 'we' like it applies to the whole family," I argued. "I know there are *plenty* of people who would be happy to see me gone."

"You may be underestimating your family's loyalty," Nate said, taking his glasses off to clean them with a handkerchief from his pocket. "A lot of them support whoever is in power, right or wrong. Others know that without you, the business would have fallen apart years ago, and they're grateful for your efforts. And believe it or not, some members genuinely do support you and your decisions." Putting his glasses back on, he leveled a look at me. "Try not to discount us all so easily."

"Yeah." I dropped my head into my hands, my brain still buzzing from that disaster of a meeting and from unexpectedly running into Sofia. For the briefest second, I *almost* wished Royce and Roger were there to help me figure out how to handle this. But I quickly brushed that thought aside. They didn't want to be part of this anymore. They didn't want to be involved with me anymore. So I didn't need them.

By the time we got back to San Diego, it was getting late. Instead of heading back to the house, I had the driver take us to the nightclub I'd opened a couple years ago. At least *that* business was doing well. Walking through the room, past the bar and the dance floor, greeting any employees I came across, actually made me feel a little better. These people liked me, anyway. That was something.

Gregorio and Nathan followed me upstairs to my office, where the music was mostly muted and we could talk. I didn't even know where to start, though. The Morettis had been part of the Council for generations. Even when we were living in New York and Dad was doing work there, we were still considered Council members. Them withdrawing from us was basically telling the rest of the world "the Morettis are no longer worth doing business with." After all we'd done for their ungrateful asses.

"Maybe it would be more effective to approach the family heads individually," Nathan said, standing near the table where Gregorio and I had sat down. He always got really still when he was thinking hard, totally the opposite of me. "Starting with Vincent. He's the most likely to sympathize and the least likely to ignore us for the sake of tradition."

"When you say 'us,' you mean *you*," I added, unable to keep my leg from bouncing nervously under the table. Nathan handling negotiations like this probably shouldn't have bothered me; it was his job, and he technically had more experience with it than I did, being older than Vincent himself. But letting him take over felt like admitting I wasn't qualified to do the negotiating myself.

"Me, on behalf of the family, yes."

"Why even bother talking to them?" Gregorio asked. "Who gives a shit what they think? We should just cut our losses and move on. Or"—suddenly, he looked excited, conspiratorial—"we show them what happens to people who talk shit about the Morettis. Get rid of 'em, one by one. We have people. We could do it."

"Gregorio, for the love of God, *think* before you speak," Nathan growled, rubbing his temples with both hands. "Do you think there's any possible scenario in which we could get away with that? You think their families would stand for it? Or are you just looking for more ways to make sure everyone hates us?"

"I'm looking for ways to make sure people respect us," Gregorio argued with a sneer. "Obviously playing nice isn't fucking working. Do you have a solution that doesn't involve groveling?"

I leaned back in my seat while they bickered, zoning out and trying to make some kind of decision. It wasn't like this was the first crisis I'd dealt with in the past few years, but it was definitely the biggest. Big enough that it could ruin our entire family if I wasn't careful. Somehow, I wound up asking myself *what would Dad do? What would Royce do?*

They wouldn't have let it get this bad in the first place, idiot.

"Look, what you two are doing right now isn't helping," I snapped, getting to my feet. "Greg, we're not fucking killing anyone. Don't be stupid. Nate, I'm not ready to start arranging any peace talks just yet. We can't act like we're just fine with the way they treated us today. They know we're pissed off. Let's leave it that way for now." He looked a little conflicted but nodded.

"Understood."

After a few more seconds of silence, I shook my head and headed for the stairs again. "I need a drink." It was a little after 10 p.m., so the club was just starting to fill up with people, and the bar was pretty busy. Still, the bartenders recognized me, so it wasn't long until one of them came over to take my order.

"You haven't been by in a few days. Good to see you're still in one piece." This girl's name was Brandy, I think. She'd always been friendly—not flirty, just friendly, which was kind of a relief. "What can I get for you?"

"Let me have a double of Wright & Brown, neat," I said. "Rye, not bourbon."

"Naturally." She winked at me and only took a few seconds to hand my drink over. "Anything else?"

"We'll see how the night goes," I said dryly. "Thanks." While she went to serve someone else, I glanced out at the dance floor and took a drink. The whiskey was pretty hot, but I preferred it that way. The club was used as a meeting place for business discussions and deals pretty often, sometimes even for other families, but this crowd seemed more like the for-pleasure kind. I didn't recognize anyone as an insider, at least.

Except for one. One I definitely didn't expect to see there. At first, I thought the erratic lights and my eyes were playing tricks on me, but no. Sofia Luciano was at the other end of the bar with a couple of other women, as if she was just part of the crowd. *As if.* I was way too cynical to believe her being there was a coincidence. Her family—no, probably her sister—must have sent her. I downed my drink, then crossed the room to confront her.

4

SOFIA

I didn't know what kind of business Myles could have with my dad, but it didn't matter. Clearly, it wasn't anything that involved me. Even though I knew he had taken over running the Moretti family, it still felt so strange to see him there in our house not tagging along with his dad and Royce, but running things himself. But he didn't seem like his usual confident self. That was what I'd always liked so much about him: his self-assurance, bordering on arrogance. It was different from his dad's or his brothers'. It was more playful and fun. But it seemed like his work might have dampened that a bit.

Not that I cared. Not that I'd missed his teasing or his cocky smile. Even when we were together in London, I knew it wasn't going to last. And considering our circumstances, it wasn't like we could pick up where we left off, in that weird friends-with-benefits limbo. No, that had only worked because we were away from home, away from our families and responsibilities. It wasn't viable in real life. In fact, if I had known he was going to be there, I probably would've avoided seeing him.

With that in mind, after Myles and his entourage had stormed out, I went to find my dad.

He was talking with the other Council members, so I didn't directly interrupt—but I did stand nearby with my hands folded, watching him intently, waiting for him to notice. It didn't take him long. Excusing himself from the conversation, he came to meet me with a smile, "Do you need something, Sofina? I'm going to be busy most of the day, unfortunately."

"Why didn't you tell me Myles was going to be here?" I asked as politely as I could manage. Papà's kind expression clouded over.

"He came purely for business reasons. It wasn't a social call." He raised an eyebrow at me. "Why does it matter? Did you run into him?"

"I did for a second. And it was an unpleasant surprise." That was only partially a lie. Some stupid part of me had gotten excited when I'd seen him, but I still would've preferred not to. "What were you all talking about?"

"Don't worry about that, *cuore mio*. I'm sure it would bore you."

I frowned. "He seemed pretty upset when he left."

"I think it's best if you don't wonder about him too much," Papà answered, more firmly than I expected. "You know how I feel about him, and he's only gotten worse in recent years. There's no need for you to involve yourself with that."

Papà had always said that Myles was reckless, and that made him dangerous. That was the reason that, despite being interested in him—when we were younger, I mean!— I never bothered trying to initiate anything; I knew my father wouldn't approve.

"Okay," I said, keeping my eyes toward the ground. Probably able to see the drop in my mood, Papà softened his tone a little and chucked me on the chin.

"Marie and Elyse are in the guest house. Lauren, too. You should go say hello. I'm sure they'd be happy to see you."

Marie and Elyse were twins, Dominic Capelli's daughters. I knew them in more or less the same way I knew Myles and his brothers, but we saw each other less frequently. Despite only being a year older than me, they had always treated me like a baby sister. Lauren Maldone, on the other hand, was only twenty-two, and because she was the Don's granddaughter, she had even less exposure to the business than I did. She looked up to me in the same way she looked up to Gemma, Marie, and Elyse. I still wasn't sure how to feel about that.

Regardless, I considered the three of them friends, so I was happy to use them as a way to keep myself occupied. When I got to the guest house, the three girls were sitting together in the living room in some sort of heated conversation, the twins apparently ganging up on poor Lauren. That exchange was paused when they saw me come in. Marie and Elyse squealed, rushing over to greet me with hugs and cheek kisses, while Lauren sheepishly made her way over and gave me a small smile and a wave. Her thick blue-black hair (dyed to cover her natural dirty blond) hung over her shoulders and partially in her face, a sort of natural shield.

"We've been waiting on you to come out all day," Marie said with a pout. "What took you so long?"

"I didn't even know you were here!" I protested quickly. "And I only got back last night, so I really needed to catch up on my beauty sleep." I certainly wasn't going to mention that I'd spent part of my morning with Arturo. Not *with* him, I mean. Nothing inappropriate. We just talked for a while. And then I saw Myles and got conflicted all over again.

"Well, at least you're here now. We're going out tonight. You'll come with us, won't you?" Marie went on. "I'll bet it's been a while since you've seen any California nightlife yourself. You must miss it."

"Well, maybe a little," I admitted. "Where are you going?" The twins exchanged a look, then gave me two versions of the same dazzling smile.

"There's a club in San Diego we've heard a lot about," Elyse explained. "We probably won't get another chance to check it out for a while, so why not tonight?"

"San Diego? You want to drive two hours there and back just for one club?" What could a San Diego club possibly have that L.A. didn't? As far as I was concerned, our nightlife was objectively superior. "Couldn't we find somewhere here instead?"

"But Sofi, Lauren's never been." Marie took a step back and pushed Lauren's hair back behind her ears like she was a little doll, either ignoring or oblivious to her blushing. "Shouldn't she see as much of Cali as possible before she has to go back to *Colorado*?"

"There's nothing wrong with Colorado," Lauren piped up, timidly indignant.

"Of course there isn't, honey," Marie agreed, then looked at me as if to say, *See?*

"Lauren, do you even want to go?" I asked.

Despite looking a little unsure, she glanced between the twins, then back at me. "Yeah. If you guys are going, I don't wanna just stay here by myself." Of course, she wanted to be part of whatever the big kids were doing. Even if it was something she wasn't interested in herself.

"Fine, fine," I conceded, "but don't complain if the ride gets boring."

"Oh, I'm sure we'll find something to talk about. Um..." Elyse looked me up and down, frowning slightly. "You'll change before we leave, right?"

"Do I need to?" I asked, raising an eyebrow at her. Maybe I hadn't dressed myself with clubbing in mind, but it wasn't like I was walking around in pajamas. There was nothing wrong with my outfit.

"No, no, not necessarily. It's just...this is a *nice* place we're going to," she said. "So we should all try to look...nice." She smiled at me sweetly, batting her eyes, and I couldn't help feeling there was something suspicious about her attitude.

"Um," Lauren started hesitantly, "I didn't really bring anything super nice. Can you guys help me pick something?" Despite being a don's granddaughter, despite the money her family *definitely* had, she'd always been a little on the frumpy side. Jeans and band T's, excessive piercings, muted colors, and rips that definitely weren't factory-made. It would've shocked me to know she even owned more than one dress.

"You're about the same size as me," I said, looking her over critically. "Or, I think you are under all that baggy fabric. You can borrow something of mine."

She looked less than thrilled by the prospect but didn't argue, willing as usual to follow our directions. That led to me picking out her outfit, Elyse doing her makeup, and Marie working her long hair into elegant curls. By the time we finished with her, we barely had time to get ourselves ready, but at least she looked club-appropriate.

Since Elyse had implied that my simple bodycon dress wasn't good enough, I changed into a slinky, sexy little gold-sequined number I'd bought during a trip to Vegas. It was tight in all the right places and probably the most light-catching garment I owned. Definitely the kind of look that got attention, which was always a plus. I pinned my hair up into a thoughtfully-messy knot on top of my head, then finished the whole thing with nude heels and red lipstick.

It should be a crime to look this good.

But it still wasn't something I wanted Papà seeing me leaving the house in, so I covered up with a shawl before I headed downstairs and gave him a quick goodbye. I met the other girls in the guest house and dramatically stripped the shawl off my shoulders to reveal my dress. "So?" I asked Elyse. "Is this *nice* enough?"

"It's perfect!" She clapped her well-manicured hands together as I gave them a little spin. She was dressed in royal blue velvet, while Marie had gone with dark green silk, both accenting their red hair. Even with Lauren seeming so nervous, we made a very good-looking bunch.

During the ride to San Diego, we shared a couple of bottles of champagne and plenty of stories. Poor Marie, the oldest child of their family, had been forced into marrying some strict and boring *capo* from a less prestigious family a few years ago, and she complained about how painfully work-obsessed he was. She mentioned being jealous of my job, of the freedom it gave me, while she was stuck at home playing the obedient wife. Elyse was suitor-shopping in the very limited range their dad had given them, and she agreed she wasn't looking forward to being tied down. I was definitely grateful that Papà wasn't *that* intent on controlling who Gemma or I married.

Between drinking and oversharing, the trip went by surprisingly quickly. Soon enough, we were pulling up to the club the twins had heard so much about, and Marlon called back to us, "Here we are, ladies. Just give me a call whenever you'd like to leave."

"Thank you, Marlon!" I said with a smile and a wave before stepping out of the car behind my friends, leaving my shawl to decorate the leather seats. On the front of the building, the word "aMoral" was written out in swirly neon text. The place looked pretty plain from the outside, but the long line at the door said that image was deceiving. Not that the line had anything to do with us. As we approached the doorman, I expected to have to use my name to get us in—since most people in San Diego knew the Lucianos through our connection to the Morettis—but Marie beat me to it. She showed him her ID with a winning smile, and he let us in without a word.

But why should a doorman in SoCal know a family from Washington? I was about to ask her, but the club's thumping music quickly distracted me. I finally realized how long it had been since I'd gone out with girlfriends like this, and enjoying that felt way more important. We made a beeline for the bar first, since the champagne buzz was starting to wear off, and Elyse ordered a round of shots.

"Oh gosh, I didn't think to ask," she said, glancing at Lauren. "Can you take shots, honey?" It had been maybe a year since we'd seen her, and back then, she was still terrified of alcohol. Lauren snorted a laugh and leaned forward against the bar, her sort of boyish body language offsetting the hyper-feminine outfit we'd put her in.

"Honestly?" she said with a mischievous smile. "I bet I could outdrink all three of you."

"Is that so?" I asked, grinning back at her. "We'll just have to test that theory." But just after our first shots were delivered—and Lauren tossed hers back without so much as a grimace—our carefree party plans were cut short when someone roughly grabbed my arm.

"Hey!" I snapped, jerking away reflexively and turning my most disdainful glare on the person to my right. Even when I recognized him, my eyes didn't soften in the slightest. For the second time that day I said, "Myles?"

"What the hell are you doing here?" he demanded. He didn't spare the other girls a single glance, keeping his glinting black eyes focused on me.

"Is this a trick question? Am I not allowed in San Diego anymore?" I asked scathingly. During our conversation that afternoon, I hadn't had the opportunity to tear into him, but in a setting like this, there was no reason to hold back. "Whatever you might think, you don't *actually* own the city."

"That's not what I'm talking about and you know it. I mean here, at the club I *do* own."

It took a second or two for that information to sink in. Since when did he dabble in this kind of business? If I had known the place belonged to him, I wouldn't have set foot in there! But that did explain why the doorman knew the Capellis.

Suddenly suspicious of exactly why Marie and Elyse had brought me there, I glanced back at them, and they quickly looked away, pretending not to be listening to our conversation. Lauren looked between me and Myles, bemused. I would definitely have to talk with the twins later about this trip. Looking back to Myles, I told him honestly, "I didn't know it was your place. You think I would travel two hours just to be in your presence? Are you *that* conceited?"

"I think you would travel two hours to scope the place out and see what you could learn if Gemma told you to," he said, crossing his arms and letting his eyes wander up and down my body. One of his eyebrows quirked up a little as he took in my outfit, and I wished I'd kept my shawl on so I could stop him gawking at me. "Or maybe even your dad. After the talk we had this morning, I won't put anything past him."

I rolled my eyes as dramatically as possible. "No one told me to come here, Myles. You're paranoid. I'm just trying to enjoy a night out with my friends."

"Don't act like this isn't something you do, getting close to important people and listening in on their business. I'm sure you've gotten real good at pretending after all that practice, but you're not fooling me."

I opened my mouth to answer, then stopped myself. For one, my work was none of his business. Besides, it wasn't supposed to be common knowledge, and who knew how many agents could be there and listening. "I'm not having this conversation here."

"Fine." Myles took a step backward and nodded toward the back of the room like he expected me to follow him. It didn't seem like he was going to leave me alone until he was satisfied with my explanation, so, despite my reluctance, I pushed away from the bar.

Giving the twins a hard look, I told them, "I'll be right back."

"Have fun," Elyse sang without looking at me. I ignored her and followed Myles to a set of stairs in the back. They led up to an office, where two men—the same two men who were with him that afternoon—were seated at a long conference table.

Myles snapped for their attention and said simply, "Get out." They left without argument, though the one with glasses gave me a searching look as he passed. Myles shut the door behind them, then surprised me by pinning me back against it and kissing me hard. His tongue licked its way into my mouth, and it was all I could do not to moan. My reflex was to kiss him back, but the logical part of my brain managed to overpower it. Just barely.

I shoved him back and slapped him across the face, struggling to calm my heart and ignore the heat he sent rushing through my veins. Damn him! "Who the hell do you think you are?" I gasped, furious with the breathless tone of my voice. Despite the red mark on his cheek, his lips still curved at the corners.

"That was the answer I expected." His dark eyes roamed slowly up my figure again. "But what else am I supposed to do when you show up looking like *that* and then let me get you alone? I only have so much willpower." Even when he tried to meet my eyes, I couldn't take them off his lips. He must have seen that because his smirk widened and he took a step closer. *Cocky bastard.*

Letting out a frustrated growl, I grabbed his lapels and dragged him down for another kiss, one he was eager to return. He tasted like whiskey, too much like that first night in London, his hands on my hips, just as familiar. For a second, I forgot all the reasons I shouldn't be doing this and admitted very quietly to myself that I had missed it. But soon enough, he reminded me where I was; as his body pressed harder into mine and his fingertips crept under the hem of my skirt, I let out a sound of protest and pushed away from him again, this time striding across the room to put distance between us.

"*Cazzo*," I forced out. Unlike my dad and brother, I kept my Italian and English separate for the most part. When I was this worked up, the barrier slipped a little. "God, I can't stand you."

"You know, you send a lot of mixed signals," Myles chuckled. I didn't need to look at him to know he was watching me closely while I tried with shaking hands to fix my hair, which had gone from thoughtfully-messy to makeout-messy. "You really didn't know this was my place?"

"No. But I think Marie and Elyse did."

"So they had some kind of agenda for bringing you here?" he asked. "Why would they care?"

"I don't know!" Whatever it was, I didn't think it was business-related. I had told them about the very confusing week I'd spent in London with him, and they knew about my many conflicting feelings toward him. Were they hoping this would push us together? It had certainly pushed us somewhere. Trying to take my mind off of whatever was between us, I glanced back at him and asked, "What did you talk to my dad about?" Still suspicious, he narrowed his eyes. "He already knows. I'm sure Gemma does too. I'm asking for myself."

After another second's hesitation, he slipped his hands into his pockets and explained, "Things haven't been going so hot for us lately. My family. A lot of people think that's entirely my fault, the Council included. Marcell basically told me today that he doesn't trust me as far as he can throw me. None of them do. They want us out of the Council unless we 'find new leadership.'"

"God," I muttered, wincing. "I didn't realize it was that bad."

"Yeah," he scoffed. "Neither did I."

"So what are you going to do? Surely you can change their minds somehow. You're persuasive." He'd had a reputation as a smooth talker since he was thirteen. When he wanted to be, at least. "If you can show them—"

"I wasn't really asking for advice," he said coolly.

"Oh. Right. Of course, you weren't. You never do," I

agreed, crossing my arms. "I should've known better than to offer since you obviously have everything under control."

"I didn't ask you because you don't fucking know anything about it," he hissed. "You've never had to worry your pretty little head about anything that actually matters; you just let your dad or your brother take care of it."

"Until just a few years ago, you were exactly the same way," I reminded him. "You thought of the whole thing as a game, something to do when you were bored."

"I *was* the same way. That's how I know it's really easy to talk shit even when no one wants your opinion." A few seconds passed in silence, and even though he tried to hide it, I could see the regret on his face. "I don't mean...I'm just talking about—"

"It doesn't matter," I said, shrugging him off, heading for the door. As I passed him, he caught my wrist to stop me. "Let go."

"Will you just listen to me?"

"No. Let me go."

"Sofi, come on."

I didn't bother answering and wrenched my arm out of his grasp to leave, stomping back down the stairs and ignoring all his little henchmen watching me. When I got back to the bar, Marie, Elyse, and Lauren were there waiting, all looking at me warily, like I might explode. The look on my face must've been pretty dark.

"So, um...how'd it go?" Elyse ventured, but I didn't answer, trying to flag down a bartender. The others were probably getting their drinks for free if the rest of the staff knew who they were, but I insisted on starting a tab. I was about to get stupidly drunk, way drunker than I should, but I wasn't going to take a single bit of charity from Myles.

"You okay?" Lauren asked, scooting a little closer to my

side. Since she was the only one there I wasn't currently pissed off at, I smiled at her sweetly.

"I'm fine. Just thirsty." For the rest of the time we were there, I made a point of seeming as unbothered and happy as possible. I drank, I laughed with my friends, I drank more, I went out and danced with any guy who caught my eye, and then I kept drinking. That was all much easier than thinking about how nice those few moments in Myles's arms had felt. It was a lot simpler to hope he was seeing me grind with some other guy and wishing he'd been less of an ass than to acknowledge how much it hurt for him to reject my concern.

By the time we were ready to leave, around 1 a.m., I was so drunk I could hardly stand without swaying. Marie used my phone to call Marlon, and I needed more than a little help getting in the car. Stupid. I knew it was stupid to do this to myself over him. He wasn't worth it.

"I'm not sure this was a good idea," Marie muttered as we were headed back to L.A. "I've never seen her like this before. It must have gone worse than we thought."

"I figured he would be happy to see her!" Elyse whispered back. "I mean, they've always been kind of snippy at each other; that's just how—"

"I can still hear you," I informed them, sprawled across the seat and staring blankly up at the ceiling. "You could at least wait until I'm not around." They fell silent, and I fell asleep for most of the ride. When we got back to the house, Lauren helped me out of the car and up to my room. Arturo was waiting in the hall again, and his eyes went wide in concern when he saw me leaning so heavily on Lauren. I took one look at him and groaned, "Ugh. No."

Lauren dropped me off at my bed, having proven that she could hold her liquor better than me or the twins, and I thanked her pitifully as I dragged a pillow over my head. When she left, I could hear her talking quietly with Arturo but couldn't make out what they were saying. Trying not to think about how utterly useless I was going to be the next day, I relaxed and let myself pass out.

5

MYLES

Three years apart, and all it took was one night for me to get stuck on Sofia again. I didn't even sleep with her, but I still thought about her every day for nearly a week. She had a lot of practice faking her emotions, but when I hurt her, I saw it. But at the time, I was too pissed off and stressed out to care. Don't get me wrong: I had thought about going after her, knocking out whatever guy had his sleazy hands all over her, trying to get her to talk to me again—but after everything I'd been through that day, I couldn't bring myself to force another conflict. For once.

I could've had the same argument with anyone else, and it wouldn't have bothered me. I definitely wouldn't have obsessed over it for the next fucking week. It was that kiss, I swear to God, that kiss that I remembered way too well. In those few seconds, it brought back every memory of her biting my lip, raking her nails down my back, losing her breath and gasping out my name. That shit wasn't easy to forget.

Even while I was sitting in my office, trying to respond to some email about work, I was fighting with myself about whether or not to try calling her. What would be the point? Even if I'd wanted to try being in some kind of...relationship with her, it wasn't like anything serious could happen between us now that the Council had officially told me to go fuck myself. That didn't leave a lot of options.

The rhythmic knock at my office door came as a welcome disruption to my brooding. "Whits, I told you, I have to work at least *one* day this week," I called.

"Yeah, but you've been working all day already," she said, opening the door and waltzing in despite my argument. And she was wrong: I had been in my office all day, but I hadn't gotten much work done. Holding up her phone, she added, "Besides, there's a movie I want to see. I can't go by myself. And it's a horror movie, so Rena probably doesn't want to go. You're kind of my only option."

"Gee, I'm flattered."

"It's whatever. Now come on, it starts in like twenty minutes!" she insisted, bouncing on her toes.

"What if I say no?"

"I'll keep standing here bugging you," she said. "And you definitely won't get any work done that way."

"I could call security to come remove you," I suggested, fidgeting with a pen from my desktop.

"Nope. All the staff like me better than you because I'm young and adorable." Starting to whine a little, she checked her phone and went on, "Come *on*, Uncle Myles, it's a classic horror matinee thing, and they're not doing more showings. I've never asked you for anything before in my life!"

"Bullshit," I laughed as I got up from my desk. "All right, all right, I'll take pity on you. Let's go." She directed me to this tiny theater I didn't even know existed. There were all of four screens, and when we got in, there were exactly six other people in the seats. I followed Whitney to one of the back rows, muttering, "Wow, what a crowd. How did you even find this place?"

"I googled 'what's the best way to get your miserable, workaholic uncle out of his office,'" she said, shooting me a sly grin.

"Cute." There were no previews, so the movie just started a minute or two later, kind of jarringly. Watching the opening credits, I leaned down and whispered, "This movie is so old! We could've watched it at home on a bigger screen."

"Shush!" She clutched her soda in both hands, eyes glued to the screen.

When she said "classic horror," she wasn't kidding; this was a showing of the original fucking *Halloween*. I'd seen it so many times that I got bored pretty quickly, leaning back in my seat and letting my thoughts wander. I didn't have to guess where they would go. What was Sofia doing, I wondered. Did she even know Whitney was in town? They had never met since Royce had made sure to keep her away from the Council. Maybe they should. I could imagine them getting along. And if it meant Sofia might go a little easier on me because Whits was there, so be it. Royce probably wouldn't like the idea. But what he didn't know wouldn't hurt me, right?

Switching my phone to silent, I slipped it out of my pocket and went back to my last text conversation with Sofia. Somehow I'd never gotten around to deleting it—but I made sure to lean away from Whitney so she wouldn't see any of the nasty shit we'd said to each other back then while we were arranging to meet up.

I didn't even know if Sofia had the same number anymore. Knowing her, she'd probably replaced her phone twice in the past three years. But I figured it was worth a shot, so I wrote out, *Hey. Guess who.* Really, that was my best opener? There were worse things I could've said, I guess. I locked my phone and turned my attention back to the movie, checking in on Michael Myers stalking some high school girls. The important people wouldn't start dying for a while.

After about five minutes, my phone buzzed in my hand, and Whits turned to glare at me. Mumbling an apology, I turned off the vibration and turned the brightness down as low as possible to check the message I'd received.

I don't have to guess, Sofia had written back. *What do you want?*

Well, that was better than "Fuck off and leave me alone."

Just thinking about you, I started, then furiously backspaced and instead wrote, *Just thinking about the other night. You got pretty plastered, so I thought I'd make sure you're still alive.*

I waited, checking my phone every ten seconds, until she finally answered, *Yes, Myles. I'm fine. Not that it's any of your business.* I couldn't help smiling at that. It was a pretty clear tell that she was being defensive when she used that setup. "Not that it matters." "Not that I care." "Not that it's any of your business." Pretty soon, she added, *Is that all you wanted?*

That seemed like a pretty leading question. But could I blame her for wanting an apology? Not really. It wasn't like that argument was entirely my fault, but she seemed a lot more upset by it than I was. So what should I say? Sorry I was a prick, you just caught me at a bad time? Sorry I snapped at you, it's just that you were trying to talk business and all I could think about was that dress—that dress looks fucking incredible on you, by the way, but obviously, that was part of the problem...

None of that would really help my case. So I finally wound up answering, *No. I wanted to let you know that even if the circumstances were fucked up and weird, I was glad to see you.* I sent that and waited a few minutes for an answer. Nothing. Ten minutes, still nothing. So I went on, *And I know I was kind of an ass to you at the club. I was taking out a bunch of unrelated shit on you. Which isn't cool.*

Ten more minutes, and still nothing. Was she just busy, or was she doing this on purpose? Did she want me to say more? Figuring it was better to be safe than sorry, I swallowed my pride and actually wrote the words "I'm sorry" before I went on,

It was weird for me seeing you all of a sudden when I was already dealing with all this work bullshit.

I mean, I wanted it to be a positive thing, us seeing each other. But I was already in such a shitty mood, so it was hard to, y'know, shift gears.

I'm not trying to make excuses or anything. Just telling you what happened.

This wasn't getting me anywhere. She still wasn't answering. Was I digging myself deeper into a hole or what? I needed some kind of feedback before I wound up totally sabotaging myself.

Hello? Are you getting these or what?

Sofia?

Can you *please* say something?

I was starting to get irritated and trying to avoid writing something more aggressive when she answered: *You're so cute when you beg.* She even added a little heart emoji at the end.

So my apology worked, at least, but that didn't stop my face from turning bright red. She *was* just stringing me along, waiting for me to say exactly the right thing. As always. At least when we were together before, she would tell me what she wanted to hear. But I couldn't be too bothered; if it meant she wasn't pissed at me anymore, that was good enough. The question was where that left us, and I was forced to ask myself again what I was trying to do with her.

As I was thinking about how to respond, Whitney leaned over and hissed, "You are being *so* rude right now." I rolled my eyes but put my phone back in my pocket for the last few minutes of the movie. Sofia could wait a while herself. As the movie came to a close and a weirdly young Jamie Lee Curtis sobbed into her hands, I glanced down at Whitney. She looked totally unfazed, even a little bored.

"So?" I asked once the credits started playing and the lights came back on in the theater. "Was it everything you were hoping for?"

"It was all right," Whitney said with a shrug. "I just watched the new one last month, so I want to see the old ones too. I think this place is playing the second one, maybe next week. Can we see that one too?"

"You want to come back here?" I asked, looking around the almost depressingly-small room.

"Come on, it's not that bad. I think it's kind of a cute place." She must have been going through that phase rich kids had where they thought cheap things were novel and somehow more interesting.

"I mean, I don't see how else you're going to get here, so yeah, I guess I'll bring you."

She insisted on staying until the credits were over, even though I promised her there was nothing to see afterward. On our way out, I checked my phone again and found another text from Sofia. *Have you been thinking about all that since last weekend? Or were you just bored today and looking for something to do?*

Oh, I could think of a few things to do with her. *A little of column A, a little of column B.*

As we got back in the car, Whitney finally asked, "Who are you texting?"

"Huh? No one." Why was I embarrassed by the question? I wasn't sure, but Whitney's smug little smile didn't help.

"Do you have a girlfriend or something? I saw what you were saying in there while you were rudely texting during the movie."

"What, and it's totally polite to read other people's private conversations?" I was just lucky I hadn't said anything suggestive. Yet.

"That's the thing about rudeness; it just causes more rudeness. So who was it?"

"You're so pushy," I muttered, refusing to look at her as I drove.

"I hear it runs in the family."

With a heavy sigh, I conceded, "Her name is Sofia. I've known her since we were kids."

"And," Whitney prompted, "what did you do to her? Why were you apologizing?"

"I just…said some shit I shouldn't have. You're not getting more detail than that, so don't ask." Neither of us spoke for a few seconds as Whitney messed with the radio, playing some kind of British punk rock from her phone. She was really taking this rebel phase seriously.

"So do you like her or something? Like, is she girlfriend material?" she asked expectantly, and I snorted a laugh.

"The hell do you know about 'girlfriend material'?"

"I'm just trying to figure out what's going on in your life, Myles," she teased in a concerned parent voice that reminded me way too much of Royce. "I feel like I hardly know you anymore."

"Oh my God, stop," I snickered. "Look, I don't know what kind of material she is, all right? Do I 'like her or something'? Yeah, definitely something. But it's complicated, so I don't know if there's any point trying to make something happen."

"Okay, well, you apologized to her," Whits pointed out, "and you don't apologize to anyone. Ever. So I feel like that says something." I reached over and shoved her braids into her face again.

"Thanks for the advice, love doctor."

But I had to admit, that was a valid point. And it was one I was already very well aware of: Sofia made me react to things weirdly. Not like myself. She was one of the only people on Earth who could make me feel guilty. Even when I knew my behavior was shitty, most of the time, I just accepted that. It was my personality. But with her, it was...different. Which was part of the reason being around her made me uncomfortable.

By the time we got back to the house, Whitney already had me 75% convinced to say "fuck work" and play video games with her. But once we got inside, it became clear that wasn't an option. Nathan was there waiting, looking even more tense than usual, and he fixed his eyes on me immediately. "Myles. We need to talk."

"Uh, okay. Let's talk," I agreed, cocking my head at him. He glanced at Whitney, who quickly took the hint and headed up to her room with a disappointed sigh. "What's going on?"

"Come with me." Nate led me down the hall into the east wing where all the non-guest bedrooms were, right to

Gregorio's room. He paused at the closed door and turned to me again. "You might want to brace yourself."

"The hell are you talking about?"

He just shook his head and opened the door. The smell of blood hit me along with the color, red smeared all over Gregorio's bed and part of the wall. He was lying propped up on the bed, barely recognizable from how badly he'd been beaten. "Holy fuck," I muttered as I stepped inside. There was a doctor by the bed trying to clean up the blood from Greg's face. When he saw me, Gregorio tried to say my name, but it came out muffled and slurred. Embarrassed, he tried to turn away from me, and the doctor snapped at him not to move.

Growing up how I did, and especially in the last few years, I'd seen blood. I'd seen stab wounds and gunshot wounds, poisonings, hangings, beatings—but this was my brother. I'd never seen any of that happen to my own brother, not like this. This was obviously done by a group, an *armed* group, and judging by the swelling of his face and his wheezing breath, he was lucky to even be fucking alive. His right hand was visibly deliberately broken. Whoever did this did it with a very specific purpose. And like hell was I going to let it stand.

"What the fuck happened to him?" I snarled at Nathan.

"Carter found him like this at aMoral. From what I can tell, no one saw it happen. But if I had to guess, all things considered," Nate said icily, staring Gregorio down, "I would say he probably picked a fight with some of the visiting Council members or their people." Greg immediately sat up to protest, but he could barely form a word.

"Gregorio, your jaw is broken, *please* stop trying to talk," the doctor begged.

"Relax," I told him. I would've put a hand on his

shoulder or something, but I didn't want to make any of his injuries worse. Looking back at Nathan, I went on, "He wouldn't."

"No? He seemed awfully set on it last week."

"He's not an idiot," I said, shaking my head. "He wouldn't have picked a fight just for the hell of it when he knew he was outnumbered. And he wasn't serious about that whole 'wipe out the Council' thing. He was just talking shit because he was pissed off." I looked at Greg, and he gave a small nod, attempting to keep his head as still as possible. It wasn't hard for me to know all that, because I was exactly the same way four years ago. But nothing like this had ever happened to me when I was his age, and it just felt like one more thing I had somehow done wrong.

That feeling only got worse when Rena rushed into the room and collapsed into tears by the bed. I wanted to try to help somehow, be there for her, but I almost felt like I didn't have the right. It was my shitty leadership that had let this happen; no one would've tried something like this if my dad were still around. If Royce were around. But with me, they thought they could get away with it.

Fuck that.

6

SOFIA

Myles took a lot longer than I expected to text me back, maybe trying to give me a taste of my own medicine. Okay, it might have been a little mean to tease him like I had, but I didn't want to make the apology too easy on him either. When he did finally answer me, the message wasn't what I expected.

Can I see you?

That was almost dangerously direct, considering our usual pattern of dancing around each other for a while. Our previous conversation had been going in a kind of flirty direction, I guess, but surely, he wasn't expecting me to drive all the way to San Diego at 9 p.m. to sleep with him?

Right now? Where?

He answered me barely a minute later. *It doesn't matter. I'll come to you. When it rains, it fucking pours, you know? There's a lot going on over here.*

If I wasn't mistaken, it almost sounded like he was directly asking for my help. Or emotional support, at least. Were things so bad with his family that he couldn't rely on any of them? Whatever had happened, if he needed me, I absolutely wanted to be there for him.

Okay. But you probably shouldn't come to the house...

...

Around eleven, I was pacing the hotel room I'd rented for the night, nervously checking my phone every few minutes. Everything about this was so strangely familiar, but the mood was significantly darker than those few carefree nights we'd spent in London. He hadn't said much about what was going on, but he was clearly upset in a way I hadn't seen him often. I just hoped I could hold back the side of me that always looked for ways to argue with him, at least long enough to help him get to a better place mentally.

At his knock, I jumped but hurried over to the door to unlock it. Myles came in looking like an utter mess. He'd lost his tie and his jacket at some point, leaving him in a half-unbuttoned dress shirt with rolled-up sleeves and...was that blood? His hair had fallen to the side, more like he used to wear it when we were younger, and he raked it back out of his eyes.

"Hey," I said cautiously, locking the door behind him. "Do you want to sit down?" I gestured to one of the two queen-sized beds, and he nodded absently as he wandered over to one of them. Kicking his shoes off, he collapsed to sit and then dropped his head into his hands. Seeing him like this was so unnerving; where was the brash, confident Myles I knew? I crawled up to sit next to him on the bed and ran a hand down his arm. "What's going on?"

"A lot," he repeated. He hesitated for a few seconds as if he was unsure of where to start or how much to tell me. "You know how many people have told me what a shitty job

I'm doing of this? How much better off we were with my dad in charge? I know Gemma's said it plenty of times." I didn't bother confirming that thought, but it was definitely true.

"Fuck what Gemma says," I told him, and he let out a dry chuckle. I still didn't know exactly what had happened with his dad, mostly because I had avoided finding out the exact details. All I knew was that Deron had gone missing, then he'd been found and confirmed dead. And ever since, the criticism of Myles's leadership had just been getting worse and worse. "You're doing everything you can, I'm sure. It's not an easy job or a simple one...at least based on the little I understand of it."

"I told you I was sorry for that."

"But you were right. I was never trained to become a boss someday. Neither were you. How could you possibly have been prepared for it if no one prepared you?" My hand was slowly moving back and forth across his shoulders, trying to offer whatever small comfort I could. It seemed like they had gotten a little more solid since the last time I'd touched them—not that that was something to think about right now! *Ugh, what is wrong with me?*

"I've been doing it for years now. Learning as I go. Trial by fire. Why am I still not good enough?" That question felt a lot broader than this conversation implied, and I wasn't sure how to answer it. I moved in a little closer to wrap my arms around one of his and rest my head on his shoulder. After a few seconds, he added, "I never apologized for bailing on you in London. Since I'm apparently in a bad mood today,"—he let out a mirthless laugh—"I'm sorry for that too." I stroked my thumb slowly against his arm.

"Why did you?" I asked. "What did I say that bothered you so much?"

"It wasn't you," he said hastily, sitting up to look at me.

Maybe this subject was an easier one to address. "Really. It was me and the way I get around you. I mean, not because of anything you do wrong. It's just—I don't know. You make it hard for me to be a selfish asshole."

I had to suppress a laugh. "And that's bad?"

"It's just not what I'm used to, so it freaks me out." He shrugged vaguely. "I feel less like myself when I'm around you—but honestly, maybe that's not a bad thing."

"I think you're more like yourself. And less like whatever it is you think you're supposed to be." That came out more dramatic than I'd intended, but I didn't take it back. "I like the way you get around me." I leaned down and kissed him softly, briefly. There was a split-second of uncertainty, then I found myself locked in a deeper kiss with him, grasping at his shoulders to stay as close as possible.

He wasted no time about dragging me into his lap, pulling my leg over to his other side so I was straddling him. Myles's kisses were never slow or gentle; he was too impatient for that. He kissed me like he wanted something, and his hands sliding up my thighs, pushing up my skirt, told me what. I wasn't about to lie and say I didn't want the same thing, but I wasn't sure if now was the right time.

"Myles?" I breathed, tilting my head back as he kissed my neck instead. "If you aren't feeling—I mean, if you're still upset—"

"I'm fine." He pulled back a little and raised an eyebrow at me. "You asked me to meet you at a hotel room. Don't act like you weren't expecting this." His hands pushed higher up my legs, underneath my skirt, and he grabbed my ass. Realizing I was wearing a thong, he grinned at me knowingly, but I avoided his eyes. So maybe I had dressed for the *possibility* that we would end up like this. He didn't have to be so presumptuous about it. Leaning in close, he ran his tongue up my neck and added softly, "Don't be shy, kitten. I promise you're not twisting my arm."

"Mm, don't call me that," I mumbled, taking in a quick gasp when he bit down on my neck.

"Or what?" he purred. This little power struggle of ours was a dynamic we'd developed on our first night together, and it was what made him so different from any other man I'd slept with. That he wasn't afraid to push me. "You seemed to like it before."

"It's been a while. Maybe I changed my mind." I slid my fingers up the back of his neck and into his hair, letting him cover my neck with open-mouthed kisses but being sure to keep an eye on him; he would leave marks all over me if I didn't stop him, and those would be a little harder to explain while living at my dad's house.

"Or maybe you're just trying to be difficult." Whenever he picked a spot on my shoulder and started to spend too much time there, sucking a little too hard like he wanted to give me a hickey, I yanked on his hair, and he growled back at me.

"Ah, ah." I sat back to look him in the eye, relishing the contention all over his face. "You know the rules. Play nice or you're not getting anything."

"Fine," he grunted, "so tell me what's okay." Satisfied that he was being obedient—for the moment—I rewarded him by sitting up to pull my loose top up and off over my head. His eyes roamed over every inch of newly-exposed skin, and his fingers dug into my legs, itching to get the rest of my clothes off.

Sliding one of my bra straps off my shoulder, I teased, "Do you want to help me with this?" Without bothering to answer, he yanked me closer and reached around me to get at the hooks. "Mph. You're so impatient."

"Can't eat candy with the wrapper still on." He flashed me another smirk as he tore my bra off and tossed it aside, then bent down to worship my breasts with his mouth, kissing down one curve and licking slowly along another. He caught one nipple between his teeth and lavished it with his tongue while sliding his hand up my waist to grope my other breast. Shivering from the sudden cold and arching my back for more, I tugged at his shirt to keep him close. His free hand reached around my backside and between my legs, fingertips rubbing slowly up and down my pussy through my panties.

"Myles!" I leaned forward a little by reflex, and he chuckled as he caught my lips for another deep kiss. With him touching me like that, I was moaning into his mouth with every breath, leaning heavily against his chest to wrap my arms around his neck.

"I knew there was a way to shut you up," he teased, and I pouted at him but didn't bother arguing. Instead, I slowly outlined his ear with my tongue, nipping at his earlobe and treating him to more soft, breathless moans. He got bolder and slipped his fingertips underneath my panties to touch me properly. I was already getting wet, and he couldn't resist pushing two fingers inside me, tearing a yelp from my lips and sending another spike of hot pleasure through me.

"Y-you could have...asked first," I whimpered, already rocking my hips down against his hand for more friction. We both knew my protesting was just another part of the game; I *loved* it when he was pushy. Which made our controlling, back-and-forth power trips all the more interesting.

"Yeah, I'm bad about that." He was sliding his fingers in and out as he spoke, slowly enough that it felt like torture. "I can stop if you want."

"Don't you dare," I groaned. Trying to work past my distraction, I focused on getting his shirt unbuttoned, splaying my hands over his chest and running my tongue up his neck. "I mean. Unless you're going to give me something better." My hand wandered down to rest on his crotch, and he sucked in a sharp breath, already rock-hard. I clucked my tongue at him with a teasing smile. "You got so excited just from touching me. You like playing with my pussy that much?"

He shivered while my hand slowly stroked him through his pants. "What can I say? I missed you." Another brief kiss, then he slipped his fingers out of me and nodded toward the bed. "Now why don't you get comfortable so I can fuck you? Or did you just wanna do it like this?" He ran his hand down my thigh, streaking my own wetness across my skin and smirking devilishly at my embarrassment.

"Like you don't get frustrated when I'm on top," I said as I crawled out of his lap to push my skirt and panties off. I let them drop unceremoniously to the floor and saw Myles swallow hard as he looked me up and down. While he hastily stripped out of his own clothes, I went to grab a condom from my purse (and check one more time that the door was locked). When I came back and handed him the condom, he made a face but took it nevertheless.

"You weren't worried about it last time," he remarked as he put it on, but he recognized this as non-negotiable. As much as I wanted him, as much as I had missed him, after all this time, I couldn't say yet that he had my full trust. So for the moment, the rule would stand.

"I know, now you won't enjoy this at all," I teased, shaking my hair out over my shoulders and running my fingertips up his leg.

His eyes narrowed. "If you don't get in this fucking bed..."

"Then what?" I asked sweetly, trying to provoke him into making a move. "What are you going to do about it?" Answering my challenge exactly the way I'd hoped, he grabbed me around my waist and dragged me into the bed to shove me down on my back. As hard as I tried, I couldn't keep from giggling as he knelt over me and pushed my legs apart.

"You're such a brat," he said, lifting my hips a little to slide the tip of his cock along my wet slit, then thrusting in, quick but not too deep. Hearing my sharp gasp of shock, he pulled back, then slid in again, a little farther, building up a rhythm and fucking his way deeper inside me. "Shit..."

I stole a look up at him and loved the way he was watching me, the dark, messy hair falling into his face, the hazy admiration in his eyes. Wanting to see more of that, to know I was doing something for him that he couldn't find anywhere else, I took his hand and pulled it up to my lips. When I ran my tongue up his fingers and took them in my mouth to suck on them, he groaned and fucked me harder, leaning over me on his free hand and pushing his fingers deeper. I gladly let him have his way, struggling to keep track of my breath while he was making this so good. I would've told him how much I liked it, even begged for more—but a lady doesn't talk with her mouth full. So instead, I just hoped my deep, wanton moans were enough to get across how well he was doing.

"Hm. I missed that too," he said, pulling his hand away from my mouth and leaving my lips shining wet.

"Wh-what?" I asked, trying and failing to keep my voice down and avoid stroking his already over-inflated ego.

"That look you get on your face when I'm fucking you."

His hand slid up my neck to grasp just under my jaw, not tight enough that I couldn't breathe, but enough to keep me grounded and force me to look at him. With a devious smirk, he went on, "It's this cute, cock-drunk, 'fuck me' look. You don't do it anywhere else." Burning hot embarrassment flooded my cheeks, while a similarly hot guilty pleasure rushed to my hips.

"You're...such a pig," I managed, but he just laughed at me.

"Tell me about it, princess." As I started to answer him, he hooked his hands under my legs and shoved them back against the bed so his thrusts went even deeper, and my sassy retort came out as a choked cry instead.

"*God!*" Since I couldn't reach him to get my arms around his neck, I stretched out and arched my back, giving him a more irritated version of that "fuck me" look he liked so much. "Ugh. You're so—aggravating. If you're that good, why don't you prove it and make me cum already?"

Myles was never one to shy away from a challenge. Without bothering to speak, he pinned my legs down harder and fucked me faster, knowing all that friction would get to me quickly. But judging by the hitch in his panting breath, punctuated with grunts and short moans, it must have been getting to him too.

"Shit." He wouldn't look me in the eye, keeping up his quick rhythm as his chest and shoulders started to shine with sweat. Even if he didn't say it, his body language told me he was getting close.

"Mm, what's the matter, Myles? You're not going to cum before me, are you?" I teased. He shot me a glare, and I let out a breathless laugh. "Here, let me help." Keeping my eyes on his, I licked my fingertips and reached down to touch myself, quickly realizing I was a lot more worked up than I'd thought. Myles hissed in a breath and bent down to kiss me hard, forcing his tongue into my mouth and keeping his hips thrusting fast against mine. My free hand grabbed at his hair again while my moans got higher-pitched, more desperate, until I practically screamed against his lips and came around his cock. His last few thrusts, slow and deliberate, said that was enough to push him over the edge too.

When he did finally let me go, his lips were red, like I assumed mine were, and we both took a second to catch our breath. I sat up shakily to kiss his cheek, drawing the corner of his mouth into a slight smile. "Good talk," I managed with a laugh. "I'm glad you asked."

"Ditto." Another quick kiss, and he pulled out to sit next to me on the bed. "Guess you'll want to take your shower now?" My smile faded as I considered. As exhausted as I was, I hated going to sleep all sweaty right after sex.

"You should come with me," I suggested, pushing myself up to a sitting position.

"Didn't I already?" he snickered.

"Ha, ha." I rolled my eyes and slowly but surely crawled out of the bed. "Fine, sit there and stay gross if you want, but I'm not sleeping next to you like that." Hoping the shaking of my legs wasn't visible, I went into the bathroom, piled my hair up on top of my head, and opened up the shower's glass door. As steam started rising in the spacious tiled box around me, I forced myself to think about what had just happened.

And I felt like an idiot. Hadn't I been telling myself for a week that this was a bad idea? But then, like he'd said before, he was there, we were alone, and my willpower could only hold out for so long. Ever since I first slept with him in London, it was impossible to be around him without wanting to do it again. Part of me very stubbornly and adamantly insisted that it was purely because of his attitude and his dick, and I wanted very much to agree with her. Another, smaller part of me had something else to say, something I wasn't ready to address yet, even after ten years of avoiding the subject.

My thoughts were interrupted by the door opening behind me, and I tensed up before realizing that Myles had decided to join me in the shower after all. As he stepped in close behind me and wrapped his arms around my waist, I shivered. "You're freezing!"

"Mm-hm." I could already hear the sleepiness in his voice, meaning he had forced himself out of bed despite his exhaustion just to stand there with me for a few minutes. That small voice I'd been trying to ignore cleared her throat pointedly, and I told her to shut up yet again. "Didn't want you kicking me out of bed for being 'gross.'"

"Good call." With little help from Myles himself, I washed the smell of sex and sweat off both of us, then prodded him back out into the bathroom to dry off. It was obvious how tired he was; he didn't bother arguing with me about any of my directions. I retrieved the spare panties and nightgown I'd brought—okay, yes, maybe I *was* expecting us to end up in bed together—and Myles grabbed his boxer-briefs from where he'd discarded them on the floor. We climbed into the other bed, and he practically dragged me into his arms. I liked his insistence too much to bother pushing him away.

7

MYLES

Sofia wasn't generally a clingy person. You might think because she was the youngest child and everyone babied her, she'd get used to being held, but she was too independent for that. Or maybe she just didn't like being touched unnecessarily. Point is, when I woke up with her using my chest as a pillow, it threw me a little. I thought about waking her up just to make fun of her, but I didn't have the energy yet. After all, she'd tired me out pretty thoroughly the night before. Demanding as ever. But damned if it wasn't worth it.

When I'd called her the night before, it wasn't because I wanted sex. I just wanted to be *with* her. I wanted to not be alone but also not be with my family and everything they expected of me. Being with Sofia didn't feel like a responsibility, like I owed her something—at least once I'd muscled through those two apologies she deserved. Now that the air between us was clear, I could enjoy being around her again. But the sex did make it a little more complicated.

It seemed like we had both accepted the fact that we wanted each other. No point trying to pretend otherwise. But us being honest about it didn't change any of the many other reasons it wouldn't work. Even as I was telling myself this shouldn't happen again, I realized I was subconsciously running my hand through Sofia's hair and enjoying the smell of her shampoo. Trying to discourage myself from getting in any deeper than I already was, I cleared my throat and carefully moved away from her, trying to put some distance between us so I could think straight.

But she noticed as soon as I moved, and she let out a whine of protest, scooting even closer. What the hell was I supposed to do with that? A few seconds later, she groaned and sat up a little to look at me. "Hm. Good morning." She smiled, and I had to look away to resist kissing her. "Something wrong?"

"No, it's just...uh, I should probably head back to San Diego soon," I said, even though I had no idea what time it was.

"Oh. Right." She made sure not to show it, but I still got the feeling she probably didn't like the idea of me leaving so suddenly. "Do you have plans or something? Something you need to get done?"

"I mean, just work in general, I guess."

"So..." She looked up at me again, and her smile had turned a little less innocent. "It could probably wait an extra hour or so, right?" Her hand slid up the inside of my thigh, and I had to force down a shiver.

"That's probably not a good idea." The tone of my voice probably made it obvious how reluctant I was to turn her down. She didn't seem discouraged, moving a little closer and reaching across me to take my hand.

"Are you sure?" she asked, pulling it over to rest high up on her thigh so my fingertips brushed the hem of her panties. I remembered that little nightgown she'd had on the night before, her hands all over me in the shower, and I let my hand wander to grab her ass as my cock twitched at the thought. How did she get to me so fast? "That's what I thought. I'll even be generous and do all the work for you." She slowly, pointedly licked her lips, and another jolt of excitement shot through me, straight to my dick. That mouth of hers was fucking incredible; if that was what she was offering, how could I say no?

Obviously, I thought as she slid one hand into my boxers to stroke me, *I can't*.

Her tits pressed up against my chest, and I leaned down to try to kiss her, but she turned away. Oh, right. She had a thing about kissing right after we woke up, one of her "rules" about sex. As much as I normally disliked being told what I could and couldn't do, this was one of the few exceptions; even beyond the fact that I didn't want to make her uncomfortable, sometimes her giving orders was kind of hot.

I settled for dropping my head a little to kiss her neck instead, trying and failing to keep my hips still while her hand quickly got me hard. I almost wondered what had put her in the mood, if she'd had a dirty dream or something, but this didn't seem like the time to ask. Not when she was pushing the covers back and crawling over to kneel between my legs. She pulled my shorts down a little, then held my cock steady with one hand and looked up into my eyes as she ran her tongue slowly around the head.

"Shit." I couldn't have looked away even if I'd wanted to as she lowered her head to lick around the base, her palm slick with saliva and pumping slowly up and down. Her tongue explored every inch of my dick like she was trying to memorize the shape, then she closed her lips over the tip, and I had to bite back another swear from how hot she was. She took her hand back and slowly dropped her head little by little, bobbing up and down to take more every time. "Fuck yeah. Just like that, kitten." She made a sound, but it came out sort of muffled; I couldn't tell whether it was embarrassment or enjoyment. Either way, she didn't stop.

There was only a brief pause once her mouth was full, then she tilted her head a little to let my cock slide down her throat, taking every inch until her lips were flush with my hips. I sucked in a quick breath but forced myself to stay still. The last thing I wanted was to hurt her when she was being so fucking good. "Holy shit," I groaned, hands clenching into fists as she carefully pulled back, then plunged back down and sent heat rushing through me again like I hadn't felt in three years. Sofia moaned deeply, seeming happy with my reaction. It was embarrassing how turned on I was already.

Her hair fell in her eyes, and she made a sound of irritation, trying to push it away without getting spit and precum in it. I reached over to help her gather it up, but she waved my hand away and sat up to wipe her mouth, glancing at me suspiciously. "What?" I asked. "You think I'm gonna hold you down or something?"

"Wouldn't be the first time," she said as she grabbed the clip she'd used to hold her hair up the night before.

"Uh, yeah, because you said it was okay last time. You know, I'm not gonna do that shit if you don't want it." She *did* know that, didn't she? Or had I fucked up badly enough that she really didn't trust me anymore?

"Of course, you won't. You know better. But you're supposed to be letting me take care of everything, remember?" She crawled back to her spot between my legs and pinned me to the bed by my shoulders to kiss my cheek. "So relax." With her reassurance and that little smile she gave me, it was hard to stay irritated—and even more so with her mouth on my cock. She really made it impossible for me to focus on anything but her.

She was as good with her mouth as I remembered. Her rhythm was slow, but because she took me so deep every time, there was still plenty of friction. I had to stop myself more than once from holding her still and thrusting into her mouth, but it's not like I was suffering. After a minute or so, she started moaning steadily along with me, and I saw her touching herself while her head bobbed on my cock. As if this wasn't hot enough already.

Based on the way her moans built up and then overflowed into breathless whimpers, I figured she came twice before I got mine, and she dropped her head again to let me cum down her throat. At that point, I couldn't help grabbing a fistful of her hair, but I made sure I wasn't pushing her down any harder. I didn't need to, the way she took it all on her own.

"Fuck," I muttered again as she carefully sat up and wiped her mouth again, visibly shaking. I tried to reach for her, to pull her back down to the bed, but she shook her head with a weak smile and got to her feet. She nearly collapsed on the way to the bathroom, probably dizzy from all that motion, and she giggled breathlessly as she straightened up. It bothered me a little that she left, even though I knew she hated leaving her face or hands "messy" after sex. I wanted her there in the bed with me. And God, the thought of leaving was so unappealing, not even because I wanted to fuck her, just because I wanted to be there.

"Ugh, my hair is such a mess," she groaned from the bathroom. She came back out drying her face with a towel and grabbed a bottle of carbonated water from the minibar. I watched her open it and take a sip, then let out a contented sigh. And I realized that I wasn't checking out her cleavage or her thighs. I was looking at her face, her eyes, her smile.

Shit.

Sofia caught me staring, and that smile widened as she came back to the bed to offer me her water bottle. I took a drink despite knowing I hate carbonated water, just because my mouth had gotten dry all of a sudden. "You okay?" she asked as she set it aside. "I left the room and you got all quiet."

"Just thinking." That was putting it mildly. I was thinking of a million things at once, and they all had to do with her. Being there with her, the two of us getting along, I felt better than I had in months. More at ease. Over the past four years, that feeling had gotten nearly impossible to find. How could I not jump at the chance for it now? "Listen, I know it's kind of awkward with the distance and all, but could we maybe...do this again? I mean, not this, not meet at a hotel room for some weird discussion about work, just—see each other. Anywhere. We could do dinner or whatever. Is that...something you might want to do?" I glanced over at her, hoping I looked and sounded casual but knowing I was doing a shit job of it. Sofia was biting her lip, smiling slyly.

"It almost sounds like you're asking me on a date, Myles. Is that what I'm hearing?"

"If I say 'yes,' are you gonna say 'no'?"

She tossed her head back and laughed. "No. I think 'dinner or whatever' sounds nice. Get back to me with more details, and I'll see when I'm available." She leaned down and kissed me briefly, and I was about to pull her into my arms when my phone rang from across the room. It was still where I'd left it in my pants pocket. But the ringtone said it was Nathan calling me, so I forced myself to answer.

"Yeah?" I said while Sofia looked at me curiously, probably wondering why I bolted out of bed like that.

"Where the hell are you?" Nathan demanded.

"Uh, I'm in L.A. Why? What's going on?"

My adviser let out a heavy sigh from his side of the phone. "Think about this, Myles: a week ago, the Council, the four most powerful mafia families in the western United States, declared that we've pissed them off. More specifically, *you've* pissed them off. Yesterday, one of our soldiers, who happens to be your younger brother, was brutally attacked, beaten within an inch of his life. So when I got up this morning and no one knew where you were, you hadn't left a note, your usual car is still here—"

"I get it, I get it," I said, running a hand through my hair. I hadn't thought about any of that or how it would look the night before. I just needed to get away, to talk to someone I'd hoped would understand. "But I'm fine, okay? I'll be back in a couple hours."

"What are you doing in L.A. of all places?" Nate insisted, sounding a little suspicious.

"Nothing. I'm about to head back." I balanced my phone on my shoulder, gathering my clothes from the floor.

"Please tell me you aren't with Sofia."

I looked at her again, and she cocked her head at me in confusion. "So what if I am?"

"If you are, you should leave. Now. I was just informed that the Lucianos were involved in the attack on Gregorio." A pause. "If she was the one who asked you to meet her—"

"That's not what happened. Look, we'll talk when I get back, okay?"

"Fine. Try not to die between now and then," he said flatly.

"Is something wrong?" Sofia asked when I ended the call.

"No. I mean, no more than usual. But I really do need to head back. The family can't do shit without someone telling them how." I was buttoning my shirt as she came to sit at the end of the bed.

"Are we...still on for that date?"

"What? Yeah, of course." Did she just assume I was going to drop her without warning at some point? Once I was dressed, I kissed her briefly—but she grabbed my shirt and dragged me back for a deeper kiss. "I'll get back to you about it soon."

"You'd better."

...

Nathan still wasn't happy with me when I got back to the house.

"So you *were* with Sofia?" he asked for a third time since I still hadn't given him a direct answer.

"Yes, all right? I was with her." I was still paranoid my clothes smelled like sex, so I was in my closet changing while he stood in my room waiting to talk business. "But I told you, I was the one who asked her to meet. And what the hell makes you think she had anything to do with Gregorio getting attacked anyway? Even if her family was involved—"

"If her family was involved, she was probably involved. She does work for them, Myles. You know that. And why did you call her to begin with? Were you trying to see if she knew anything about what happened?"

I didn't answer. Nathan only had a vague understanding of my relationship with the Lucianos. If it had been Royce or Roger I was talking to, they would've known exactly why

I'd called Sofia, and they would've known it had nothing to do with her family. "Tell me about this information you got," I called back to him, picking out a watch that matched the rest of my outfit. *Looking* put-together went a long way toward making me *feel* put-together. "You said the Lucianos were 'involved.' What does that mean?"

"It means the people who attacked Gregorio were members of their family. We don't have names, but we checked the club's security footage for the period when the attack took place," Nathan explained, mercifully dropping the Sofia subject for now. "It was around 7 p.m. There isn't much traffic around that time, so we ran all the license plates in and out. All of them were ours except one. That one belongs to Marcell Luciano."

Maybe it wasn't the most definitive proof I'd ever heard, but it was pretty damn suggestive. "But why would Marcell order something like that? He was a dick to me at the Council meeting, sure, but I didn't do anything to him personally. Greg didn't do anything to him. If he was going to attack anyone, it should've been me."

It should've been me...

"You're harder to get to," Nathan pointed out. "Maybe it was intended as a warning. Maybe they're planning to go after you next. Who knows? Regardless, I think we can say with some certainty that the Lucianos are our enemies at this point."

And that made me trying to date one of them a lot more complicated.

"Uncle Myles?" If it weren't for her using the word "uncle," I wouldn't have recognized Whitney's voice; I wasn't sure I'd ever heard her sound so small and weak. Shrugging my jacket on, I came back into my bedroom to see her in the doorway, looking uncharacteristically nervous.

"Hey, Whits. What's going on?"

"She was worried about you," Nathan said. Normally, Whitney hated it when anyone else tried to speak for her, but in this case, she just nodded. "She was the first one to realize you weren't here this morning."

"My judo class was canceled, so I wanted us to do something today," she explained. "But you weren't in your office. Or in your room. Or in the dining room or by the pool or at the range. I asked all the staff and Rena and Nathan, but no one knew where you were. And I knew what happened to Gregorio. And I thought..." I could see tears welling up in her eyes as she sniffled to try to keep them at bay.

"Hey, hey, it's okay," I said, coming over to kneel in front of her. "Look at me. I'm totally fine. I didn't mean—"

"Where were you?" she snapped, suddenly turning her fear into anger. *She's a Moretti, all right.*

"I was..." Was telling the truth dangerous here? Obviously, I wasn't about to say exactly what went on with me and Sofia, but if I mentioned her, would Whitney assume it on her own? The absolute last thing I wanted was to have the birds-and-the-bees talk with my thirteen-year-old niece. "I was with Sofia. I needed someone to talk to, and she was the one who came to mind." I heard a scoff behind me and could picture Nathan shaking his head. Whitney's glare softened a little.

"You could've said something," she said, scrubbing away any lingering tears from her eyes.

"Yeah, I probably should've. I'll keep it in mind next time."

"There shouldn't be a next time," Nate muttered, and I rolled my eyes.

"Why not?" Whitney asked. Before he could answer, she

jabbed a finger at him and added, "And don't say 'it's complicated.' I'm so bloody tired of hearing that."

"Even if it is?" he asked.

"Still, it's not a real answer. 'It's complicated' is just an excuse for you not to properly explain. *Or* it means you think the person you're talking to—that's me right now—is too dumb to understand." She had reclaimed all her usual attitude and stuck her hands to her hips, giving him a challenging look. "Is that what you think?"

"All right, kids, that's enough," I said, getting to my feet and waving them both off. "Whits, you said you wanted to do something today, right? Since I was an inconsiderate shithead, pick whatever you want, and we'll do it." All her sass dissolved immediately into a grin, and she bolted down the hall, probably to get her laptop and figure out what was going on in town.

"Please don't forget that you have a job," Nathan said, following me out of my room. "I'll be looking into exactly who was involved in the attack. Once we have names, we'll need to do something about it."

I couldn't imagine Sofia had been involved at all. But if she was…I couldn't just ignore it.

8

SOFIA

Antoni might've had his mom's eyes and his dad's nose, but that pout on his face, he definitely inherited from me. Nadine had asked me to help quiz him on some of the lessons he'd been getting from his dad and grandpa, but it was obvious he hadn't been absorbing a whole lot of information from those lessons. We asked him about the family's structure, and he shrugged. We asked if he remembered the rest of the Council, and he shook his head. We asked if he knew about the jobs anyone in the family did, and his face finally lit up as he explained all about my work—as a flight attendant. Not what I did for the family as an informant but the ins and outs of flying. Of course.

Nadine eventually got so frustrated that she left the two of us alone to talk, probably going to look for my brother and complain to him about how impossible his son was being. My nephew still had one of his little models in hand, and he played with it absently, pretending nothing was wrong.

"What's going on, kiddo?" I asked, sitting next to him on a couch in the sunroom. "You're so good at memorizing details. But you don't remember anything *Nonno* teaches you?"

He shrugged vaguely again. "It's boring stuff. My brain doesn't want to hold onto it."

Or maybe he just didn't want to know it. Trying to test a theory, I asked, "Come on, Toni, don't you want to be a good *sotto capo* like your dad?"

He blinked and frowned. "Dad's not a sotto capo. He's a regular capo. We only have one sotto capo, and it's *Prozio* Leon." He paused as he realized what he'd said, then quickly turned his eyes back down to his model, staring at it even harder and refusing to look at me.

"So you do remember," I concluded. Antoni didn't respond. "If you know all that, why do you act like you don't?" Again, he didn't answer, so I sat back with a sigh, sneaking a glance at my phone. Myles had texted me back, *I really don't think that's a good idea*, so I frowned and unlocked my phone to answer.

It had been another week or so since that night we'd spent in the hotel. In that time, I had only seen him twice—once at aMoral, then again at a restaurant in L.A...which led to a hotel later on—but we'd been talking every day. That morning, I had suggested he come over to talk with Papà since this whole Council thing was obviously still stressing him out. It wasn't like the two of them were strangers, and I knew my dad was reasonable. Myles could explain himself, and then Papà could talk to the rest of the Council on his behalf. Then, if everything went according to plan, we could patch up the relationship between our families, and it wouldn't be an issue that Myles and I were together.

In theory.

But for some reason, Myles was against that idea. I knew interactions like these could be delicate, and talking in person wasn't always the right way to go about solving problems, but what could it hurt to try? I texted back, *Why not? It could help. The rest of the Council trusts him. If he trusts you... shouldn't that be enough for them?*

Setting my phone down, I looked to Antoni again. "Talk to me, kiddo. What are you thinking?"

After another few seconds of silence, he finally spoke. "Dad doesn't have time for me. He's always busy. Zia Gemma said he'll spend more time teaching me if he thinks I don't get it."

Gemma was the one who told him to play dumb? Why would she do that? I couldn't believe it was out of a genuine desire to get him more quality time with Danny. Did she *want* Nadine to get frustrated with him? I couldn't figure out what she got out of this. But regardless, it sounded like there was a lack of communication between Danny and Antoni, and someone needed to do something about it. Gemma's solution didn't seem to be working. So that meant it was up to me.

"Even if he's busy, he still has time for you," I insisted. "I bet he would be happy to hear that you already know all this. Don't you want him to be proud of you?"

"Yeah. But if I tell him, then he'll think he doesn't have to teach me anymore."

"No, he'll just have new things to teach you," I assured him. "There's a lot to learn if you're going to fill his shoes someday. And the more you learn, the more you'll get to spend time with him because you'll be working *with* him. Doesn't that sound fun?"

"Maybe," Antoni said dubiously, rolling his little plane back and forth across his palm.

"Come on, I know you must be bored hearing the same lesson over and over again."

He nodded firmly at that.

"Then let's talk to your dad so you can keep learning new stuff."

Even though it was very slight, very hesitant, he did smile. "Okay. That sounds good."

...

The next day, I persuaded Danny to step away from work in order to have lunch with me, Nadine, and Antoni. I figured Gemma was probably too busy to go with us. Also, I didn't want her there. Marlon escorted us to one of our favorite restaurants in town, one that may or may not have been owned and operated by our family members. (Personally, I think restaurants are more useful in our business than nightclubs, but to each their own.)

Nadine seemed a lot more relaxed now that we were out of the house and both her boys were within her sight. She had always done her best to be the proper wife of the don, only marginally involved in the business but always around when Danny needed her to be. Most of her energy went into raising Antoni into the heir our family needed—but this afternoon was supposed to be a break, and she seemed grateful for it.

I regaled the three of them with some of the few kid-friendly stories from my job, and Danny jumped in here or there when someone he knew popped up in my retellings. He also had a few stories of his own, including some new ones about our Council guests, who had flown back home the week before. Despite the fact that he came up often in my mind, I didn't mention Myles. I didn't want to spoil Danny's good mood just before we had our discussion about Antoni. And besides, since Myles had agreed to come over and try talking to Papà, we would have plenty of time with him later.

"So, Antoni," I said casually, glancing over at him while he ate a plate of spaghetti with impeccable manners. "Can you remind me who Nonno's sotto capo is?"

"Come on, Sofi," Danny said with a frown. "Don't make him—"

"It's Prozio Leon," Antoni said, folding his napkin in his lap while his parents gawked at him.

"What about some of our other capos?" I prompted.

"*Cugino* Martin, Prozio James, Prozio Carter—"

"And all your dad's soldatos?"

Nadine and Danny listened in shock while Antoni rattled off all fourteen members of Danny's crew, first and last names, and relation to us where applicable. He seemed bashfully proud of their reaction, stealing nervous little glances at me while I smiled to encourage him. "Did you... teach him all that?" Nadine asked.

"He already knew it," I told her, shaking my head.

"Dad's told me a bunch of times," Antoni admitted. "I thought...if I pretended I didn't know it, you would spend more time teaching me. I'm sorry for lying." Nadine looked conflicted between frustration and confusion.

"I know I'm not here very often, so I can't really throw stones," I said, taking a sip of my water. "But it kind of sounds like Antoni doesn't get to spend as much time with you as he would like, Danny. And obviously you're busy, but maybe he could be around while you work? That might even help him learn more." My brother was frowning slightly, looking guilty.

"You could've said something," he told Antoni.

"Zia Gemma said it would bother you. So it was better to not say anything."

Gemma, again. What was she playing at? Danny exchanged a look of confused suspicion with me but turned his attention back to Antoni. "Next time, don't worry about bothering me, okay? I still wanna know what you're thinking." He reached over and ruffled Antoni's hair, and although he quickly smoothed it back into place, he was smiling again.

"Okay."

Once we got back to the house, I held Danny back from going inside. "Do you know why Gemma would tell him not to 'bother' you?" I asked. "Why would she go out of her way to keep him from speaking up?"

"No idea. But frankly, I can't claim to know what she's thinking even half the time," he said with a dry smile. "She has plans wrapped up in her plans, stuff us mortals just can't comprehend."

"Ha, ha." I rolled my eyes. Obviously, he wasn't taking this seriously—and maybe I was taking it *too* seriously. Maybe she was just being her controlling self, trying to keep every single aspect of the house in check. Like he said, it was pretty much impossible to tell.

Deciding that it was probably not a big deal, I headed up to my room and saw I had a text from Myles. *Otw.* That was from twenty minutes ago, so it would only be about an hour and a half before he got there and could start patching things up with Papà. Maybe he could stay for dinner. He and Danny would talk about cars and suits and shoes, then probably get into an argument and laugh at each other. It could be like before, back when we were all close. And just like before, he and I would make eyes at each other across the table, and then after dinner…

My imagination was completely running away with me. This whole little fantasy of mine was based on the assumption that he could show up and talk to Papà amiably, that they would get along and understand each other and he wouldn't say anything combative or offensive. When it came to Myles, that was sort of a lot to ask for. So instead of fantasizing, I just hoped, prayed, *begged* that this meeting would go well.

When I checked out the window again and saw Myles pull up in his beloved red Lamborghini, I hopped up and went downstairs to meet him. But when I got outside, I found Arturo waiting near the door, arms crossed, looking menacing. "Um, Arturo? Is something wrong?"

He threw me an over-the-shoulder glance. "You should go inside, Sofi. I have a trespasser to deal with."

"A trespasser?"

Myles smiled at me as he came up the walkway, but he quickly turned his attention to Arturo instead. "You're one of Marcell's guys, yeah? Did I do something wrong already?" He was joking, but Arturo didn't laugh.

"This is private property, you know. Don Luciano isn't expecting you, so you shouldn't be here."

"*I'm* expecting him," I pointed out, crossing my arms and trying not to get too indignant. Didn't I have at least a little authority here? "I invited him here."

Arturo blinked at me, frowning. "What? Why?"

"What does it matter to you?" Myles asked, looking him up and down disdainfully.

"It's my job to protect the family. Sofia's included in that, and you aren't the type of person she should be dealing with," Arturo answered with a sneer. Myles barked out a laugh.

"I didn't realize that was a judgment bodyguards got to make for their betters." Turning to me, he added, "Do you even know this guy?"

Arturo scoffed, and I suddenly realized this conversation was headed in a very bad direction. "She definitely knows me."

Myles's dark eyes narrowed, and he turned to me looking for an answer, which I hadn't quite formed yet. So he turned back to Arturo and took a step forward to growl, "What the fuck is that supposed to mean?"

Seeing the smug look on Arturo's face, I decided I had to step in before he could answer. "It means that Arturo and I used to be involved. In the past."

"Used to be?" he repeated, looking sort of bemused.

"Yes, used to. It's been about a year since then," I pointed out for both of them. As cute as it was for Myles to get all jealous and possessive over me, the last thing we needed here was more conflict. Myles's irritation faded quickly into amusement as he observed the look on Arturo's face.

"Oh, that's adorable," he said with relish. "You didn't even know she traded up."

Arturo drew up to his full height, a couple of inches taller than Myles's, and answered, "I wouldn't call *you* an upgrade."

"Of course, you wouldn't. Remind me again: who the hell are you?" Myles asked, cocking his head to one side, oblivious to my frustrated sigh. Even when he knew how ill-advised it was, even when he knew it wasn't appropriate to the situation, he just couldn't resist escalating a conflict. "Because the way I'm understanding it, you're pretty much nobody. You should consider yourself lucky she ever even looked at you. You didn't really think anything was going to happen between you two, did you?"

"Plenty happened, trust me."

"That's enough, both of you!" I snapped, wishing I could keep my cheeks from flushing as they were talking about me like territory to be marked. "Myles, you're not here to fight with anyone. Arturo, I asked him to come myself, so there's no reason for you to lock him out."

"These are Marcell's orders, Sofia. Sorry, but he outranks you." Arturo's gray eyes had turned cold, our relationship apparently going back to all business since he couldn't sleep with me anymore. While I was mustering up my best argument, the front door opened behind us, revealing Danny and Gemma both with sour looks on their faces.

"What are you doing here, Myles?" Danny asked, taking a step in front of me like he thought he was protecting me. Myles hadn't done anything wrong—other than being his snarky self—and they were acting like he'd killed someone!

"Ask your little sister," he said, nodding toward me. "I told her this was a bad idea, but she insisted I come. I guess Marcell's not on board with the plan."

Danny looked askance at me, so I took a step toward Myles and explained, "I wanted him and Papà to talk. Without the rest of the Council here. The Morettis have been our allies, our *friends*, for fifteen years! We can't throw that away just because Myles isn't his father."

"Or his brother," Gemma added, lips pursed.

"That doesn't mean he's not fit for the job," I hissed back at her. "Just because he doesn't have the experience that Deron did—"

"Wait." Danny held up a hand to stop me. "Is that why you think Dad's cutting ties with them?"

"Isn't it?" I asked. Danny raised an eyebrow at Myles, but when I looked back at him, he was avoiding my eyes. "What? What's going on?"

"I think you should go, Myles," Danny said, ignoring my questions.

To my surprise, Myles nodded. "Yeah, sure."

"What? Hang on!" I caught his arm as he started to walk away. "You don't have to leave. This is important."

"No, it is. But you need to know the whole thing before you keep advocating for me." He hesitated for a second, then leaned in and kissed my lips softly. "Listen to your brother. I'm sure he'll give it to you straight. Then, if you want, you and I can talk about it." I wanted to fight with him, to demand that he stay and explain himself—but he seemed so sad all of a sudden. It wasn't a mood I'd seen him in often, and I didn't know how to respond other than to let him go. As his car headed down the driveway, I rounded on my siblings.

"*What* is the big secret?"

Danny nodded toward the house. "Come inside and we'll talk. Thanks, Arturo." I went in with my siblings, not sparing a glance to my father's bodyguard. Since that was apparently all he was anymore. Despite Myles's advice that I should listen to Danny, Gemma decided she needed to be a part of this conversation too. The three of us sat together in the sunroom, and Danny took off his jacket to hang it over the back of the couch. "Do you know how Deron Moretti died?"

Already, I disliked where this was going. "No. I haven't heard the full story," I admitted. I had been actively avoiding hearing the full story, in fact. Nevertheless, I forced myself to ask, "What does it have to do with Myles?"

"Everything," my brother said. He explained about Royce, Roger, and Myles thinking their dad had something to do with their mom's death all those years ago. Supposedly, Deron had gone into hiding because he knew his sons were out for his blood. Then he showed up again a year later, demanding the boys hand over all the money the business had made under his rule. Deron had kidnapped

Royce's current wife, his girlfriend at the time, and was using her as a hostage.

"So the three of them went to make the deal with him," Danny went on, "but it went south. The details are sort of fuzzy since they were the only ones who walked away from it, but—"

"Myles killed him," Gemma said coldly. "He murdered his own father. And the guards there with him, I hear. Shot them all in cold blood." I stayed silent for a few seconds, wide-eyed, while Danny gave her a dirty look.

"You don't have to be so blunt about it."

She rolled her eyes. "She's not a baby anymore, Daniel. You can't keep treating her like one. She asked what happened. And what happened is Myles Moretti pulled a gun on his own flesh and blood."

"But why?" I asked when I finally found my voice. I couldn't imagine Myles would've done something like that without a good reason. Could I see him doing it? If pressed...yes. But not without provocation. Not in cold blood. "Deron must have done something. Was he threatening them?"

"He did have that woman hostage," Danny agreed vaguely, but he made it sound like that didn't matter. "Look, I know you want to see the best in him, but Myles isn't the little boy you grew up with anymore. Not everyone deserves the benefit of the doubt."

"He did it because he didn't want to go back to being a nobody in his own house." Gemma leaned back in her chair and crossed one leg over the other, watching me calmly. "You know how Deron treated him. How everyone treated him. He was a child and didn't know anything about the ins and outs of cosa nostra. Then he spends a year running the show, gets used to everyone pretending like he's worth something—"

"Stop it." I bit back a sneer, knowing it would look too much like hers. I couldn't begin to imagine Myles killing his dad just so he could stay on the throne. After the way I'd seen him before, how exhausted he looked. That question, *why am I still not good enough?* I didn't even know if Myles *wanted* the job.

"And the only reason you're so intent on sticking up for him is that you two have so much in common," my sister went on, tapping her fingers slowly on the arm of her chair. "You know what that feels like too. Being the baby, not contributing anything useful. You don't want to believe that he's worthless, because if *he* is, that means—"

"Enough," Danny growled warningly, and she rolled her eyes once again. Turning back to me, he went on, "His abilities as a don are irrelevant. He can't be trusted. *That's* why we have to cut things off with him. With all of them."

"I feel like we don't know the whole story," I said, arms crossed tightly over my chest. "I have to ask him about it. There must have been more going on."

"Sofia. You need to stop seeing him." Danny's voice was surprisingly stern, and so were his eyes when I looked up at him. "He's dangerous."

"He wouldn't hurt me." The thought was almost insulting somehow.

"Why not? You think he cares more about you than he did about his own dad?"

"Why are we acting like this is unprecedented?" I asked, straightening my spine and setting my jaw. "It's not like no one in this family has blood on their hands." I looked at my brother pointedly.

"But not our own blood," Gemma pointed out. "No one

here has ever killed a member of our own family. It's not the same thing."

"We don't tolerate people who threaten us. If Deron was making threats of his own, then Myles was protecting himself and his brothers. His *family*. Are you saying we're supposed to excuse offenses like that if they come from our own flesh and blood? Like that makes it okay somehow?" I demanded. "If Deron turned on them first, then I think...I think Myles was right to put a stop to it."

"Careful," Danny said quietly, not looking at me. He was hunched forward, resting his elbows on his knees, hands folded together. "You shouldn't say shit like that." What, was I about to be punished for insubordination or something? I wasn't even allowed to speak my mind around my siblings? I had expected indifference and judgment from Gemma, but Danny had never been so cold to me before. After a few seconds of empty silence and feeling too much like an unwanted guest in my own house, I got up and headed toward the stairs.

"I'm going to stay somewhere else."

"What?" my brother called after me. "Where are you going to go?"

"I don't know. I'll get a hotel room. An apartment or something. I don't know. I just don't want to be here."

"Sofia." He chased after me, catching up to me on the stairs and grabbing my arm to stop me. "Don't leave. You belong here with us. Is this really just about Myles, or is something else going on? Whatever it is, we can talk about it."

Can we?

"What if it about Myles?" I asked. "If that's the case, there's nothing to talk about. Clearly, everyone in this house has already written him off, and I don't want to. I won't."

"Whatever you think is going on between you two, I promise he doesn't care as much as you do. When I say you should stay away from him, I'm not speaking on behalf of the family, and I'm not thinking about our reputation. I know I can't stop you from doing what you want." He let go of my arm and took a step back. "No one can, once you've made your mind up. But as your big brother, who cares about your feelings, I'm telling you that trying to…fix him or whatever it is you're doing, it's not going to end well."

What could I say? I wanted to appreciate his concern, but it was based on this unshakeable belief that Myles was some kind of monster, and I refused to believe that. With a sweet smile, I told him, "I'm gonna go pack, okay? I'll come back and visit in a few days. We can have lunch again or something."

His face visibly fell, but he nodded. "Yeah. Okay."

I packed a couple of suitcases, and some of our staff members helped me carry them downstairs. Marlon even volunteered to drive me to the extended-stay hotel I had booked. An apartment wasn't really practical, I figured, since I wouldn't be able to stay for at least six months at a time. No, a hotel suite would be fine. I considered getting a place in San Diego, but that felt like too much, especially after the sort of weird note Myles and I had ended on that afternoon.

Once everything was arranged, I headed for Papà's room to tell him goodbye. But instead, I found Gemma waiting in the hall outside his office. She looked up at me disinterestedly when I got close.

"So you're really going through with this little tantrum?"

"It's not a tantrum. I think it's best for me to have my own space for a while. That's all."

"Right. So you can invite him over without worrying about *Papà* scolding you?"

"It's none of your business who I invite where," I told her, nodding toward the door. "Is he in?"

"He's busy. You shouldn't bother him just to say you're leaving because we were mean to your Moretti boyfriend."

"I kind of feel like you might be jealous that I have a Moretti boyfriend and you don't," I told her with an innocent smile, and she scoffed. "Is that why you're so against me seeing Myles? Because it would make you pursuing Royce seem even more pathetic? Or you don't like the idea of me succeeding where you failed?"

"Trust me, little sister, I would *love* to see you succeed at...anything, really," she said, shifting her weight to jut her hip out like she did when she was trying to make a point. "Even if it's a terrible choice like this one. Let me know how it turns out once he gets tired of you. I give it a couple of weeks at most. Assuming he doesn't decide to just kill you at that point."

My hands clenched into tight fists at my sides, and I forced myself to turn away from her. "I'll just call him later." I didn't bother telling her goodbye, knowing she didn't care whether I was there or not.

9

MYLES

I had to hold back a wince every time I saw Gregorio around the house. The swelling around his face had gone down, but he still had a couple of nasty cuts that were always visible, not to mention the cast on his hand. Apparently, I was the only one of my brothers who had gotten Dad's ambidextrous gene; Gregorio struggled pretty often with just his left hand. If the whole thing hadn't fucked me up so much, I might've joked with him about getting some badass scars out of the deal. But even though it was my go-to for just about any situation that made me uncomfortable, I couldn't bring myself to make jokes this time.

He was still trying hard to act like it wasn't a big deal, like his jaw didn't twinge any time he tried to talk, like the whole experience was more of a nuisance than anything traumatic. But he spent a lot of time in his room, I think because he was too embarrassed to be seen at less than his best. That good old Moretti pride.

When I went back to the Lucianos' place, I should've stayed and asked Daniel what the fuck they were playing at.

I should've told him about the evidence Nathan had found and demanded that he explain it. He really had the fucking nerve to stand there and look at me like *I* was the scum of the Earth when he and his people had just attacked my kid brother without provocation. I *should* have blown up in his face about it—but I didn't, because I got too distracted with Sofia. I had been intentionally avoiding talking to her about how Dad died because I was positive it would change how she saw me, and then this kind-of relationship that was starting to happen between us would get cut off for good. I wasn't looking forward to her reaction after Daniel explained the whole thing to her, but it was also objectively shitty of me to keep hiding it from her.

Only once she found out, she didn't dump me immediately. She didn't call and say she couldn't do this anymore. She didn't send me a long string of texts about how important family is and how she can't be with someone who doesn't understand that. (All of which I had considered possibilities.) No, she just texted me again that night after I'd gotten back to the house and stressed out about it for a couple of hours and said she was sorry for wasting my time.

She apologized to *me*. Said her family was obviously not interested in hearing me out, and maybe she was stupid to think they would be. She really did think her dad would be willing to talk, but if he'd already decided I wasn't allowed anywhere near the place, that wasn't an option.

Don't worry about it, I wrote back. I'd been sitting at my desk trying and failing to work for an hour, so this was a welcome distraction. *I knew it was a long shot anyway.* Then, even though I really didn't want to, I went on, *So did you and Daniel talk?* While I was waiting for her to answer, I got a call instead. Oh God, she wanted to talk about this now? Over the phone?

But my nerves settled when I realized it wasn't Sofia calling but Royce. And then my nerves went through the roof again. I swiped to answer and hoped my voice sounded casual. "Hey."

"Hey. What's going on over there?" he asked. "Rena told me something about Gregorio getting attacked? She made it sound like it was *bad*. I mean, I know she tends to exaggerate when it comes to violence, but she seemed pretty freaked out."

What was he doing talking to Rena in the first place? Why would she call him just to talk about this? "Yeah, that was like a week ago. I mean, it happened. He's fine." That was a huge overstatement, but I really didn't have the time or patience to explain the whole situation with the Council and the Lucianos and everything. Besides... "What do you care anyway? Whatever's going on over here, it's not affecting you." There was a tense silence.

"I care because my child is staying with you, Myles," he pointed out coolly. "And if there's even a chance that she's in danger—"

"She's not in fucking danger! You know I wouldn't let anything happen to her." We'd already had this conversation. I had spent hours on the phone with him, trying to convince him I was capable of keeping Whitney safe. That yes, I really would be responsible and take care of her. Yes, I literally would protect her with my life. Why any of that was even a question for him, I wasn't sure, but I *thought* I'd convinced him. Was this why Rena called him? To warn him that Whitney wasn't safe with me?

"I would've thought the same about Gregorio. The fact that something *did* happen to him means that you obviously don't have as much control as you think."

I wondered sometimes if my brother kept a list somewhere of all my supposed inadequacies so he could pull them out and read them to me any time I started feeling too good about myself. The first bullet point was probably something about how I would never be as good at this job as he was.

"Look," I said, trying so hard to keep my tone even that it came out flat. "I wouldn't be keeping her here if I thought it was bad for her. All right? If I felt like she was going to get hurt, I would put her on a plane back to you, even though she'd probably be kicking and screaming the whole way."

"What makes you say that?"

"Ask her yourself." I really didn't feel like getting in the middle of the rebellious teenager and her oblivious parents. "My point is, I'm not going to put *your child* in danger just to prove I can protect her. Can you just—just once in your life—trust me?"

Another moment of silence. "Okay," Royce said finally. "I don't doubt that you want to keep her safe."

"Just that I'm capable of doing it."

"No. I'm—" He let out a frustrated sigh. "It's not you. I would worry no matter who she was with; if she's not right in front of me, I worry."

"You should try to cool it with that," I said, leaning against my desk, dropping my chin into my hand. "She's not three anymore, and she's not as helpless as you think." And there I was getting in the middle of it anyway. Rather than arguing with me, Royce changed the subject.

"She told me you're seeing Sofia." *Little snitch.* "What's going on there?"

There was almost a smile in his voice, like he was trying to do the typical big brother thing and give me a hard time. That ship had kind of sailed already. He was the one who christened it, in fact. So I wasn't really interested in that sort of familiar banter shit. "I don't know. Nothing, officially. We aren't on the best terms with the Lucianos right now."

"Did something happen?"

"It doesn't matter. I'm taking care of it, okay? I need to go." I didn't *need* to do anything, but talking to him was exhausting.

After ending the call and taking a second to clear my head, I checked my texts again and found an answer from Sofia. *We did, but you and I can have that conversation later. Right now, we should be celebrating.*

Confused, I wrote back, *Celebrating what?*

It only took a second for her to answer. *Me finally moving out of my dad's house.*

That wasn't any less confusing. *Moving out? Like for good?*

Like I said, we can talk about it later. I think you should ask me to dinner. That way, we'll have plenty of time to talk...and then you can come see my new place. She tacked on another one of those heart emojis at the end, and I couldn't help smiling at the suggestion.

Okay. Do you want to have dinner with me, Sofia?

I don't know, she wrote back. *I'll have to check my schedule.* What a brat. *When were you thinking? Tonight?* Given it was already around nine, I figured that was probably a joke. Was I willing to drive another two hours to meet her in L.A. again if she insisted? Absolutely. Would it probably be better to wait a couple days? Also yes.

I mean, if that's the only time you're free. Saturday might work better, though.

She responded immediately, *UGH.*

Two whole days? That's cruel. I could just imagine the pout on her face. I was about to write back and tell her that if she needed to see me that bad, I could come tonight, but she beat me to the punch. *I guess if that's the only time you have free. I'll try to be patient. But I'm sure I'll be miserable by the time you get here, so it'll be up to you to cheer me up.*

My smile turned into a devious grin. *Don't worry, princess. I won't leave until you're completely satisfied.* I was looking forward to it already.

"Myles." Nathan came in with a stack of papers in one hand and Gregorio tailing behind him. He dropped the papers on the desk in front of me. "These were the ones responsible for the attack. I've gone through them with Gregorio, and he recalls seeing all of them there."

About damn time. I didn't want to actively give him shit for it, but it did take him a lot longer than expected to get these names. Nate was usually quick about that kind of thing. But then, the Lucianos weren't on the same level as the idiots who usually crossed us. I looked through the files, each one with a name, a photo, how they were related to the Lucianos, and what role they played in the family.

"Hang on." I picked up one sheet with a sneer, recognizing the name and face. *Arturo Fidelle.* The same asshole who wouldn't let me near the door at the Lucianos' villa that afternoon, and more importantly, the one who apparently slept with Sofia. When I singled him out, Gregorio let out a growling scoff, and I looked up to see him glaring at the paper with contempt. "This guy was worse than the others?"

He nodded and answered with some difficulty, "He was...in charge, I think." Holding up his broken hand, he added, "Did this. And...fucking laughed about it."

I leaned back in my chair and pushed the page forward. "Then he's the one we'll make an example of." *Thanks for giving me an excuse to kill you, fucker.*

"Just him?" Nathan asked. "And the others get off scot-free?" I turned to Gregorio.

"What do you think?"

He straightened up a little, seeming surprised I was asking his opinion. He didn't often get much say in running things, but in this case, it was the least I could do. He was the one who suffered. He should get to choose how we got our payback. Stepping forward to push the other pages out of the way, he stabbed his finger onto Arturo's photo.

"Just him. And make sure it hurts."

"We can do that."

...

Somehow, even though I knew Sofia wouldn't like it, planning Arturo's death didn't make me feel guilty in the slightest. I couldn't decide what I hated him for more: fucking my girlfriend (I could think of her that way, couldn't I?) or attacking my brother. Either way, he was going to pay for both. I didn't have any plans to do it myself. He wasn't worth my time, and I convinced Gregorio it wasn't worth his either; the guy wasn't even a made man, just an associate. But I had a couple of my best men lined up for the job, and they had Greg's orders. *Make sure it hurts.* The plan was for it to go down Sunday.

Some part of me—that sounded weirdly like my oldest brother—said this was a bad idea, that it was only going to make things worse, that I should try talking to Marcell again. But I brushed it off. I had already tried talking to him, and he'd rejected the idea completely. Besides, I wasn't about to let that bastard get away with what he'd done. So whatever happened afterwards, we were at least making it clear that fucking with the Morettis was bad for a person's health.

Gregorio and I stayed up late Friday night, sitting in my office, drinking and talking out the plan. Okay, I did most of the talking, but that wasn't really unusual to begin with. Maybe it was the couple glasses of whiskey I'd had, but I started thinking again that this shouldn't have happened to him in the first place. I'd done way too much apologizing lately to start thinking about doing it again, but I still hadn't really addressed it with him.

"Hey, so..." I started, swirling the alcohol in my glass just for something else to focus on. "We haven't really talked much about what happened."

"Yeah, I haven't really talked much at all," he said, smiling just slightly. Any wider than that probably hurt more.

"I'm serious. I know you want to act like it was no big deal, but—"

"Then let me keep acting like that." His kind-of smile had disappeared, leaving him looking a lot more bitter than I was used to. The alcohol must have made talking a little easier on him since he didn't pause or hesitate like usual. "I don't *want* to talk about it. I don't wanna have 'that conversation.' Mom keeps trying to talk to me about it too. I'm fine, okay? Just...leave it at that."

I took another drink and nodded. He and I were way more alike than I wanted to admit. That was my response to shit I didn't want to deal with too: brush it off as a joke, and if that doesn't work, get defensive and shut the subject down completely. And it worked to a point, but it was a temporary solution at best, and a fucking emotional handicap at worst. That was something my brothers and I had all inherited from our dad in one way or another. Even though we all knew it probably wasn't healthy, even though we all knew it would catch up to us eventually, it was the only way we knew how to be.

But whatever. It wasn't like I was dying to have a heart-to-heart with him anyway. *Just ignore the problem until it goes away.* So instead, I raised my glass. "To getting even."

"And then some," Gregorio agreed, knocking back the rest of his drink.

...

I woke up the next morning to punk music blaring from down the hall. I couldn't remember exactly how much I'd had to drink, but it was apparently enough to make my head throb with every drum beat and cymbal crash. What the fuck was Whitney doing playing that shit loud enough that the whole house would hear it? Maybe I would send her back to London after all...

Staggering out of bed, realizing I hadn't even bothered getting undressed before I passed out the night before, I trudged down the hall to pound on her bedroom door. "Whits! Can you knock that shit off? People are trying to sleep!"

She opened the door, letting the music flood out even louder and making me flinch. "It's almost noon," she pointed out, raising an eyebrow at me. "Were you still in bed?" Shit, was it that late? "Besides, it's gonna be way louder than this tonight. You should get used to it." With a wide grin, she started hopping and dancing around her room, singing (or screaming) along with the music. Since it didn't seem like she was going to do it, I came into her room and turned off the wireless speakers on the dresser. They looked way too small to be putting out such an ear-splitting volume. Whitney's dancing immediately stopped, and she pouted at me.

"What the hell are you talking about?" I asked, pushing my hair back out of my eyes and trying to clear my head now that it wasn't too loud to think.

"The concert?" she said, like I was being an idiot for asking. "Tonight? L.A.? Tar and Sugar? Did you forget?" The crushed look on her face made me feel like shit even while I was still trying to remember what it was I'd forgotten.

Oh. Suddenly I did remember her bursting into my office all excited just a few days after she'd first arrived. She had found out one of her favorite bands—some all-girl UK punk group, Tar & Sugar—was playing in L.A., and she pretty much *informed* me that we were going. When I tried to argue, she reminded me that I had promised to take her to L.A. sometime, so this was going to be that sometime.

Too bad that wasn't on my mind when I asked Sofia out. Like an idiot, I'd apparently double-booked myself for the night. And since Whitney's plans were made first, Sofia was the one I had to disappoint. Unless...

"No, I didn't forget," I scoffed. Whitney's eyes narrowed. "Okay, maybe I forgot, but I remember now. We're still going, don't throw a fit. But I was thinking maybe... Uh, would you be interested in meeting Sofia?"

Her brown eyes widened. "Tonight? Would she go with us?"

"I mean, I can ask. I don't know how into it she'd be, but it's worth a shot." I actually knew for a fact that Sofia was the kind of girl who was more at home in a club than at a concert, especially a punk rock concert. But something told me she'd jump at the chance to meet Whitney, even if it meant going somewhere there would be lots of loud, drunk, and disorderly people.

"Well, I guess if she wants to go. And if you can get another ticket this late. Then I guess it's fine. You two better not be *gross* the whole time, though," she warned, wrinkling her nose.

"I'll keep that in mind," I said, rolling my eyes as I left her room and went to call Sofia.

10

SOFIA

AFTER I GOT OFF THE PHONE WITH MYLES, I WASN'T QUITE sure what to do next. Don't get me wrong: I was still happy I'd get to see him, and I was more than a little excited to meet Royce's daughter. I'd heard plenty about her, but because she'd lived in England most of her life, we'd never actually met. I was definitely curious as to how a Moretti child raised to not be a Moretti would've turned out.

But a punk rock concert? Honestly, I knew next to nothing about the genre. It just wasn't my thing, never had been. All those sweaty, rowdy people mashed together, standing room only, three times louder than any nightclub or bar? No, thank you. Still, I was planning to go just the once, and I wasn't about to show up looking completely out of place.

Realizing this wasn't something I could tackle on my own, I called the only person I knew who might have some experience in this area: Lauren Maldone. Her confusion was obvious in her voice when she answered. "Sofia? Did you call me by accident or something?"

"No, it was intentional," I laughed. "I wanted to ask a favor if you have a minute."

"Uh, sure? What's up?"

I explained a little about Myles, about Whitney and the concert, and about how I wanted to look like I belonged but just wasn't sure how to do it.

"I mean, I know that band," Lauren said. "They're kinda poppy for my taste, but they're okay. You just want help picking what to wear? You've never asked for my opinion on that before." I might've imagined it, but it almost sounded like there was a little contempt in her voice. But then, the Capelli twins and I had been a little harsh about her look in the past, mostly because it was so different from ours. Maybe that wasn't quite fair.

"I need help from the ground up," I confessed. "Shoes, clothes, makeup, hair—I'm totally clueless here. And I figured since you usually look..."

"Sloppy?" she supplied, still sounding a little miffed.

"I was going to say 'casual.' I mean, you don't really care what you look like."

"...thanks?"

"I'm sorry! That came out wrong." God, what was wrong with me? I wasn't at all used to *asking* for help. Usually, someone offered, or I could demand it rather than request it. "What I meant was you don't care what other people think about how you look. You don't dress for anyone but yourself." And wasn't that the whole point of punk?

"Not unless someone makes me," she agreed, forcibly reminding me of all the times we had insisted on dolling her up, like her own preferred clothes weren't good enough. In hindsight, yeah, that was pretty obviously insulting. It was kind of surprising to hear her sticking up for herself at all, but maybe doing it over the phone was easier. Or maybe she had lost some respect for me after she saw me get so wasted over Myles.

"You know what? I shouldn't have bothered you for something like this," I said, trying my best to sound pleasant and contrite. "I'm sorry. I'll just let you go."

"Hang on," she said abruptly. There was a pause, and I just hoped she was going to take pity on me. "Maybe I can help a little. Why don't you video chat me or something, so I can see what you're working with?"

I probably thanked her a hundred times over the next hour or so as I shared my vague idea of what I might wear and asked every question that came to mind. It quickly became apparent that I would have to go shopping if I was going to pull this off, so Lauren helped me make a list of what to look for.

"Fishnets?" I asked with uncertainty. "You don't think that's too much?"

"Not for this band. They do mesh all over the place, and I'm sure their fans do too. And plaid! You have to have something plaid."

"Oh, what about makeup? Should I get a lighter foundation? Is this the kind of aesthetic where you're supposed to be pale?"

"Eh, I wouldn't bother. It's punk, not goth." She laughed, but not in the chilly, mocking way most of my friends did. Everything about this conversation felt a lot more helpful and a lot less judgy than a sartorial discussion with, say, the Capelli twins. "And you can't leave your hair that neat, either. It's too long to try to spike it, so just make it a complete mess. Like, out of your face, but other than that, go wild."

"Okay," I said, looking over all the notes I'd taken. "Okay,

I think I should be good to go. Thank you so much for your help."

"No problem. You can text me or whatever if you end up needing something else. And you should send me a picture once you put the whole thing together!"

"If it comes out looking even halfway decent, I definitely will."

...

Around 9:30 that night, I was pacing around the living room in my temporary suite. My job had given me quite a lot of experience with hotel rooms, but I didn't often opt for extended-stay suites like this one. It was more like an apartment than a hotel, and I'd settled in pretty quickly, so at least I was comfortable while stressing out about the evening. The worst case scenario was that they would both think I was trying way too hard and looked ridiculous. I'd already sent a picture to Lauren, and although she assured me I looked great, I still had my doubts.

I was fighting with myself about toning down my outfit when the knock at my door finally came, startling me out of my own thoughts. I checked through the peephole and saw Myles dressed only a little more casual than usual; his well-tailored suit was missing a tie, the first couple of buttons on his shirt undone, sunglasses hanging from his chest pocket despite it being so late. Oh God, he was going to laugh at me for looking so childish.

When I opened the door, his eyes visibly widened in shock as he took in my ripped mesh tights, purple plaid shorts, and loose, long-sleeved crop top. Refusing to be bashful in the slightest, I thrust my hands to my hips and demanded, "What?"

"I didn't expect you to take this so seriously," he said, an amused smirk playing about his lips.

"I don't know what you're talking about. This is my usual wardrobe." I grabbed my purse from the counter and stepped into the hall to pull the door shut behind me. But Myles didn't step back, keeping me trapped between him and the door.

"It looks good," he said, lowering his voice a little so the words felt more meaningful. He reached up to rub his thumb over my dark purple lips, and I had to resist the urge to take it in my mouth. "I always like it when you get a little messy." As he leaned down to kiss me, slow but deep and thorough, I realized that touch was probably to check if my lipstick would smear. As if I'd make such an amateur mistake.

"Well. It's a good thing you approve because I'm not changing," I answered, clearing my throat and trying to pretend he hadn't gotten me hot and bothered within five minutes of showing up. As we walked out to the car, I remembered that he would have to go back home with Whitney after this, that he wouldn't get to stay the night, and I bit back a groan of frustration. I was going to get that man in bed, even if it meant I had to drive to San Diego myself the next day.

When we got to the limo, he let me in first, and Whitney was waiting inside. Much to my relief, she was dressed similarly to me, with hot pink leggings under torn black jeans and an off-the-shoulder t-shirt. She even had the guts to spring for black lipstick, which I was a little too chicken to try. "Hi," she said brightly, sitting forward to look over my outfit. "You're Sofia, right? I'm Whitney. I love your shoes!"

"Oh, thanks," I said, glad I'd decided to take the chance on the platform booties. They were definitely my favorite part of the outfit. "Yours are adorable too." Her sneakers gave new meaning to the word "hi-tops," reaching almost up to her knees.

"Ugh, and you said *I* was gonna be gross," Myles said, shooting Whitney a look, and she stuck her tongue out at him. I suspected he was just jealous that he wasn't getting all my attention for once. On our drive to the concert, Whitney gave us a brief history of the band we were seeing, how they'd gotten together, broken up at one point, then gotten together again. They weren't the most popular all-girl group, she granted, but they were still one of the best. By the time we got there, I was actually sort of excited to see them play.

The whole time we were talking, I couldn't help thinking Whitney looked strangely, distantly familiar. Not like we'd actually met before, just like I'd seen her somewhere. Surely, she had never been at aMoral for me to glimpse her there. It was only when we got out of the car, when I saw the purple mixed into her black braids and her careless, sort of lanky body language, that I finally realized why.

"Out of curiosity, Whitney," I started as we made our way through the ticketing lines, "when did you get into town?"

"Uh, I dunno," she said with a shrug. "A couple of weeks ago. Why?"

"I think you and I might have come in on the same plane. Because I'm pretty sure you shoved me out of your way after you climbed over the seats to get out ahead of everyone else." I gave her a sly look, and she tensed up for a split-second before flashing me a grin.

"You must have the wrong person. None of that sounds like anything I would do," she assured me, and Myles snorted a laugh. "Er, but if I had, I would probably be sorry. Hypothetically."

"And if you were, I'm sure I would accept your apology. Hypothetically," I agreed with a wink.

"That's the thing about standing out so much, Whits," Myles told her, flipping all of her braids up and over her head so she had to shake them out and straighten them again. "People notice you."

She pursed her lips in a pout. "Who says that's a bad thing?"

I was relieved to find that even though the concert was taking place outside, there were at least seats, meaning there would be a measured distance between us and the others in the audience. The bad news was that our seats were at the very front row, on the left but right next to the pit. Still, I kept my discomfort over any of it from showing on my face, continuing to chat with Whitney—or rather, listen to her chatter—about the band. The audience quickly filled up with other people varying from Mild Punk to Two-Foot-High-Orange-Mohawk Punk.

When the opening act, a band called Basement Foxtrot, come out and started playing, the place erupted into screams and cheers even louder than I'd imagined. The music was at about the same volume, and I had to force myself not to grimace. No, this definitely was not my scene. But at least Whitney looked happy, dancing a little in her seat and singing along to each chorus. Myles seemed totally unaffected by the noise, sitting back in his chair and absently tapping his foot. I resolved to grin and bear it, pushing down the urge to complain.

After the opener and the applause that followed, there was a moment of merciful semi-quiet while the crew set up for the main act, and I couldn't help letting out a relieved sigh. Suddenly realizing how tense my body had gotten, I tried to relax.

"You okay?" Myles asked. I had to bite back a firm "*no*."

"I'm fine." Trying to take the focus off me so he wouldn't give me another opportunity to whine, I glanced across him to Whitney—and found she'd left her seat. "Where...?"

"She went up to the pit." Myles pointed her out where she stood by the railing, bouncing on her toes in excitement. "I swear trying to get that kid to sit still is a fucking ordeal." This seemed more like a casual observation than a complaint.

"Is she okay over there?" Did people mosh at shows like this? She was so small, it would be easy for her to get lost or hurt.

"She's fine," Myles said, waving off the concern like it was silly. He was generally a pretty carefree person, so maybe the answer shouldn't have surprised me. But it didn't make me feel any better.

Soon enough, the headlining band came out, a group of four women all dressed in the same punky style as me and Whitney but noticeably more on the sexy side. Their frontman (frontwoman?) was a busty redhead in a tube top and a chain-decorated vest, and she was the one to step forward and introduce them. She then started their first song with an aggressive guitar riff. The others quickly joined in, and the pace picked up to the cheering of the crowd— including Whitney, who was hopping and screaming with all the other fans.

Hoping I didn't look as miserable as I felt, wishing Myles wasn't watching the show so intently now, I sat back in my chair and crossed my arms. It was my fault, of course, for agreeing to go when I already knew I wouldn't enjoy it. Myles eventually noticed my discomfort and leaned over to ask loudly, "Do you want to move or something? There are seats farther back." He had to practically shout in order for me to hear him over the music. I shook my head.

"I don't want—" Nope, not loud enough. I tried again, "I don't want to leave Whitney on her own!" He made a face but nodded and sat back again. But he at least seemed sympathetic with my discomfort; he ran a hand slowly across my tense shoulders, then down my back, trying to help me relax. It was a sweet gesture, at least.

A few more songs in, during an instrumental interlude while the singers took a break, I saw that Whitney had found someone to talk to as well. She was having a sort of shout-chat like ours with a guy who looked closer to my age than hers. The sight instantly gave me a bad feeling, and I nudged Myles to get his attention.

Nodding toward Whitney as she shifted her weight from one foot to the other, laughing and gesturing as she spoke, I asked, "Should she be talking to someone like that? He looks a lot older—and honestly, I don't trust anyone here." Myles glanced in their direction, then looked back at me and shook his head.

"Don't worry. She can handle herself." He was her uncle. He knew her better than I did. But she was so small, so sweet and friendly; if the guy wanted to take advantage of that, I felt like there wouldn't be much she could do to stop him. I almost wanted to go over there and shoo him off on principle. He had no business chatting with a thirteen-year-old in the first place.

"What if she thinks he's just being friendly and tries to... I don't know, go somewhere with him? I really think you should do something," I insisted, but still, Myles disagreed.

"She's not stupid. And she's not gonna go anywhere. I mean, you can keep an eye on her if you want, but I promise she doesn't need it."

I decided I *would* keep an eye on her since he apparently wouldn't. What was he thinking? Did he just not want to bother dealing with the guy? Myles so rarely backed down from a fight that I was shocked he wasn't jumping at this chance. As I watched, the guy oh so casually reached up to brush Whitney's braids back over her bare shoulder, and I was on my feet immediately, ready to go tell him off. She jerked back slightly and tried to slap his hand away, but he caught her wrist with a sympathetic smirk.

I kept my eyes locked on them as I marched over, but I still wasn't sure exactly what happened next. One moment, the guy was holding onto Whitney's wrist, laughing as she tried to wrench her arm away. The next, he was on the ground, and Whitney was stomping a hi-top into his stomach, shouting a much more colorful string of insults that I would've expected.

"Whoa, whoa, all right, that's enough," Myles said, finally jumping up to intervene. He grabbed Whitney around her waist with one arm and picked her up while she continued to shout and try to kick the guy who had touched her. "Whits, you made your point. Relax." He walked past our seats, getting a little outside the crowd before he set her back on her feet. Even then, she was visibly shaking with rage. But as I came closer to check on her, I got a better look at her expression—wide-eyed, tense, tearful—and I realized she might be shaking for a different reason.

"Whitney?" I leaned down to try to meet her eyes. "Are you—oh!" To my surprise, she threw herself against my chest, wrapping her arms tightly around me, practically hyperventilating while she struggled to calm down.

"Bastard," she growled, her voice choked with tears. "Fucking dirty son of a bitch! Can't just grab someone like that. And he wouldn't let go. And he laughed at me." Her hands clutched at two fistfuls of my shirt, her face buried against my shoulder. Unsure of what else to do, I held onto her and told her softly that she was okay, she was safe, and no one else would touch her. When I chanced a look at Myles, he looked nearly as shaken as she did.

As much as I told myself it wasn't his fault, I was still furious with him for not stepping in sooner. Maybe he was right; maybe she *could* handle herself. But she shouldn't have to. After a few minutes, her shaking slowly calmed, and she disengaged herself from my shirt, looking embarrassed. "Hey," I said, pushing her braids back behind her ear. "Do you want to leave?"

She shook her head, flinging her hair everywhere as she rubbed her eyes too hard. "No. They haven't played my favorite song yet. I want to stay to the end." And she turned back toward the stage without another word, arms crossed tightly over her chest.

"Hey, Whits—" Myles reached for her arm, but she jerked away from him, not even bothering to look in his direction. He took a step back and put his hands in his pockets, giving her space and looking miserably guilty. She was quiet for the rest of the show, watching from a distance where we stood, though she managed to get back enough energy to cheer and clap for an encore. I had stopped paying any attention to the band at that point, staying focused on her. Even if she didn't want to talk about what had happened, that fear on her face wasn't easy to forget.

Yet, when the show finally ended and she turned to face us again, her grin seemed totally sincere. To my surprise, Myles managed an equally natural smile. "So? All your hopes and dreams fulfilled?" he asked.

"Almost. I need at least one shirt before we can leave."

I wasn't quite sure how to respond. She led us to the

merch booths and navigated out of the crowds laughing, talkative again, like nothing had happened. Did she just not want to think about it? Was it possible she'd gotten over it already? "I'm starving," she said once we got back to the car. "Do you know any places that are open this late?"

Realizing she was addressing me—the only native Angeleno in the group—I tried to shift gears from my worries about her. "I can think of a few. Is there something, in particular, you want to eat?"

"Hamburgers," Myles supplied. "It's all she ever eats."

"Not *just* hamburgers," Whitney protested. "Any kind of burger is fine. Turkey burgers. Shrimp burgers. I'm flexible." A burger-exclusive diet and she was still that tiny? Her metabolism must have been insane.

Deciding it was probably best not to take the two Morettis to a Luciano-owned restaurant, I picked a little 50's-style diner that Nadine was always raving about instead. It was a cute 24-hour place, a bright, neon-laced beacon among the quieter stores surrounding it. Whitney and I must have stood out pretty starkly with our dark makeup and flashy clothes, but our waitress didn't bat an eye as she took our order.

"So, Sofia," Whitney said, sitting across the table from me and Myles and looking between the two of us. She folded her hands on the table, oddly businesslike, and asked, "What's going on here?"

"Uh, what do you mean?"

"Whits, can you not?" Although Myles groaned, he was still smiling.

"I'm just trying to figure out what your intentions are with my uncle." She somehow managed a serious tone despite Myles cracking up at the idea.

"My intentions, huh? You know he's the one who invited me out, right?"

"But you said yes. And he's come here to see you a couple of other times lately," she pointed out. "So are you dating or…? What? That's what I mean: what's going on?"

"You know, I'm honestly not sure myself," I confessed, stealing a glance in his direction. "We've sort of been in a weird not-knowing place for a while now. Years. *I* would say that we're dating at this point. What do you think, Myles?" Whitney and I both turned to him expectantly.

"I mean, I don't know what else to call it," he agreed with a shrug.

"Wait, what do you mean years?" Whitney asked. "How long have you two known each other?"

"You're thirteen, right?" I asked, and she nodded. "Then I've actually known him for longer than you have." Her mouth dropped open as the waitress came back over to deliver our food. Myles and Whitney both had hamburgers, while I'd opted for a ham and Swiss omelet. Picking out a chunk of honeydew from my little side of mixed fruit, I added, "I know your dad too. Or I did, before he moved." Whitney frowned past a mouthful of French fries.

"How?"

Before I could answer, Myles spoke up for me. "Her dad was friends with ours." That was the simplest possible explanation, I guess, but it wasn't the full story. Was there a reason not to tell her exactly who I was, who my dad was? I looked to him for some explanation, but he kept his eyes on his plate. Well, if he didn't want to go into it, we didn't have to…but I would be looking for an answer about this later.

"Yeah, so we kind of grew up together," I went on. "Myles and I always got along because we have a lot in common." I tried my best not to think about Gemma's assessment of all our similarities.

"Like what?" Whitney asked.

"Can we change the subject?" Myles grumbled, cutting me off again. Why was he suddenly getting irritated? I was almost tempted to keep pushing on the topic just to annoy him more, but that didn't seem like something to do in front of Whitney. So instead, I followed his suggestion, my attitude turning a little chillier.

"*Okay.* Whitney, you live in London, right?" I asked, hoping it was clear that my frustration didn't apply to her.

"Yeah," she agreed between bites of her burger, seemingly oblivious to the tension between me and Myles. Or maybe just ignoring it. "But I like it better here."

"Really?" Myles seemed surprised by the statement. "Why?"

"I have more family here," Whitney said with a shrug. "And it's more exciting. With the...business and all."

"Oh, I would pay money to see your dad's face if he heard that," Myles said. He had a point. Considering Royce's feelings on the subject—that cosa nostra was inherently evil and worth leaving the country over—hearing that his daughter actually enjoyed being involved in it was pretty shocking.

"I can't tell him. He'd freak out. Mum was already mad about me even coming to visit," she explained. She had started doing some kind of motion with her hand, and I felt like it was an extremely weird fidget until I realized that Myles's hands did the same thing when he played with his butterfly knives. Like uncle, like niece, apparently —only Whitney didn't actually have a knife on her person at all times. "I tried asking him if we would ever move back and he got all mad and stressed. It's not like he would have to be in charge. You're taking care of it." Well, at least someone had confidence in Myles's leadership abilities.

"Yeah, I think that's a lost cause, kiddo. Your best chance is probably moving back on your own once you're eighteen."

"If I do, will you give me a job?" she asked with a playful smile.

"Well, obviously. You're kind of heir to the throne, so I wouldn't have much of a choice."

That statement only made Whitney's grin and her eyes grow wider. "That means Nathan has to listen to me, right? You should tell him that."

"All right, Simba, calm down," Myles said, rolling his eyes at her. "I'm still in charge for now, so it's not like you're taking over tomorrow."

"But someday." She nodded like this was a surefire thing. "Now I'm looking forward to it."

"So am I," I admitted with a laugh. "I can't wait to see where you take the family."

Once we realized it was past midnight, we reluctantly admitted we should probably be going. Whitney was visibly less energetic during the ride back to my place, and because the mood between me and Myles had gotten a little weird, we didn't talk much. When we reached the hotel and I got out of the car, he followed, and we stood awkwardly in the parking lot for a few seconds.

"So...this didn't go quite like I was expecting," he said. "I mean, you were obviously uncomfortable the whole time, and—"

"Not the whole time. And I don't regret going. It was nice to meet Whitney. I feel like she takes after you a lot."

"Yeah, it's gonna cause problems for her in the future," he muttered. "I guess I should get her home."

"Right. We'll have to reschedule that dinner date, though."

His lips quirked into a faint smile. "Yeah." He kissed me, but it was brief, simple, totally void of passion. I wasn't sure he'd ever kissed me like that before, in a way that didn't feel charged with desire. Maybe it was because he felt guilty for what happened to Whitney. Or for hiding things while we were at the diner. Whatever the reason, I hated it. But like he said, he needed to take Whitney home. So that would be an argument for some other time.

I took a step back and waved as I watched them leave, then turned to head back to my rooms. There had been ups and downs to the night, but I felt Myles and I had ended on a distinct *down*. Even as I was unlocking my door, I was regretting not fighting with him. Or not getting the opportunity. Lost in thought, I pushed the door open—and choked in a gasp when I found Gemma sitting in my living room.

"What are you doing here?" I demanded, coming inside and setting my purse down. I didn't have nearly enough patience to deal with her at the moment. Seated in the corner of the couch with her long legs crossed and her face illuminated by her phone, my sister looked up at me with no urgency at all.

"I came to check on you, obviously. Can't a girl worry about her misguided little sister?"

"Get out."

"Has he gotten tired of you already?" There was an almost-smirk in the corner of her mouth. "Is that why you're so upset? Or are you just mad he didn't get to stay the night?"

"Get *out*," I growled again, pointing to the door. She didn't move.

"You got to meet Royce's daughter, didn't you? What is

she like? A real Moretti like her dad? Competent? Or more like Myles?" Her smirk had widened, making it clear she was enjoying tormenting me a little too much.

"What do you want, Gemma?" I didn't have to ask how she knew I had met Whitney or how she'd gotten a key to my room. With her connections—which might have been even more extensive than Danny's, given how much effort she put into making them—she always seemed to know things that were none of her business. "You just want to hurt my feelings? Is it really that simple? Because you disapprove of my boyfriend, you want to make me feel bad?"

"Disapprove is a very mild word for how I feel about him," she said, finally getting to her feet. "And I couldn't care less about him as your boyfriend. But because you're my sister, because you're a part of my family, this relationship you're pretending to have with him is a liability. Suppose things get worse between you two and he decides you're more useful as a hostage than as a *girlfriend*. Dad would do anything he asked if it meant keeping you safe." She said this with blatant contempt, seething with anger over the fact that our dad cared about me.

"You're delusional," I told her plainly.

"*You're* a fucking moron," she growled, striding over to meet me in the kitchen, "if you think there's any possible scenario where you and Myles end up living happily ever after together. Things aren't going to get any better for him, little sister, and if you aren't careful, you might just get caught in the crossfire."

Was my own sister explicitly threatening me now? I had always known Gemma was ambitious, conniving, even ruthless. Everyone knew that about her. And of course, she and I weren't close by any means, but...she was still my sister. And of all the times in my life that she'd insulted me or criticized me or fought with me, she had never really scared me. Until now.

"Please leave," I said quietly, not taking my eyes off hers. Her gaze stayed cold, hard, dangerous for a second longer, then softened. Maybe she saw the fear in my eyes. Maybe she'd remembered, all of a sudden, that I actually was her sibling. She straightened up and brushed her hair back over her shoulder.

"I'm telling you you're safer if you stay away from him." Her tone was even, controlled, and she left without another word. I managed to shakily lock the deadbolt before my eyes blurred over with tears.

11

MYLES

I was totally lost about how to address what happened with Whitney. She got quiet as we headed toward home, but I couldn't tell if that was because she was tired or because she was thinking about earlier. Either way, the guilt in my stomach was gnawing at me too much to keep ignoring it.

"Hey, Whits."

"Hm?" She didn't look at me, staring down at her shoes instead.

"What happened earlier, at the concert—"

"I don't want to talk about it." Of course, she didn't. "I'm fine." Of course, she was. This felt a lot like the conversation I'd had with Gregorio—or tried to have—only in this case, I was talking to a little girl, not an adult. A little girl who was incredibly tough, so much so that she thought she was invincible and then had a rude awakening. One I could've prevented.

"I don't think you are."

She tensed up in her seat, her hands clenched into tight fists where they rested on her legs. "I said, I'm *fine*."

"Then why do I feel like you'd break my arm if I tried to touch you?"

"Don't!" That came out as a shout, and she withdrew to a corner of her seat, still without looking in my direction once. Quietly, she added, "Don't touch me." I didn't try to move closer, didn't sit up or do anything that might stress her out any more. Maybe I wasn't great at emotional sensitivity, but I had learned a thing or two about psychology. Enough to know that trying to force her past this would only backfire in the worst possible way.

"I'm just trying to talk to you," I told her calmly.

"I *don't* want to talk about it," she repeated, and even past her defensive anger, I could hear the tears in her voice.

I know, kiddo. I really do. But we're going to anyway.

"You got scared." My hands were folded in my lap, legs stretched in front of me, and I left them like that. "That's okay. That shitbag shouldn't have grabbed you. That wasn't your fault."

"I know."

"Plus, you put him in the fucking dirt. The minute he touched you, you let him know it wasn't okay."

"He laughed at me." She dug her fingernails into her crossed arms. "He saw me get scared when he wouldn't let go. And he laughed. I'm not supposed to get scared."

"It's okay—"

"No," she insisted, her eyebrows drawn, her face tense. "Why was I afraid? Other people have tried to fight me. I dropped him, just like I dropped them. *Why* was I afraid?"

"He wasn't trying to fight you," I pointed out. Whitney's face went blank. She blinked, sending tears rolling down her face, and she wiped them off distractedly.

It seemed like that was what had really fucked her up about the situation. That guy thought he was in control, thought she was helpless. And his attitude made her think the same thing for a second. Whitney was used to having some authority, used to being respected. Suddenly feeling powerless must've been a pretty intense shock.

"Nobody's going to touch me without my permission again," she said matter-of-factly.

"For their sake, I hope nobody's stupid enough to try."

"Can we stop talking about it now?"

Based on that question, I doubted the conversation was completely over, but at least she had gotten to the point of moving forward instead of dwelling on it. "Yeah."

After a few seconds of silence, she spoke again, and her tone sounded a little more normal, not tight with confusion and pain. "I probably freaked Sofia out."

"I don't think so. She was probably just worried about you."

"Why were you being weird when we started talking about her?"

"Oh, is it my turn for talk-about-shit-you-don't-want-to therapy?" I asked dryly.

"Yup." She seemed a lot more relaxed now that it was *my* baggage we were talking about. Go figure. "Let's have it. What's the big deal?"

"Sofia's family is part of the Council." Technically not a lie. But admitting exactly which family would be a problem. Like most of our family, Whitney knew we were in active conflict with the Lucianos. Which was why I didn't tell anyone I was seeing her; Nathan was the only one who knew the whole story, and he still disapproved as much as ever. What if I told Whits that Sofia was a Luciano and she called me a traitor? I wouldn't know how to deal with that.

"So what?"

"So, they don't like me. They don't want me anywhere

near them or theirs. Eventually, we're going to have to address that. In the meantime, talking about it just makes me feel like shit." Again, all true.

"Well, I think you made *her* feel like shit instead. Is that better?" Jeez.

"Of course not."

"We should go back, then."

"What? Back to her place?"

Whitney nodded. "So you can apologize. Didn't you see how sad she looked when we left? You can't just leave her that way."

I definitely did see that, but I didn't know how to fix it in just a few words. "Okay, that sounds like maybe *I* should go back, and you should get back to the house and sleep."

"No." She frowned hard again. "I want to go too. If you go, I want to go. I don't..." She paused and looked toward the partition like she was afraid the driver might overhear. Was she scared of Jerome? That was someone she knew, someone she'd been around plenty of times; they got along fine. And she was afraid to be alone with him now? *Shit.*

After what she'd been through earlier and the conversation we'd just had, it seemed like a dick move to tell her "sorry, you don't get a say." With a resigned sigh, I lowered the partition and asked Jerome to turn around. He seemed a little confused but didn't argue with me. We'd already gotten twenty minutes out, so it was nearly 1 a.m. by the time we got back to Sofia's place. I just hoped she wasn't already asleep. I tried calling her, but she didn't answer. So I knocked, and we waited a minute or two. I was about to try calling again when the door finally unlocked and opened.

Sofia looked confused, but it didn't seem like we'd woken her up. In fact, she was in a bathrobe, like she was about to get in the shower. She'd already taken all her makeup off. "Hey?" she said, looking between me and Whitney, who was stifling a yawn every minute or so. "Did you guys forget something, or...?"

"Myles has some things to say to you," Whitney said smugly, nudging me with her shoulder.

"Thank you, Whits. I can take it from here," I said, then quickly added to Sofia, "I mean, if you're okay with it. We can leave if—"

"No, it's fine." She took a step back and gestured for us to come in. "But it's getting really late. I have an extra bedroom if you want to get some sleep." That was directed at Whitney.

"You have two bedrooms? In a hotel?" she asked, punctuating the questions with another yawn.

"Well, I moved in on short notice, and there weren't any one-bedrooms left." Sofia led us through the kitchen and to the door on the right side of the living room where a little guest bedroom was set up complete with a TV on the dresser. Whitney didn't waste any time making herself comfortable, yanking her shoes off and crawling into the bed. She turned the TV on and relaxed, totally at home already.

"Goodnight," she said before I closed the door.

"Night, kiddo." Shutting the door blocked out the sound of the TV completely. It was surprisingly good soundproofing.

Sofia was waiting for me in the doorway on the left of the living room, which led to a bigger master bedroom. She sat on the edge of the bed while I shut the door behind us. "So?" she said, arms and legs crossed, a little more guarded than I expected.

"Uh, Whitney pointed out that I was being 'weird' earlier. At the diner."

"You were," Sofia agreed.

"And she figured it probably made you feel shitty."

"It did." She nodded. Before I could say I was sorry, she held up a hand and asked, "Why were you being that way?"

"I didn't want Whitney to know about your family. I mean, that you're one of them."

"One of *them*?" she repeated indignantly.

"Yes, part of the family that hates my fucking guts so much that they think I'm a threat to be around." My tone was a little sharper than necessary, but she already knew about this. The question was whether she knew about all of it. "The family that hates *my* family enough to jump my brother and beat the shit out of him for no reason." Her eyes went wide.

"What are you talking about?"

"I'm talking about your dad's people attacking Gregorio outside my club. Happened about a week ago. You didn't know?"

"Myles, of course, I didn't know." She was somewhere between outraged and hurt by the accusation. "I can't even imagine my dad ordering something like that. Are you sure it was him? How do you know?"

"One of his cars was there when it happened, so we looked into it. And it turns out your little boyfriend, Arturo, was the one leading the whole thing."

"Oh, for God's sake," she groaned, "he's not my *boyfriend*, and he never was."

"So you just fucked a few times? Is that supposed to make it better?"

"No. This is not turning into something where I'm in the wrong." Her arms were crossed again, even tighter this time. "You were the one who came back to explain yourself."

"Have I not done that already?" I started pacing in front

of the bed, shoving a hand through my hair, trying and failing to stay calm despite the chaos going on in my head. "I told you, I didn't want Whitney to know you're a Luciano. You heard her yourself: she likes being part of the business. She understands what's going on between your family and mine, and she's loyal to our side."

"So what? Does being with me mean you're betraying them somehow?"

"Yes!" I let out a noise that was almost a laugh, almost hysterical. "I'm risking all their lives by coming to you, by sharing anything with you. I'm making it so fucking easy for you to use me. That's the way they would see it, anyway. That's sure as hell how Nathan sees it. And I don't know what it is about you that makes me okay with that."

"You know, it's sort of funny," she said after a few seconds. "My sister was here saying the same thing to me earlier. That being with you is hazardous to my health. That our relationship is a 'liability' to the family. You could be just as dangerous to me as I am to you. Maybe even more so. But here you are, standing in my bedroom, and I'm glad you're here. I'm not afraid of you. I'm not on my guard. I'm certainly not thinking about your family. I'm just waiting for you to remember why you came back and make up for that weak kiss you gave me earlier."

This time, my laugh was brief but genuine. "Fuck what Gemma says, right?"

"And what Nathan says too," Sofia added with a smile. God, I liked that smile.

Sofia wasn't involved with her sister's plotting or her brother's duties or her dad's attacks. She wasn't reporting everything I said back to them. She wanted me there because she wanted *me*, and what a wild fucking idea that was. That she actually, genuinely wanted me, that I wasn't a second or third choice, and that she wanted me badly enough to put up with her family's bitching about us being together. She wanted me enough to figure out a way around all my bullshit excuses for why it shouldn't happen.

I walked over to the bed and slid both hands through her hair, tilting her head up toward me. And I kissed her right this time, every bit as bold and possessive as she wanted, until I had her whimpering against my lips and clawing at my jacket to get me closer. Even when I pulled away from her, her hands stayed clenched on my lapels.

"I'm sorry," I told her, "for acting like I did tonight. And generally being a prick. I'll try to work on that in the future."

"Mm." She licked her lips thoughtfully. "I don't think I can accept that apology just yet. Ah-ah-ah..." She held up both hands to stop me before I could get irritated. "All I'm saying is that I think a more thorough apology is in order. You were throwing around some pretty hurtful accusations."

"Right." I rolled my eyes and leaned down to put my lips to her neck. "So what do you have in mind, princess?"

"Well, I *was* on my way to the shower," she said, glancing toward the open bathroom door. "Maybe there's something you can help me with in there."

"Your wish is my command." I took a step back and gave her a half-bow, gesturing to the door.

"Careful, or I might get used to that." She untied the robe on her way to the bathroom and shrugged it to the floor to show—damn it—she was already naked. I stripped down quickly to catch up to her, and while she was leaning halfway in the shower trying to get the water temperature right, I couldn't resist the urge to slap her ass. She squealed and turned a glare on me over her shoulder.

"Oops," I said with a grin. "My hand slipped." She rolled her eyes and stepped into the shower, grabbing my hand to pull me along. She ran the water a little hotter than I would've, but I ignored it and focused on mapping out her body with my hands, following every dip and curve while she tilted her head back against my chest. Talk about trust. Sofia was totally relaxed in my arms, giving me free rein to do whatever I wanted with her. She even rubbed her ass back against my dick, slippery and hot all over, trying to wear my patience a little thinner. At least, that's what I assumed she wanted, knowing her.

"Mm." She tensed up when my hand came to rest on her throat, reaching up to grip my wrist but not trying to push me away. My hold tightened a little, just enough that I could feel her pulse, and she dragged in a slow breath to let it out as a whimper. "Myles..." I loved the way she said my name, a little breathless, a little helpless.

Sliding my free hand down to her hips, I spoke into her ear: "Open your legs for me, kitten." It was more of an offer than an order, but she still obeyed, shakily stepping her feet a little wider apart so my fingers could slip between her legs and explore her. Her pussy was hot and slick already, and not from the shower. I made sure to take my time about touching her, tracing her lips with my fingertips, dipping them just barely inside, then sliding them slowly around her clit until she whimpered and shook in my arms. When I finally took the pressure off her throat, she gasped in a deep breath, then it came out as another soft whine.

"I'm gonna...pass out if you're not careful," she mumbled.

"You can tell me if it's too much."

"Well. I didn't say that."

I chuckled and led her over to lean her back against the wall. "Here, if you're worried about it. Just stay there and let me take care of you." She bit her lip in anticipation.

"I'll be sure to pay you back for being so sweet."

"Yeah, I bet." I worked my hands and my mouth slowly down her body: my lips on her shoulder, my hands sliding down her waist, my tongue flicking her nipples, my fingertips digging into her hips. By the time I got down to kneel in front of her, she was panting, open-mouthed, her breathing deep and slow while she watched me with hazy eyes. I knew I couldn't do much with her legs closed, but that was the idea. I wanted her to beg. So I didn't bother pushing her legs apart as I ran my tongue along her hipbone and the crease of her thigh. Dropping my head a little, I pushed my tongue into the gap between her legs, barely able to reach anything and knowing it must be driving her crazy.

"Mph," she whined, squirming her legs. "This isn't a very good apology if you're going to keep being so stingy." Oh right, this was supposed to be more for her enjoyment than mine. So maybe waiting for her to ask was a little cruel.

"All right, I get it." Without warning, I lifted one of her legs up and put it over my shoulder, wrapping my arm around her thigh to encourage her to rest her weight on me. Despite being a little shaky, she did, and she slid both her hands into my hair. With her spread open right in front of my face, it was too easy to lean down and stick my tongue inside her, making her squeak and tug on my hair to keep me close.

"Mm, that's much better," she moaned. Talking back would've meant taking my mouth off her, which I was beyond unwilling to do. So I just hummed my agreement and pressed my mouth harder against her pussy, tonguefucking her slowly and enjoying every appreciative little mewl she let out. How did every single part of her manage to turn me on? Even just the taste of her, the feeling of her squeezing around my tongue, was already getting me hard.

When I pulled my tongue out of her and trailed it upward to glide over her clit, she dropped her head back and ground out, "*Oh*, God..."

As much as I wanted to tease her about it, I wasn't willing to give up the now-constant sounds of pleasure dripping off her lips. It seemed like if I wanted to, I could make her cum like this—in fact, it almost seemed like she might insist on it. But while I was getting caught up in how hot she was on my tongue, how smooth and soft, she eventually used her grip on my hair to push me away, tilting my head back so I would look up at her.

"If you're going to fuck me," she panted raggedly, "you'd better do it. *Now*." Not much room for argument there. Once I got to my feet, she immediately dragged me in for a rough kiss, shivering when she tasted herself on my tongue. Her hands slid down my chest and stomach to stroke my cock, as if I needed the extra help. I jerked away from her with a gasp when her hand slid down to cup my balls. With a very obvious smirk, she said innocently, "My hand slipped."

"Uh-huh." I yanked her closer to me by her hips to grind against the softness of her thigh. "You have condoms here or what?" As far as I knew, she had her own birth control in place, so the condoms had always been more of a control thing. Without hesitation, she shook her head, flinging wet black hair everywhere.

"Don't bother." Bracing her hands against the back wall of the shower, she glanced at me over her shoulder and shook her ass. "Come get me, baby." I didn't need to be told twice.

Trying to ignore the sudden jump in my heart rate, I stepped in close behind her and pressed the tip of my cock barely inside her, just enough to hear her sigh. Then I gripped her hips firmly and pulled them back against mine, groaning as her hot cunt slid over my cock. Sofia's breath caught for a second, her back arching with me buried so deep inside her. Goddamnit, she was good. Itching for more friction, I pushed her forward, then dragged her back again. The way she took me, the way she gasped and sighed and even giggled breathlessly, it wasn't long before I found myself pushing her forward and fucking her into the wall.

"Oooh, God, yes," she managed, scrabbling at the tiles, struggling to stay upright. "So—so good! Fuck me—harder!"

"Yeah, you like that, princess?" I growled right back, my hand fisted in her hair to keep her still. Not that I needed to; judging by how clouded her eyes had gotten and the high, desperate pitch of her voice, getting away from me was the last thing on her mind. My other hand rested against the wall by her head, and she was grasping my wrist tightly. "Tell me."

"Yes! I...I like it. I want you to...touch me. So I can cum for you."

"Oh, you're gonna cum already, huh?" I couldn't help grinning at the unnecessary stroke to my ego. Not to mention how much I liked it when she got this way. When she wanted me bad enough, all her brattiness disappeared and she was willing to beg. I slid my hand out of her hair and down between her legs but didn't touch her yet. "Say please."

Sofia let out a squeal of frustration. "Please!" When my fingertips touched her clit, slipping wetly across feverish skin, her legs shook and nearly buckled. "Yes, yes, just like that...!"

"Go ahead and cum for me, princess. Cum all over my cock." Even though she bit down on her lip to keep from screaming, I could still feel her pussy squeeze and throb with her orgasm—but I didn't give her a second to rest, keeping up my rhythm through it to see how overwhelmed she could get without tapping out. Despite her moans turning deep and ragged, she wasn't asking me to stop yet. Knowing I was getting close too, I asked, "Can you give me one more, kitten?"

"Mm-hm." She nodded weakly. Even as tired as she must've been, she still had the energy to blush.

"I'm gonna cum in you," I told her, rubbing her clit lazily along with my rough thrusts, "and you're gonna take it. Aren't you?"

"Mm-hm!" Her nod was a little more enthusiastic this time, whether because she actually wanted it or because she wanted to please me. Either way, it was satisfying. "Yes, baby. Give it to me."

She pushed her ass back against me, bending over a little more to let me go deeper. And so I could focus on keeping my hips moving, she reached down to take over touching herself, tightening up around me already. A little harder, a little faster, my hands gripping her hips hard enough to bruise—then she came around me again, and I was forced to cum with her. I kept her close against me, tilting my head back and groaning deeply while I finished inside her. A couple more slow thrusts and I finally pulled out to watch my cum drip down her leg.

But without me supporting her, Sofia's weak legs quickly gave out, and I had to grab her before she fell. Shit, I had really worn her out. The way she shook in my arms, I almost felt guilty. Then she turned around to face me, wrapped her arms around my neck and kissed me softly, and the look in her eyes was so painfully affectionate that I couldn't feel bad anymore.

"You okay?" I asked, letting her lean on me as much as

she needed to. Even if I'd exhausted myself too, I wasn't having trouble standing like she was.

"Yeah. That was…a lot," she admitted, but she was smiling.

"Tell me about it. Honestly, I'm impressed you stayed standing the whole time."

She swatted my chest weakly, pouting. "I'm tougher than you give me credit for."

"Uh-huh. You want my help bathing, tough stuff?"

"'Need' is more like it. But since it's your fault I'm so tired, I think it's your responsibility to help me," she said. "So get to it."

"Yes, ma'am." As much as I liked it when she got all submissive, I definitely preferred her usual prissiness. Repaying her for the multiple times she'd done the same for me, I helped her wash off the scent of sex and sweat, replacing it with some orange-tangerine body wash shit she had in the shower. When we got out, she managed to dry herself off, but she barely made it back to the bed before collapsing.

"Oh. Wait." She sat up just a little and gestured to the dresser. "It's probably better not to sleep naked when we aren't the only ones here. Can you grab a nightgown for me?" I did what she said, but she still narrowed her eyes at me. "*And* panties?"

"So demanding."

She wriggled into her clothes while I grabbed my boxers from earlier and came to meet her in the bed. She didn't waste any time getting close to me. Apparently, she'd gotten a lot more touchy-feely since our first few nights together. At least, when it came to me.

"So, were you satisfied?" I asked, and she raised an eyebrow at me. "With my apology."

"Oh! Yes. Definitely," she giggled. "Although I feel like there was a point where that 'your wish is my command' attitude pretty much disappeared."

"Probably the point where you kept begging me to fuck you," I teased, and she pursed her lips at me. "I mean, if you wanted me to stop, you had a funny way of showing it."

"Shut up," she said, pushing my shoulder again. "And go to sleep, you jerk." Still, she didn't argue when I pulled her close. I felt like the moment was missing something, like there was something I should be saying. But I didn't know how or what, so I settled for another kiss instead.

12

SOFIA

Even if I never would've said it out loud to him, I always enjoyed waking up next to Myles. He looked so uncharacteristically innocent in his sleep, and I couldn't help but run my fingers through his hair. I was tempted to go right back to sleep at his side to enjoy being close to him a little longer—but it was already 10 a.m., and I imagined that Nathan would be worried over Myles and Whitney not coming home last night. That man worried every chance he got. But then, maybe that was a good counter to Myles's carefree personality.

I leaned in to plant a kiss on his cheek and ran my fingertips over his shoulder. "You should be getting up, Mister Moretti. I'm sure you have work to do today." He grunted and turned away, trying to ignore me like he always did when I woke him up. With a sigh, I got up and headed to the closet to get dressed. When I came back, I nudged Myles again gently. "Last chance. Don't make me do this the hard way." His eyes cracked open just enough to glare at me, then he stubbornly closed them again. "I warned you."

When I pulled the curtains open and sunlight flooded over the bed, Myles let out a strangled cry and turned over to bury his face into the pillows. I barely heard a muffled, "fuck" before he finally started to sit up. Absently brushing back his messy hair, he muttered, "You're a slave-driver. You know that?"

"Cry me a river," I said without a hint of sympathy. "I bet Whitney won't throw such a fit. Should I go get her up?"

"Ugh. Yeah, I guess. Hang on," he added before I could leave the room. "Don't touch her or anything. She's probably still fucked up about last night." I nodded and shut the door behind me so he could get dressed. After crossing the living room to the other bedroom, I knocked at the door gently. No answer. So I knocked a little harder and called Whitney's name. Still nothing. Maybe she was an even heavier sleeper than Myles. I cracked the door open and peeked inside to find the covers thrown back and Whitney gone from the bed.

Oh, God. I quickly checked the closet and the bathroom, but she wasn't there. Why would she have left? Where would she have gone? "Myles!" The panic in my voice must have reached him; he met me in the living room with his shirt barely buttoned.

"What? What's wrong?"

I was almost afraid to even say it out loud. "Whitney's missing." His eyebrows furrowed for a second, then relief washed over his face.

"God, don't scare me like that."

"Your niece is missing in a hotel with God knows how many floors and rooms and people, and *that's* your response?"

"Knowing her, she probably just went to get breakfast." He shrugged and continued doing up the buttons on his shirt. "You know she's a person, right? With a brain? She's just a small one."

"That was what you thought at the concert too," I reminded him, still not convinced that we shouldn't be mounting a search party right away. He winced at the memory.

"Yeah, and *that* was bad judgment on my part," he agreed. "But this is different. She'll be back soon, trust me."

"I don't know what you were thinking last night." I sat down on the couch and looked up at him critically. "Why didn't you step in sooner?"

Myles let out a heavy sigh. "Look, you don't know her very well yet, but she hates being babied. She hates anyone speaking for her. She hates it when people assume she's not capable. If I *had* gone over there and told her she couldn't talk to the guy, she would've gotten pissed at me."

"But she also wouldn't have gotten traumatized."

"Oh come on, 'traumatized'? That's an exaggeration." Even as he was saying it, he didn't seem fully convinced.

"Myles, you didn't feel how hard she was shaking. And God, that look on her face..." I shook my head, trying to replace the image with the smiling girl I'd seen at the start of the night. "Surely, her getting mad at you for a minute is better than her going through something like that again. You're the adult. *You* have to decide when she needs help, even if she doesn't want to admit it."

"I'm not her dad, okay?" he snapped. "I'm not the guy who worries about her constantly and assumes she can't do things on her own. Sometimes people go through traumatic shit. And then they keep living. Especially if she wants to get involved in the business someday, I wouldn't be doing her any favors by keeping her sheltered."

Well. That was one way of looking at it. I had grown up

pretty sheltered myself, but I couldn't say whether that had made my life any harder. Regardless, he was the one taking care of Whitney. She was his niece, not mine. I just hoped he would be a little more mindful in the future. And that he'd always be there to jump in when necessary.

I was brought out of my thoughts by a scraping sound at the door, and Myles went to check who it was. Grinning at me over his shoulder, he said, "Told you so." He opened the door to reveal Whitney, still dressed from the night before and with her makeup half-intact, her arms full of packaged pastries and hands grasping three tiny Styrofoam cups of orange juice. "Well done, Whits."

"I had to look for forever to find the stuff," she said, depositing everything carefully onto the counter. "This place is huge!"

"You scared me a little running off like that," I admitted, sure that my tone was lighthearted so she wouldn't feel guilty. Still, she blanched slightly.

"Sorry. I didn't want to wake you guys up, but I got tired of just sitting here."

"It's not a big deal," Myles assured her, reaching out like he might flick one of her braids, but pulling his hand back just as quickly. "I told her you'd be back. And with muffins!" He reached around her to grab one, and I didn't miss the slight tension in her shoulders before he stepped back. *I think 'trauma' is exactly the right word.*

"I'll make some coffee." Luckily, the kitchen was big enough that I could maneuver around her without worrying about getting too close. "Er, Whitney, would you prefer tea?"

"Ugh." She snorted. "That's a stereotype. But yes, definitely."

The three of us ate a very healthy breakfast of preservative-filled danishes, sugary orange juice, and cream-drowned coffee and tea. Around noon, Whitney remembered she had plans to watch a football game with Gregorio later. It was Italy vs. France, so obviously (the way she put it) it was vital that she saw how it turned out. And it started at 3:00 p.m., meaning they needed to leave "like, now." She was gathering her things up and pushing Myles toward the door within minutes.

"Hey, instead of griping at me," he said as he was putting his shoes back on, "why don't you call Jerome and tell him we're ready to head out?" Whitney groaned as if this were a huge imposition, but she got her phone out and went into the hall anyway. Myles went to follow her but paused at the door to look back at me. "Thanks for letting us stay. I know last night was kind of weird in a lot of ways."

"I'm used to it. Our relationship has been 'kind of weird in a lot of ways' too long for it to bother me anymore."

He smiled genuinely. It wasn't dry or ironic, not sarcastic or cynical, and it did things to my heart that I was terrified of admitting. "Good to know I'm not the only one who's given up fighting it."

"As long as you don't give up fighting *me*, that's fine," I told him with a sweet smile.

"Even if I tried, it wouldn't last long. You have a talent for getting under my skin." He reached for my waist to pull me closer, but we were interrupted by Whitney's voice from the hall.

"Jerome's on his way! We need to go!"

Myles sighed and stole a quick kiss before opening the door. "I'll see you later." Despite being utterly unsatisfied with that goodbye, I kept my smile in place as he left. A few seconds passed, I resigned myself to cleaning up our mess from breakfast. As I was tossing empty plastic wrappers into the trash, there was yet another knock at my door. Apparently, I was very popular lately.

But when I opened the door, I realized it was the same visitor as before, coming back to my door for the third time. Before I could ask why he was there, Myles snaked his arms around my waist and pulled me in for a kiss so passionate I couldn't help smiling against his lips. He was grinning too when he let me go, keeping his eyes locked on my mouth.

"Dinner," he said firmly. "Wednesday. I'll pick you up. Okay?"

"If you insist."

"I absolutely do." Another brief kiss, and he walked away again, leaving me in a much better mood this time.

...

"Wait, he came back after they dropped you off?"

"Yes! Both of them did, actually." If you had told me a month ago that I would end up living in a hotel suite away from my family by choice, sitting on my couch video chatting with Lauren Maldone about my punk concert date with Myles Moretti, I would've thought you were completely insane. Yet there I was, and not a single part of it bothered me. Lauren had asked for an update about how the concert had gone, and my instinct was to call and spill the whole story. She was either genuinely interested or very good at pretending. "He said Whitney told him he was being weird —and he was, without a doubt."

"Yeah, it definitely sounds like it, but I don't get why." Even once I explained the whole Moretti-Luciano feud, she still didn't seem to understand. "I mean, it's not like *you* did anything against them. You didn't attack anyone. Why should you get blamed for what the rest of your family did?"

It was a little crazy how different Lauren's upbringing was from ours. Maybe it was just her distance from the don, or maybe the Maldones had a different perspective on this stuff than we did. It really seemed like she didn't subscribe to the whole blood-is-everything, your-family-name-is-who-you-are concept, which was so incredibly refreshing when I was constantly surrounded by people who did.

"I don't know. It's a weird, complicated thing. Principles, I guess. I mean, don't get me wrong, I love my family, and I wouldn't turn on them for anything. Or anyone." Letting out a conflicted huff, I tilted my head to the other side. "But if he's right about what they did to Gregorio? And the way they completely shut Myles down without giving him a chance? How am I supposed to support that?"

Lauren was shaking her head sympathetically. "It must be a really weird position. Obviously, I don't know Myles nearly as well as you do. But he seems cool. The couple times I've met him, he's been really...I don't know, just chill. Different from most of the dons' kids."

"Yeah," I agreed distractedly. "He is. Different."

After a brief pause, she added, "And you're obviously *really* into him."

I frowned indignantly. "I don't know about all that. I like him, sure. We have fun, I guess. But 'really into him' feels like a stretch."

"Sofia." Lauren almost looked amused by my denial. "You moved out of your family's house because they didn't want you to be with him." Maybe, but that was just a tantrum. Wasn't it? "You're still seeing him despite your sister telling you it could put your life in danger." Well, maybe that was partially to spite Gemma. "And after that fight you guys had when I was visiting? It obviously messed with your head a lot. Whatever kind of feelings you have about him, you can't act like they're not strong ones."

"All right, all right," I groaned, still struggling to pretend this was a casual thing regardless of all evidence to the contrary. "Look, let's talk about something else. *You* wouldn't happen to have any guys in your life you're keeping from me, would you?" I'd never gotten to do the teasing-older-sister thing, and frankly, Gemma had never given me an example, but I liked to think I knew how it should go. As intended, Lauren flushed a little and tilted her head to hide behind her hair.

"Oh, no. Uh, I'm not really good with that sort of thing," she said with a nervous laugh.

"There's no one you're interested in?"

"I don't know. It doesn't really matter." It seemed like her mood had gone from flustered to resigned in seconds, and I suddenly regretted bringing this up.

"What do you mean? Why not?"

"You know where I'm at in my family. My grandma's the don, but my mom's not her heir. She's not the oldest," Lauren pointed out, shaking her bangs partially out of her eyes. "I'm not really part of the business. I'm pretty sure the only reason I get to go places and meet people is so she can marry me off eventually. I'm basically a walking peace treaty waiting to be signed."

I couldn't tell whether she was being hopelessly pessimistic or if that really was her situation. It made sense, I guess. Huge families like the Maldones were bound to have lots of kids, and they couldn't *all* be heirs to the throne. Some of them would end up working for the family in different ways, like the cousins I had who were capos or soldatos. And some would be used as bargaining chips to secure the loyalty of smaller families. Like Marie Capelli and her marriage.

"Hey, who knows? I might get lucky and get too old to be traded off." Lauren forced a laugh. "It's not a big deal. Just the hand I was dealt, you know? That's what my mom always says." It wasn't fair. Some people in our families didn't want the hand they were dealt. They didn't ask to be brought into the game in the first place. And it wasn't like they could opt out, not without a ton of grief—as Royce and Roger could attest to.

"Well, that doesn't mean you can't keep your eyes open. Maybe if you end up finding someone you like, your grandma will realize you're not available for bargaining anymore."

Her smile lingered somewhere between doubt and pity. "Yeah. Maybe."

It really wasn't fair.

...

Wednesday morning, I got a call from my brother, and I answered it excitedly. The two of us hadn't spoken since I'd left the house last week, mostly because I wasn't sure if I could comfortably visit the house anymore with Gemma there. But in spite of my delighted greeting, as I sat up in bed to talk to him, Danny's voice was cool as he asked, "Have you heard from Arturo?"

Right to business, I guess. "No. Why would I have?"

"Don't act like you two haven't been close in the past."

"Yeah, in the past." There was no point reminding him

that I really was seeing Myles and it wasn't just a passing fling. "We're not really close anymore. You sound upset. Is something wrong?"

"He's missing. He left the house Sunday night, and no one's seen him since," Danny explained. My face drew into a frown. It really wasn't like Arturo to miss a shift. Even if he was injured, even if he was sick, it never kept him from showing up to work. He was all about his duty to the family. So if he was missing, that must mean—

Suddenly, my blood ran cold, and I nearly dropped my phone. What was it Myles had said?

I'm talking about your dad's people attacking Gregorio outside my club.

And it turns out your little boyfriend, Arturo, was the one leading the whole thing.

He said that Gregorio was attacked for no reason. And if that was the case, I knew for a fact he would want to get even. And it was obvious he already hated Arturo because of my history with him. I almost couldn't process the possibility, but some part of me felt very firmly that there was no question about what had happened.

"Sofi? Sofi!" I realized Danny was still on the line and shook myself out of my thoughts to answer him.

"Is anyone else missing?"

"Not that I know of. Why? Do you know something?" His tone had turned suspicious, like I might have been involved in it somehow.

"No." It wasn't technically a lie.

"Sofia, if Myles is behind this—"

"Do you know anything about Gregorio Moretti being attacked?" I asked, hoping the change of subject would shock him into giving me some of the answers I desperately needed.

"What? No. Are you saying that's why—"

"Does Gemma know? Can you just...can you two look into it? If Papà really did send some of our people to hurt him, then..."

"Where are you even getting that idea? Did Myles say that?" Danny let out something between a sigh and a growl. "He's playing you. He's trying to turn you against us. And you're almost giving me the impression that it's working."

"Why would he make something like this up?" I was asking myself as much as Danny, suddenly very unsure. Of everything.

"As an excuse to have one of our men killed?" The words were so chilly they nearly gave me frostbite.

I shook my head slowly, vaguely. He wouldn't. He wouldn't just kill someone without a reason. And the fact that I had been with Arturo couldn't possibly be enough of a reason. "Will you just ask Papà about it? Or don't ask him. Just look into it on your own. See if he had a group sent to Myles's nightclub last week. If that's the case, if Arturo was with them—"

"Hang on. Are you trying to say Myles might be justified in taking him?" His voice was utterly incredulous, like I was crazy. "I don't know anything about an attack on the Morettis. Surely if it happened, I would be aware of it. Dad hasn't said anything about it. Hasn't even hinted at being hostile toward them; he just wants to be done with them. Even if he did have some kind of grudge, attacking them would mean blood for blood, which he wouldn't risk."

Everything he was saying made sense. It all sounded logical, and knowing my dad, I knew Danny was right. He wasn't the sort of person, the sort of boss, to attack anyone over an indirect offense—like Deron's death. There was no reason he would've had Gregorio attacked. But I couldn't imagine that Myles was lying to me either. He must have just been mistaken. But if that misinformation meant he'd wrongfully kidnapped Arturo, or worse...

Danny must have heard my panicked breathing bordering on sobs as I tried to sort all this out in my head. His voice was a lot gentler as he said, "Sorellina, I'm really worried about you. I don't know what Myles has been telling you, but it sounds like nothing but lies. It's okay to decide you're in over your head. It's okay to come home."

It wasn't okay. God, nothing was okay. I took a deep breath, trying hard to tamp down the nervous fear swirling in my stomach. This whole situation would've been so much easier to sort out if the two sides would just agree to *talk* to each other. But since I was dealing with a bunch of grown men who insisted on acting like children, it seemed like I would have to be the go-between. Fine. They needed someone to mediate? Fine!

"I'm going to talk to Myles," I said calmly. As my brother started to protest, I kept talking like I didn't hear him, "Whatever's going on, obviously no one has the full story. So I'm going to figure it out."

"But you're still trusting his word. That's exactly how he's manipulating you."

"Stop." A pause. "I know you're going to worry no matter what I say, but I promise: I can handle him. I'll get back to you once I know what's actually happened." And I ended the call.

The conversation I had to have with Myles was not going to be an easy one. But I had never been scared of him before, and I wasn't about to start now. This wasn't just about him or me; it was about a conflict between our families that could very easily turn into a war if it wasn't stopped. And if I had to play both sides to stop it, then I would.

...

I spent the rest of the day planning out exactly what I would say to Myles, including the questions I needed answered and the counter-questions I needed to ask if his answers didn't check out. I didn't think he would lie to me outright, but he had a nasty habit of withholding information, even when he knew I should have it. Like his plans to kidnap Arturo, for instance—assuming that was what had happened. One of the many pieces of this puzzle that didn't quite fit.

I texted him that afternoon asking when he was coming to pick me up, and he responded with a cheeky remark about how he could come over right away if I was that desperate to see him. I couldn't bring myself to be playful and instead, suggested that it might be best for us to have dinner at my place rather than going out. If he noticed I was being somber, he didn't acknowledge it. He agreed that he would pick something up and meet me at my suite at 9:30. When I told him I couldn't wait, it was honest, just probably not in the way he expected.

The hour before he got there was spent making sure I was composed, from my attitude to my thoughts to my looks. I wore a red silk pencil dress he'd mentioned liking before and matched my lipstick to it perfectly. I was careful not to go too far since technically it was just dinner at home, but I put in enough effort to impress him. After critically observing every aspect in my closet mirror, I decided I was finally ready to do what I did best: look pretty and get information.

Myles arrived at 9:42 with takeout bags in both hands. "Sorry I'm late," he said as he set them down on the counter. "Who knew lobster takes so long to cook?" Finally sweeping his eyes up and down my figure, he let out a low whistle. "Damn it, you look good. Is this some kind of special occasion I don't know about?"

I smiled as he pulled me into his arms, focusing for a second on the genuine peace I felt when he held me. As he leaned down to kiss me, I considered throwing my whole interrogation plan out the window. *Just have dinner with him. Drink wine. Stop worrying. Kiss him again. And again. Get him in bed.* For the first time, I genuinely resented my family's business for forcing me into this position.

But I remembered the discomfort in Danny's voice, the stress on Myles's face, the threats Gemma had made, and I reminded myself why I couldn't just enjoy him. "You know I can't have you seeing me at less than my best."

"As if you need all this"—he gestured to the hair, makeup, and outfit I'd worked so hard on—"to look your best." *Damn it, stop making this difficult.*

"Did you really bring lobster?" I asked, peering at the bags he'd brought in.

"I figured why the hell not," he said with a careless shrug.

For the first hour or so, I let it be a mostly normal date. I poured wine but didn't drink much from my glass. We ate and chatted and bantered, but the normalcy was underscored with nervous anticipation the whole time. Once we'd finished dinner, I let myself get quiet and my uncertainty show on my face.

"Hey." Myles reached across the counter to rest his hand on mine. "Something wrong?"

"We need to talk."

He swallowed hard as I got up and nodded toward the living room. "Yeah, okay." I sat in the corner of the couch with him at my side, holding his hand and absently fidgeting with it. "What's up?"

"I went by the house today," I lied, trying to keep it as neutral-sounding as possible so he wouldn't jump to the conclusion that I was asking on behalf of my family, even if I was. "To have lunch with my brother and his son."

"Antoni, right?"

I forced a smile. "Yeah." I had mentioned Antoni to him before, of course, talked about his recent dad-doesn't-have-time-for-me moment. "Anyway, while I was there, I noticed that Arturo wasn't around." Myles's smile immediately disappeared, replaced with suspicion and irritation. "I asked around if anyone had seen him. And they said he went missing on Sunday. Hasn't been back to the house since." He took his hand out of mine and leaned away from me slightly on the couch, his eyes wandering away from mine. I persisted: "And then I remembered you saying something about him being involved in Gregorio's attack. So I wanted to ask if you know anything about him going missing."

Even now that I'd put the ball in his court, Myles didn't answer me right away. And when he did, it wasn't really an answer. "What do you care?"

"How can I *not* care? No family likes to lose one of their own. And when they do, they usually want payback." This wasn't anything he didn't already know. "So if you were involved in one of my dad's guys disappearing, I feel like that's something I should know."

"Is that what this is about? You getting payback for whatever happened to him?" He could keep trying to make this about me and Arturo as much as he wanted; I wasn't biting. "Besides, I don't know what makes you assume it was deliberate. *Gli incidenti accadono.*"

Accidents happen. In any other situation, I would've thought it was cute to hear him speak Italian. But that particular phrase was something he'd taken from his dad. It wasn't an explicit confession, but the way Deron used it, it might as well have been.

"You're not giving me a straight answer. All I want is to know the truth. Because it involves my family. Because it involves you. Because both of those parties are pretty damn significant to me."

"What, so you should know everything that involves either of us? You sure you *want* all that information?" he asked, draping his arms over the back of the couch.

"Can you please just answer me?"

"You didn't see what the guy did to Gregorio. It would've made you fucking sick. You wouldn't be defending him if you were there."

"Myles."

"Yes, all right?" he snapped. "Yes, I know exactly what happened to him, and I know it wasn't fucking pretty. I also know he's not going to be showing back up at the house any time soon. I know, because I'm the one who made it happen. Because I wanted payback too. Happy?" I took a deep breath to keep myself calm and followed up with my next question.

"How do you know it was him?"

"Gregorio recognized his fucking face. Said he was the one in charge, and he thought the whole thing was just hilarious."

I couldn't imagine Arturo enjoying hurting anyone, even someone he thought was an enemy. Gregorio was only 23, and as far as I knew, he hadn't done anything wrong. How could anyone take pleasure in that? But then, there was the darker possibility that Myles had made up the attack altogether.

"Do you…" I knew he wouldn't like this question. "Do you have any pictures of what happened? Videos from the club, maybe?"

Myles stared at me in disbelief. "Are you serious right now? You want *proof*? No, I don't have any goddamn pictures. Maybe I can get you some x-rays if you really want. Would that be good enough to convince you that Arturo fucking deserved what he got?" I hated it when he got this way. Angry and defensive and eager to take out his frustration on anyone who tried to talk to him about it.

"I just don't understand," I told him plainly. "You know my dad. You know he wouldn't have ordered something like this—"

"I thought I did, sure. That was before he completely sold me out to the Council."

"—and if he didn't order it," I went on, "then he'll think of what you did to Arturo as an unprovoked attack." Silence for a second.

"That might worry me if I didn't already know he was responsible. Gregorio *saw them*. Pointed them out to us. And everyone responsible is part of your family." It definitely didn't seem like he was lying. Whether he was right or not, it was clear that he genuinely believed all this was true.

"I'm only asking because *I'm* worried for you. The rest of the Council doesn't like you. You know they want to see you removed. If they hear about this and they're able to spin it the right way…" I stopped as his hands clenched tightly on the cushion behind him.

"It doesn't matter how they 'spin it.' It was retaliation. That's a fact. He came for us first. I wasn't going to just let that slide."

Sensing a segue into the next unpleasant topic, I asked quietly, "Like what happened with your dad?"

Myles's eyes went wide for a split-second, but his expression quickly went back to drawn and hard. He shoved to his feet and start pacing the living room. "So that's what all this was? Just a warm-up for the 'why'd you kill your dad' question?" He scoffed out a mirthless laugh. "This is really not the conversation I thought we were about to have."

"I don't know what happened with your dad," I admitted, keeping my spine straight, hands folded in my lap. "But I want to. If you're willing to tell me."

"What happened is he crossed a line, and I did something about it," Myles said, casually slipping a butterfly knife out of his pocket and starting to play with it, trading it back and forth between his hands, tossing it and catching it now and again. Somehow, it seemed to keep him calmer. "What happened is he was a selfish, manipulative asshole who turned on the people he was supposed to protect. My brothers. Me. My mom." His face darkened even more. "And I knew he wasn't going to stop. He wasn't going to change. If we gave him the opportunity, he was going to do the same damn thing again. So I didn't give him the opportunity."

"He was threatening you, right? The three of you?"

He nodded. "And Deanna. Had a knife to her throat." He looked at the blade in his hand for a second, then flipped it and kept talking. "As if trying to ruin our lives wasn't enough. He really would've killed her. Like he killed our mom. No one else was willing to do what needed to be done. So I did it. As usual. *I* killed him so my older brothers didn't have to get their hands dirty. So my younger brothers wouldn't have to go through the same thing in ten years. So my niece wouldn't have to worry about her mom being used as leverage." He stopped pacing and flipped the knife closed again, not looking even remotely in my direction.

"Nobody fucks with my family," he said finally. "No matter where it comes from. I won't stand for it."

I hardly knew how to answer him. Gemma really thought he'd killed Deron just to stay in control? Looking at him, comparing him to the man he was three or four years ago, it was clear what a toll the job had taken on him. Maybe it was attractive when he first started, but he had obviously learned that being in control was *hard*. But it was exactly like he said: if not him, who would've done it? Royce and Roger were too insistent on getting out, too determined to have their own Perfectly Normal Lives elsewhere. While Myles had stayed to take responsibility. At any time, he could've decided it was too much, that it wasn't fun anymore so he was no longer interested. He could've abandoned his family and run off to live his own life. But he hadn't. How anyone could see that and think of it as selfish or malicious, I couldn't understand.

My other questions had fled my mind, leaving me silent and embarrassed. Guilty.

"That's...admirable," I said, and he scoffed. "I'm serious. It's a choice you made, a choice to do a job that involves a lot of work, constant criticism, and not much thanks. Not every man would've done that."

"Is this the part where you try to convince me I should give it up?"

My brows furrowed. "Why would I do that?"

"It's what happens to the men in my family, apparently. A woman falls in love with you and then convinces you you're 'better than this.' That you 'don't need it.' Maybe that woman comes from a family that would benefit from your career ending. Who knows?"

Raising my chin defiantly, I asked, "What makes you think I'm in love with you?" Slipping the knife back into his pocket, he finally turned back toward me with a knowing smirk.

"The fact that that was the part you got hung up on."
Arrogant bastard.

"I don't care anything about persuading you to give up your position."

"Then what's the point of all this?" he asked, gesturing to the remnants of our dinner, then to me. "You obviously have a point. You wouldn't have just started this conversation for the hell of it. So where was it going?"

"I told you, I'm worried about you. You're in a dangerous position, and I feel like it's only getting more dangerous by the day. I don't want to see you get hurt."

"There it is." He nodded as he swaggered slowly across the room back to me. "That's the logic." Adopting a falsetto voice, he went on, "'I don't want to see you get hurt. It's too dangerous. Just give it up and be with me.'" I couldn't help feeling he was acting a lot drunker than he actually was. Maybe it was just the stress of the conversation. Stopping in front of me, he ran his fingers up the side of my neck, forcing me to shiver and pull away.

"I told you, that's not my angle."

"Then what is? Why are you bringing up your 'concern' to me?" He kept his eyes on mine, his hands in his pockets. "I can't change what's already done. If the Council wants to lynch me for it, they're going to. So what do you want me to do?"

"I just want you to know!" I insisted, pressing my fingertips into my temples. God, he was irritating! Here I'd thought I was in control of the night, of the conversation, and once again he was proving that even though each of us liked to pretend we were governing the situation, any time we were together, we were both totally powerless.

"Hey." He bent down, trying for a kiss, but I turned away. I was having a hard enough time trying to sort out my thoughts without him clouding my head even more. Still, he reached up and slid his fingers into my hair, not forcing me to look at him but leading me gently. So I did. And he kissed me.

I said before that Myles's kisses were never gentle, but that wasn't quite true. Since we'd been together lately, *actually* together, he had been proving that he had quite a repertoire I just hadn't been exposed to before. This one was slow and very deliberate. He licked my lips gently, letting me part them by choice rather than being pushy and forceful as usual. And the way his tongue moved against mine, the way he tilted my head back a little and grasped at my hair like he wanted to hold me but not hurt me—God, it was all so much softer than I'd come to expect from him.

When he let me go, my hazy eyes stayed fixed on his lips until he leaned down a little more to meet my gaze. He seemed pleased as usual with my reaction, with how weak his kisses made me. Keeping his voice low, his eyes on mine, he said, "Now tell me you don't love me."

I had to blink the dreamy fog from my eyes when I realized what he'd said, and my helpless gaze hardened into a glare. That only seemed to entertain him more. I was about to open my mouth and tell him that no, I didn't love him, and if that was what he was going for, he would have to put in some more effort to make it happen. But the words didn't come out. His hand was still in my hair, his thumb rubbing across my neck.

I wished he hadn't said the word at all. Because now it was all I could think about. That, and his skin on mine. *Love* and how badly I wanted another kiss. *Love* and how angry I was with myself for upsetting him earlier. *Love* and how I really, genuinely wanted him to be safe, how unexpectedly cold I felt at the thought of him getting hurt.

My scowl softened, and Myles's smirk vanished. Wetting my lips, I leaned forward and started, "I—"

"Whoa, hey, wait a minute!" He jumped back, pulling his hands away like I'd burned him. With a shaky, nervous laugh in his voice, he managed, "I was just fucking with you. Quit taking everything so seriously. Can't I make one fucking joke after all this heavy shit we've been talking about...?" He crossed the room to the kitchen, putting as much distance between us as possible, and downed the contents of my half-full wine glass.

Once again, I didn't know how to respond. He was joking? That was really all that amazing kiss and the intense look in his eyes amounted to? He was just fucking with me? But maybe it shouldn't have surprised me that he didn't want me to be serious. He wanted a sneer and a snippy retort because it meshed with his own naturally casual attitude. Because it didn't make him think too hard. It was easy. Conflict was easy for him. So what if it was the wrong thing to do? So what if I wanted something else?

We can't be anything other than what we are.

Deron used to say that. He and my dad agreed on a lot of things, but that wasn't one of them. I had always been told that self-improvement was a choice. And Myles was told not to bother trying.

I took in a slow breath and got up from my seat on the couch. Myles had backed himself in the corner of the kitchen like he thought I might attack him, but I turned toward my bedroom instead. Pausing in the doorway, I said without looking at him, "You've been drinking. You shouldn't drive home tonight. You can stay here or get your own room. I don't care."

He didn't answer. So I closed and locked my bedroom door behind me. In some ways, the night had been a success. I had gotten some of the answers I was looking for, at least. I'd learned a lot of things, in fact. And I wished I could wipe the whole thing from my mind.

13

MYLES

The ice in Sofia's voice could've frozen over the whole West Coast. *I don't care.* No plainer way of saying it than that. And I still stood in the corner of her kitchen, cowering like a fucking child, shell-shocked over the look I'd seen in her eyes. Why did it scare me so much? Why was I afraid?

The whole night had thrown me completely off whatever I was expecting. Honestly, when she gave me that big, serious "we need to talk" speech, I thought *that* was about to lead to the I-love-you conversation. And then it absolutely didn't. I still had no idea why she was so insistent on talking about business, about Arturo and the Council and my dad. I didn't know at all, but it definitely put me on the defensive, and then I was determined to be a prick the rest of the time. Bringing up that shit about my brothers and their wives. Comparing her to them. I really didn't expect her to take that stupid love line seriously. I thought she'd make a face at me and tell me she couldn't believe how full of myself I was. Her actual response was... I didn't know how to handle it.

Standing alone in her kitchen, staring at her bedroom door, I wondered if she was planning to come back out. If she would hear me out if I tried to talk to her. Did it matter? I wouldn't have known what to say. *Sorry for baiting you about your feelings and then turning chickenshit when you actually had them?*

"Fuck..." She was right about one thing; I knew I shouldn't drive home after, what, three, four glasses of wine? But I couldn't force myself to stay there, either. In fact, I felt like a trespasser at this point. So I grabbed my keys and my jacket and went to book a separate room so I could pass out and let sober me handle it in the morning.

...

Unfortunately, I was still at a loss when I was sober. I knew I *should* go back to Sofia's place and talk to her. That was the only solution, the only way I could fix what I'd fucked up. But I didn't. I couldn't. I still didn't know how to explain myself to her, and what good would it do anyone for me to go there and just trip all over myself trying? Normally, thinking on my feet and talking—about pretty much anything—was one of my biggest strengths. But not in this case. This time, I needed time to think, to figure out how to approach it.

So I drove back to San Diego without saying a word to her. When I got to the house, for once, no one was waiting to greet me. No Whitney trying to drag me away from work. No Nathan trying to drag me to it. No Gregorio in the living room to nod when I walked in or Rena with a hesitant smile. Nothing to take my mind off what a shithead I'd been. Maybe I deserved to stew over it for a while. I locked myself in my bedroom to shower and change clothes. Might as well be productive while I was brooding.

It wasn't like I didn't care about Sofia. I couldn't even

pretend that was the case; I'd had it bad for her since we were freshmen in high school, and it had only gotten worse over the years. But it was always in those words. I "crushed" on her or "liked" her or was "into" her. Love never came into the equation. And I hated to have the typical mafioso attitude of "love is a weakness." I especially hated thinking of my dad's "love is a weapon" ideology. But if I was honest, yeah, it *was* pretty damn inconvenient. From what I could tell, at least. After all, before Royce met Margot, he was the perfect Moretti scion without a single flaw. Two wives later, he wouldn't go anywhere near the business. And Rena? For whatever reason, she genuinely loved our dad, and what good had it done her?

It just wasn't good for business. Why couldn't I just be with Sofia without making it into some kind of official commitment? I wanted to be with her. Sure, I loved how I felt when I was around her. Why couldn't that be enough?

...

Days passed, and for the most part, it was business as usual at the house. Gregorio seemed to be in a better mood since Arturo was out of the picture. Nathan was still keeping an eye on the other Council families, but none of them had made any moves. Whitney still went to her judo classes. But now she flinched any time someone got close to touching her without warning her first. No, scratch that: she flinched any time a *man* got close to touching her without warning. We hadn't talked about what happened again since the night of the concert, but it was obviously still on her mind, subconsciously if nothing else.

And Sofia was no longer answering any of my calls or texts. Just complete radio silence. Nothing worked. I tried provoking her. I tried being sincere. I tried telling her that ghosting me like this was childish and not going to solve anything. I tried asking if my one fuck up that night was really enough for her to cut me off completely. Nothing. And my mood got worse with every day she ignored me. Everyone noticed it, but no one said anything. Most of them had no idea I was seeing her in the first place, so they probably just thought I was being pissy for no reason.

Then out of the blue, not in response to any of my many messages, I got an email from Sofia.

Can we talk? I want to see you.
-Sofia

That was it. No demands. No apologies. No indication of whether she was still pissed. But if she wanted to see me, that must mean something. It was a chance to talk, at least. We arranged to meet at my office at aMoral on Saturday night. A public place, more or less, so we weren't on good enough terms for actual privacy yet.

I cleared everyone out to give us space, and at 11:20, the door finally opened. "Took you long enough," I called from my desk. Were jokes even okay? Fuck, I was so lost. But when I heard the door lock and looked up, the long-legged brunette in my office was not the one I expected. "Gemma? What the fuck are you doing here? Where's Sofia?"

"She won't be coming," Gemma said pleasantly, wandering around the room and looking it over. "She asked you to come here on my behalf."

"Yeah, right. Since when do you two work together?"

"Let's say our family has been through some losses lately, and it's brought us closer together."

Did she mean Arturo? Was that what she was there to bitch at me for? Whatever it was, my guard was up. "And what does that have to do with me?"

"Everything, considering you're the person who caused those losses." She slowly sauntered toward my desk, watching me like a predator.

"I don't know what you're talking about," I told her, keeping my expression patently bored.

"That's interesting. Because I happen to have evidence that you do." Reaching into the purse at her hip, she pulled out her phone, then tapped and swiped a few times. When she held it out toward me, I was surprised to hear my own voice from the speakers.

"Yes, I know exactly what happened to him, and I know it wasn't fucking pretty. I also know he's not going to be showing back up at the house any time soon. I know, because I'm the one who made it happen. Because I wanted payback."

"What the fuck?" Was there recording shit set up in Sofia's apartment? Had Gemma put it there? No way would Sofia be okay with that. "You bugged your own sister's rooms?"

"Me?" She tilted her head back and let out a cool laugh. "No, Myles. Sofia did that herself."

"Bullshit." This was obviously some kind of ploy to turn us against each other, and I wasn't buying it for a minute. For all I knew, Gemma was the reason Sofia hadn't been responding to me. I wanted to believe that, at least.

"Oh please, don't take my word for it." She obviously expected me not to believe her because she had another recording ready to play.

"I'll talk to Myles. I promise: I can handle him. I'll get back to you once I know."

My eyes narrowed. Sofia's voice hardly ever got that cold, but it was definitely her. Some small part of my brain reminded me how weirdly insistent she had been about me answering the question about Arturo explicitly. No. Bullshit. She wouldn't.

"So this leaves us in sort of an awkward position," Gemma said, standing on one hip. "I have pretty damning proof here that you had one of our men killed, and all because you were jealous of his relationship with Sofia. Honestly, I didn't think even you were that petty."

"Hold the fuck up. However you got that recording, if you listen to the rest of it, you'll hear about how your dad had my brother attacked," I growled, sitting forward in my chair. "Arturo was involved. *That's* why I got back at him."

"I did hear that part. Do you have any proof that our family was involved in Gregorio's unfortunate accident?"

I started to mention the security video and Greg's eyewitness account, but those were both pretty shaky. They wouldn't be definitive enough to put in front of a jury—or a Council, for that matter. "What do you *want*, Gemma?"

"You, gone," she said flatly.

"Why? What did I ever do to you? Is this payback for Royce ignoring you your entire life?"

She rolled her eyes, obviously not affected by my jabs. "It's nothing personal, Myles. Strictly business. You're terrible at your job. You're ruining the Moretti name. We can't be associated with someone weak, which means some bridges will have to be burned. Whether my father likes it or not."

Wait.

"What?" She was there *against* Marcell's wishes? At the Council meeting, he seemed happy enough to feed me to the wolves. Did she have something to do with that? "You bitch. You were the one who had Gregorio attacked."

"Ha! Those are big accusations from such a little boy." The way her lips curled smugly, I knew I was right. "Why on

Earth would I have Gregorio attacked when I hate you so much more?" It sounded more like a genuine question, like she was expecting me to figure it out.

"I don't know. Why don't you tell me?" I got up to lean both hands against my desk, but she looked unimpressed.

"And here I thought you prided yourself on being so clever."

I rolled my eyes. "I'm harder to get to. Or maybe your guys went after the wrong target."

"Try again." She was obviously enjoying this, her dark red lips split into a grin.

"I don't fucking know! What, people would notice more if it was me?" She raised her eyebrows like I was on the right track. "You wanted it to be kept quiet. So no one would look into it."

"Except you, valiant, protective, guilt-ridden big brother. And by 'you,' I mean your consigliere, of course. Nathan, right? He's the only competent one left in the house." She put her phone back into her purse and crossed her arms. "Besides, if you were beaten to a pulp, Sofia's interest in you probably wouldn't have held long enough for me to convince her that I needed her help getting rid of you."

Sofia had told me about Gemma warning her. But she said she didn't believe any of it. What the fuck was going on? "Stop trying to pretend she's involved in any of your bullshit schemes. Everything that's happened has been because of you. Your dad and brother probably weren't even involved. Just how much effort have you gone to to get rid of me?"

"Well, you're right to think I do most of the work in our house." She made a show of looking over her fingernails. "When the men of the house are too afraid to make a move, I have my crews take care of things behind the scenes. But Dad and Daniel came around eventually. They certainly understand how dangerous you are to us now. You're more trouble as an ally than as an enemy. Sofia took a little more convincing. Maybe if you hadn't broken her heart, just like everyone told her you would, we wouldn't be having this conversation."

"I should fucking kill you right now."

Gemma's eyes sprang open, her smile widening further. "Myles. Did you just threaten my life?" And suddenly I realized she was probably wearing a wire, recording this conversation too. How did security not catch that? "Well, if that's not enough to convince the other Council members you've outstayed your welcome, I don't know what will be."

"Get out of my building," I snapped, forcing down the urge to pull my gun on her. As much reason as I had to take her out, it would only make the situation ten times worse.

"I'm going," she said on her way to the door. "But you should really think about doing the same. I give it a day or two at the most before the rest of the Council gets here in force. They can't just let a mad dog like you run free, after all." Her self-satisfied laughter echoed back up the stairs as she left.

"Fuck."

Sofia wasn't part of this. Sofia wasn't part of this. Sofia wasn't part of this.

No matter how many times I said it to myself, there was still some part of me that was drowning in doubt. She wouldn't have turned on me because I hurt her. She wouldn't have sold me out to Gemma of all people. But why was she asking all those weird questions in the first place? Why did she *make* me say what happened to Arturo? She hardly ever wanted to talk about work in detail like that. Could Gemma have gotten to her earlier on? And what was with that recording, her promising she could "handle" me?

"Fuck, fuck, fuck!" Desperate to break something, I shoved everything off my desk and threw my chair to the floor.

"Myles?" I reached for my gun by reflex when the door opened again, but it was just Nathan, looking over all the shit I'd just thrown to the floor with concern and confusion all over his face. "Is everything okay?"

"No. No, it's fucking not."

...

"For the last time, Whitney, this isn't up for debate." I was trying hard to be patient with her, but she was really pushing it. After a night of frantic research, I'd explained the whole situation to Rena and begged her to take Whits out of town to keep her safe. Maybe I was the only one Gemma was throwing under the bus, but I didn't think for a second that anyone in the house would be safe if the Council's men showed up to take me out. Like I expected she would be, Rena was horrified by the news but agreed to take Whitney, along with her younger boys Kurt and Patrick, out to the safe house we had outside Dulzura. She'd tried to insist that Gregorio come with them, but he was firm about staying. And of course, so was Whitney.

"I can help!" she insisted, teary-eyed and panicked. "I don't want to leave you here! Come with us!"

"I can't. If you're with me, you'll be in danger." The story of a Moretti's life. "Go with Rena. Take care of her."

"I don't want to go!"

"Whitney, we don't have time for this." Despite knowing she wouldn't like it, Nathan reached for her arm, and she scrambled back.

"Don't touch me!" When she was already so worked up,

pushing her seemed like the worst possible idea—but Nathan was in a pretty bad place himself and was probably just trying to get her to safety as quickly as possible. This time, he succeeded in grabbing her arm, then yanked his hand back just as fast, hissing in a breath. His shirtsleeve was torn, his forearm bleeding, and Whitney was clutching one of my butterfly knives in one hand. "I said. Don't. Touch me."

Shit. She was in a lot worse shape than I'd realized. One more thing that was my fucking fault, that wouldn't have happened if I'd had better judgment. "Whits." I knelt where I was without trying to get any closer. She was shaking again, holding the knife close to her chest. "No one's trying to hurt you here. You know that. This?" I pointed to the knife. "Not okay."

"I need it," she said quietly. Turning a glare on Nathan, she added, "Obviously."

"Not around friends you don't." I held my hand out, but she didn't budge. "Come on, kiddo. I really need to know you're safe if I'm gonna make it through this. I'll call you guys once it's safe to come back." *Or someone will.*

Another second of stillness and Rena came over to rest a hand on Whitney's shoulder. "Let's go, honey," she said gently. Finally, Whitney stood up straight, then expertly flipped the knife closed and held it out to me.

"You don't have any others, do you?" I asked. After a second of pouting hesitation, she reached into the side of her shoe and handed over another knife. We would really need to have a talk about this later. Surely there had to be some kind of middle ground between Royce's policy of "no risks ever" and my obviously-flawed "do what the fuck you want" attitude. "I'll get back to you guys soon, okay?"

"Don't die," she said flatly, glancing up into my eyes.

Once Rena and the others had left, we sent away all the staff and filled the house with soldiers instead. While Nathan was bandaging his arm, I told him, "You know this bodyguard thing isn't your job. I mean, if you want to leave—"

"My job is whatever the hell you tell me to do," he reminded me with a dry smile, pulling his sleeve back down over the bandage and buttoning his cuff. "Besides, I'd like to see you live through this. And you're forgetting exactly how long I've been in his business." He pulled a 9mm pistol out of the holster on his hip and looked it over to be sure it was in working order.

Gregorio was sitting in the living room with us, holding his .40 in both hands. He'd only gotten his cast off recently, but we'd spent the past few days at the shooting range reminding his hands how to handle a gun, and his aim was as sharp as ever. *That*, I did teach him. But he'd never had to fire at a living target before, so this was probably freaking him out.

"You okay?" I asked, and he nodded without looking up from his gun. "I'm not really expecting anything to happen here."

"Right. Just...covering your bases. I know." I had told him that already in another equally useless effort to reassure him. I was going to switch tactics when my phone rang, and at least four of my men drew their weapons.

"Well, now we know who's on-edge." I was only relaxed enough to joke because I'd been waiting on this phone call all morning. "Daniel."

"Talk fast."

"It's what I do best. So I had a chat with your sister last night—the older one, not the younger one—and learned some pretty interesting things about your operation. 'Your' meaning the Lucianos', not yours personally. So first, I want to ask you: are you aware that she has capos and crews who answer directly to her?"

There was a pause as he processed everything I'd just said. "Wait, Gemma? She's not even a capo herself. She doesn't have the rank to command anyone."

"Well, she must have invented one for herself, because apparently, she has people 'taking care of things' behind your back. And your dad's, most likely. So this is all news to you, right?"

"Assuming any of it's true, yes."

"Look, why don't I give you a few names and you can look into it yourself?" I listed off the names of all the guys involved in Gregorio's attack. All of them were Lucianos so we'd assumed they worked for Marcell, but apparently, they were working for Gemma instead. "She also made it very clear that she's trying to sabotage my whole operation here. I'm sure I don't have to tell you how much she hates me; she's probably said it plenty of times herself."

"Yeah, that's no secret."

"No, the secret part is how hard she's been working to get me thrown out of the Council and hated by...pretty much everyone. You know, telling people how I killed my dad just so I could stay in charge, that kind of bullshit?"

"She has said that," he conceded.

"Yeah, that's not the only dirty rumor she's spread about me—and honestly, I wouldn't even care, if any of them were true." Nate and I had stayed up all night researching all the different ways Gemma had been badmouthing me, the rumors she'd spread to other families, some based on truth, some blatant lies. She really had been doing everything in her power to drive my reputation into the ground since right after Dad's death. She'd seen it as an opportunity and took full advantage of it. But she'd made the mistake of 1) telling me about her plans like some kind of fucking comic book villain, and 2) assuming I was too stupid to do anything about it. "Thing is, my dad didn't even want to come back to his position here. *My* position. He wanted to disappear into the black market or some shit. So yeah, killing him wasn't about job security."

"Myles, why are you telling me all of this?" He sounded like Royce when he got frustrated.

"Because your sister is setting me up to get fucking destroyed by the Council," I said plainly. "And I assume that's something you're unaware of. Considering she's stepping out of line *and* pretty much framing me, I thought it was something you'd like to know." And God, I could only hope it was something he wanted to stop.

"Hang on. Gemma's doing *what*?"

14

SOFIA

I'd been waiting on Myles to call me for nearly a week, and he still hadn't tried once. Was he really that freaked out by the conversation we'd had? I couldn't bring myself to try and contact him, too embarrassed and afraid of being rejected outright. But going without seeing or hearing from him for so long was starting to drive me crazy. Lauren was right: I *was* really into him.

When I went to call him, looking through my contact list, I couldn't find his number. My text conversations with him were gone too. I wouldn't have done all that, no matter how irritated with him I was. When I went to make a new contact, I saw that his number was even blocked. What the hell? Had someone been messing with my phone? Was that why I wasn't getting calls from him?

Suddenly a lot more hopeful with the possibility that he *had* been trying to contact me, I called him immediately. Pacing around my suite, I waited nervously through a couple of rings before he answered, "Yeah?" Oh. He sounded a lot colder than I expected, all things considered.

"Hey." It was hard to decide exactly what my tone should

be. I was happy to hear from him, of course, but there was still some lingering discomfort from before. I settled on "hesitantly friendly." "Have you been trying to call me? I just saw that my phone blocked your number for some reason."

"Oh, by accident, huh?" He obviously didn't believe me. I guess it did sound a little unlikely.

"I'm serious! When have I ever just ignored you? I've been hoping you would call me, and we could talk about what happened last time we saw each other."

"What, you mean your interrogation?"

My stomach squirmed slightly with guilt. Technically, he wasn't wrong. No matter how good my intentions were, I had been looking for answers from him so that I could share them with my family. Of course, after what I'd learned that night, I knew that confirming Danny's fears about Myles taking Arturo wouldn't do anyone any good. So I'd kept the information to myself. But deceiving him in the first place still made me feel awful.

"I didn't really think of it that way." Even that was a lie. "And I'm sorry if it came across that way."

"Cut the bullshit, Sofia. I know you were getting information for Gemma."

"What? Why would you even think that?" He knew as well as anyone how bad my relationship with my sister was, especially lately. If he had been talking to Gemma, then things between us were even more complicated than I thought. "I don't work with Gemma. Even when I do gather information, it's for my dad or Danny. I don't know what she does for the family, and I don't want to. It doesn't have anything to do with me."

"Yeah? Then why were you promising her some shit about how you can 'handle' me?" he demanded.

I was totally lost. What was he...? I had said that to

Danny during our phone call. But how would Myles know anything about that?

"That wasn't—Have you been talking to Gemma or something? It sounds like she's screwing with both of us." This conversation would've been a lot easier in person. Without being able to read his body language, all I had to go by was his tone, and that wasn't giving me much hope.

"Yeah, I bet."

"Why are you acting like this?" I was trying to be patient with him, knowing we had both been a little freaked out by that whole weird love conversation, but he didn't have to be such an ass about it. And why the hell would he ever believe Gemma's word over mine? "Can you please stop deflecting and just talk to me? I'll come meet you at the club or something."

"Look, I don't really have the time right now. Your sister's using that recording you gave her to set me up, so the Council's soldiers will probably be here any minute. If I live through that, maybe I'll get back to you later."

"Wait! Myles, what—?" He ended the call without waiting to hear me argue.

Everything he'd said left me totally nonplused. First, what recording was he talking about? It was obvious Gemma had spoken to him, and for whatever reason, he'd actually listened to her. If she had a recording, if she had played my conversation with Danny for him—oh God. That night I came back from the concert, after I'd been gone for hours, she was there waiting in my room. If she could get in, what was stopping her from setting up a bug somewhere? Fuck my privacy, fuck my unwillingness to help her; she'd gotten what she wanted anyway.

Meaning she had Myles on tape saying that he'd killed Arturo. "Goddamn it." And he thought I was involved?

That I'd set him up? I tried calling him again, but he ignored me.

Whatever it was Gemma was hoping to get out of this, she'd taken it too far. I was going to demand an explanation, and God help her if it wasn't a good one. I took a cab back to the villa and scurried inside as it was starting to rain. Right when I got through the door, I could already hear a shouting match going on in the den.

"—no fucking right to do what you did! How long has this been going on, Gemma? How long have you been pulling strings and taking actions you *knew* Dad wouldn't approve?"

Oh. It sounded like Danny had beaten me to grilling her, but it also sounded like he had more information than I did already. Hoping to pick up more of what was going on before I joined the conversation, I crept a little closer to the den to listen.

"I've been doing what I had to for our family to thrive," Gemma argued, her volume just below yelling. "I've been taking the actions you and Dad wouldn't approve of because they were necessary! You can hate me for it if you want, but it's still a fact that we're better off because of my plans."

"And what about the Morettis?" Danny asked, grabbing my attention and sending my heart into my throat. "What were they, collateral damage? Don't pretend you haven't had it out for Myles since day one."

"No, only since he proved he couldn't be trusted."

"Bullshit! There's no way you went to all this trouble to get rid of him because you're genuinely afraid he's going to turn on us."

"He already did! He killed Arturo! Does that not fucking count?" Gemma barked.

"He killed Arturo because *you* sent him to attack Gregorio! You knew Myles would retaliate, and you wanted to use it again him."

I had to cover my mouth so they wouldn't hear my horrified gasp. If Gemma had been the one to order the attack, then my earlier conversation with Danny only made more sense. Of course, Papà didn't know anything about it. Of course, he wouldn't have set something like that in motion. But obviously, we couldn't put anything past our sister. I couldn't have moved if I'd wanted to at this point. I stood rigidly still and listened with rapt attention.

"Stop lying to me," Danny growled. "You need to tell me exactly what's going on here so I can fix the fucking mess you've made."

"I already told you: it's what needs to happen. Myles has to be removed from power, and now the rest of the Council knows it for sure. If that means one of the younger sons taking over for him, fine. If it means the Morettis disappear altogether, *fine*. But I won't stand for things to stay the way they are now. I won't let Dad try to make them our allies again if Myles is still the one calling the shots."

White-hot anger flooded through me, and I stormed into the den before I could stop myself. "Who the hell do you think you are?" Shock and relief flashed over Danny's features when he saw me, but Gemma looked crazed, panicked, and even afraid. "You won't *let* Dad fix things with the Morettis? You're saying he would've talked to Myles, and you were the one who stopped it?"

"Someone had to." She spoke with conviction despite being outnumbered and visibly shaken. "You should both be thanking me. The Morettis might have been our allies once, but now that they're out of the Council, they're competition. Meaning they need to be put down before they can do any more damage to us."

"They're only out of the Council because *you* told Dad not to endorse them, you fucking psychopath!" I was ready to claw her eyes out with my own hands, but Danny held me back. Still, I struggled to get past him, to hurt her like she'd hurt Myles, like she'd hurt me. "All of this is your fault! That's why you told me to stay away from him. Because you were so fucking set on seeing him dead, and you'd rather let me go down with him than give up. You're crazy. You're... I can't even..."

Suddenly I was having trouble breathing, and I staggered out of Danny's arms to collapse into a chair and cover my mouth with both hands. How could she do this? My own sister? Did she really hate Myles that much—or was this just about power for her? Somehow, that seemed a lot more likely. It was just about being in control of something, about proving she could outsmart him. Proving how useful she was to the family. *Good God.*

"Dad's going to be back from the Council meeting soon." Danny was addressing Gemma, his voice much more controlled as if to contrast my screaming. "And he's going to hear all about this. Everything. If you have even a shred of respect for him or for our family, you'll stay right here and wait."

"Daniel," she said as he started to walk away. "Please don't do this. Whatever you think about me, however Myles has managed to mess with your head, don't just take him at his word. He *is* dangerous. Trying to work with him won't turn out the way you want."

"Why?" I asked, shooting her a glare. "Because you won't let it?"

"I don't have a choice," Danny said. "My family was responsible for half the criticism and difficulty he's gone through over the past three years, even if I didn't know about it. And if he's going to get anywhere near the Council safely, he'll need our support. He's going to come back with me, and we're all going to have a chat with Dad." Kneeling in front of me, he touched my arm to get my attention. "You were right, apparently. I didn't have the whole story. I know you must want to hear everything, and I know Gemma probably won't explain it to you, but I can't right now. I need to get in touch with Myles and—"

"It's fine," I said tersely, shaking my head. "Just go."

After a brief hesitation, he got back up and told Gemma on his way out, "Don't make this worse than it already is." The front door slammed behind him, leaving Gemma and me frozen in tense silence. I had no idea where to even start. There was so much going on in my head that I was almost numb.

"Did you bug my rooms?" I asked finally.

"Yes."

"Did you tell Myles that I knew about it? That I helped you?"

"Yes." My sister's voice was as low and flat as mine, as if neither of us really knew how to have this conversation. Or maybe we were exhausted from shouting.

"Why?"

"So he would cut you off. If he thought you'd betrayed him, he would refuse to see you. And if you aren't around him, you can't be part of what's going to happen to him."

"I absolutely do *not* believe that you did it out of concern for me," I said, finally looking at her again. "That you were doing some kind of big sister duty, trying to keep me safe." She smiled at me coldly.

"You've always been so clever." Her voice dripped with sarcasm. "I was keeping you safe. I *am* keeping you safe. But no, it's not because you're my precious little sister or because

I feel some kind of instinct to protect you. We both know you're Dad's favorite. You always have been. If something happened to you, his sweet little Sofina, Dad would be devastated. If he were depressed and sullen all the time, he'd start looking weak."

"Oh right, I forgot. You only ever do anything for the sake of the family, right? You know best how to take care of us and keep us strong?"

"I don't expect you to understand. You're a child. That's all you'll ever be. Pampered and pretty and spoiled, and what else matters, really?" She took a seat in the chair across from me, crossing her legs and resting her hands regally on the chair's arms, looking like she was playing at being a boss herself. With that cold look in her eyes and the firm set of her jaw, it wasn't hard to imagine. "You don't know anything about doing things for the good of others. You certainly don't know anything about making sacrifices."

"What sacrifices have you made, Gemma?" I sat up to straighten my posture, folding my hands in my lap and crossing my ankles primly. If she was doing the evil-queen villain act, I could match her in dignity, at least. "What have you given up for the sake of the family?"

"My entire life. Do you know why I started pursuing Royce in the first place?" It wasn't really a question. "Because Dad told me to. He always talked about how nice it would be if I wound up with Royce, if I could marry us into the Moretti family. He made it sound like such an accomplishment. Like he would've been so *proud* of me for snagging a big fish like Royce Moretti."

"So what? That's why you became obsessed with him?"

"It was never about him," she said, shaking her head. "Yes, he was capable and competent. More than that: he was proficient. He was perfect for the job he was supposed to be doing." She must have realized she'd gotten a little wistful, as she cleared her throat and turned her gaze cold again. "But it was more the fact that he was Deron's son. His heir. And if he would've just cooperated, that could've been the end of it."

"The end of what?" I had never cared much about her fixation on Royce. I still didn't. But if she was sharing things freely, it was very possible I could learn something useful by keeping her talking.

"My obligations. My efforts. My working so goddamn hard all the time." Her hands gripped at her chair's arms. "You know, with the Morettis on the decline, our family is the most powerful one on the West Coast. I was the one who made that happen. Myles helped, mostly by being so impulsive and temperamental. A child. Just like you."

"So that's what this whole hostile takeover is about. Us—no, you—'winning' against them. If you can't join them, beat them." She really was fucking crazy. "It's too bad Danny found about your little evil plans. Now he's going to reverse them, and all your hard work will be for nothing."

Gemma's lip twitched into a sneer, but she quickly glossed over it with another smile. "We'll see about that. He might just be too late already. Word travels fast, and if the Council has already approved Myles's death, there won't be much dear Danny can do for him."

How could she talk about all of this so calmly? I couldn't stand staying seated or in the same room with her for a second longer. I stood and left with as much grace as I could muster, hoping she wouldn't see my distress.

There had to be something I could do to help Danny. Something I could do to help Myles. I knew both of them better than they knew each other, and there would probably be some lingering hostility they'd have to work through.

Between Myles's aggressive, antagonistic personality and Danny's issues with being disrespected (even playfully), there was too high a chance of them getting into an argument somehow. We couldn't afford that. If I went, I could mediate for them, being the only person with a stake on both sides.

But I didn't even know where they were. *God, think, Sofia.* It would only make sense for them to meet somewhere neutral. Not the Moretti house. Not aMoral or one of our restaurants. Where would Myles feel safe? Where would he think was appropriate?

I only had to think for a minute before the answer came to me. I couldn't be positive, but my intuition told me there was only one option. So I acted right away, stepping out under the canopy over the front door and calling a cab to take me to San Clemente.

...

When we were younger, our dad would meet Deron Moretti at one of three places: the Moretti house, our villa, or a beachside town between the two, San Clemente. If the meetings took place at our house or theirs, they were friendly. Discussions of the two families' separate businesses, family updates, Gemma trying her best to win Royce over—that sort of thing. The meetings in San Clemente were more formal, and they were for the purpose of business only. During those few hours, Papà and Deron were businessmen first, friends second, which meant they happened most often during a disagreement between the two. And they chose the most neutral setting possible: a church.

The priests of Our Lady of Mercy Catholic Church had a

history of involvement with cosa nostra, but they weren't actually a part of it. They had always encouraged feuding families to convene at the church, talk their differences out, and come to an agreement without resorting to violence. They offered religious counsel and took confession if asked, but mostly they offered the building as an absolutely unaligned setting for resolving disputes. There was an unspoken law that violence was forbidden inside the church; even when negotiations went sour, the parties would leave the building before attacking each other.

I'd only been there a few times, myself, but I knew of it, and I knew Myles did too. Given his flair for the dramatic and Danny's respect for tradition, that was the only place that made sense. The cab driver seemed a little hesitant to drive me an hour out to another town, but he'd seen the villa and probably knew I wouldn't have trouble paying for it. He tried a couple of times during the drive to make small talk, but my terse, flat answers must have discouraged him.

The church was toward the edge of town, conveniently partially isolated. I recognized the little building from a distance once we got close and asked the driver to drop me off a few hundred feet away. Everyone was probably on-edge enough without seeing an unexpected, unfamiliar car pull up to the door. Although he seemed a little unsure about leaving me, I assured him it was fine and gave him a generous tip for having driven me so far. I started briskly toward the church as the cab made a U-turn and went back the way we came.

I was too far away to see anything through the narrow windows, and it was almost eerily quiet on the road. If it weren't for both cars sitting outside, Myles's limo and ours, I wouldn't have known anyone was there. Then when I was within about a hundred feet of the church, I heard the unmistakable pop of gunfire, a single shot followed seconds later by a burst of others.

"Oh, God." I broke into a sprint as fast as I could manage, thankful to be wearing flats and pants. I got close enough to recognize Myles, Nathan, and Gregorio rushing out of the building to their car along with two others, guns drawn, and my heart clenched at the sight of a dark red stain spreading down Myles's shoulder. This was supposed to be peaceful. It was supposed to be *helpful*. What could have gone so wrong? By the time I reached the church, Myles's car was disappearing down the road. Struggling to catch my breath, I met one of Danny's soldatos, Sergio, at the door.

"Sofia? What are you doing here?" When I tried to step past him, he blocked my way. "You shouldn't go in there."

"I need to talk to my brother," I said, trying and failing to shove him out of my way. So I shouted past him instead, "Danny! What's going on? Tell your men to let me in!"

"Sofia, please, he doesn't need—"

Another soldato appeared in the doorway behind him. "Let her in, Serge." Although he looked conflicted, Sergio stepped out of my way and allowed me to rush inside to find my brother. When I did, I let out a horrified scream. Danny was sitting on the floor, propped up against one of the pews, sitting in a pool of blood that I could see growing every second, blood flowing out of a gunshot wound just below his heart. I barely managed to force his name out before I dropped to the ground next to him, shaking him gently, trying to get him to look at me.

"Why are you...here?" he asked through shallow breaths, glaring at me weakly.

"I came to help. Why are you all just standing there?" I shouted at the surrounding soldatos. Seven men, half his crew, and they weren't doing a single thing to stop him from bleeding out. "Help him!"

"I told you to stay at home," Danny muttered.

"You told Gemma to stay at home."

The breath he let out was almost a laugh, and he smiled very slightly. "You're so difficult. You shouldn't...have to see this."

"You can gripe at me later. We need to make sure you're safe first," I told him past the painful lump in my throat. Looking at the others, I begged, "Get him in the car! He needs to get to a hospital!"

"Sofia..." One of his older guys, Martín, who I knew for a fact had medical experience, shook his head at me. "There's no time. He has minutes at the most."

"You're not even going to try?"

"Listen." Danny rested a hand on mine where they were clenched on his shirt. I tried to disregard the cold wetness of blood against my skin and focus on his words. "You need to...tell Dad about Myles. It has to come from you." Myles? That was what he wanted to talk about right now?

Suddenly, I felt sick, either from the overpowering scent of blood or the realization that Myles must have done this. But why? Why would he have turned on Danny when he was trying to help? My tears escaped and rushed down my cheeks as everything I thought I understood suddenly came into question. Why could nothing go the way it was supposed to?

"I'll tell him." My voice was choked, my throat tight. Even if I didn't understand any of it, I would tell our dad what had happened. Maybe he could make sense of it. "Don't worry about that." Danny's grip on my hand tightened a little.

"You should...stay. And help Nadine. With Antoni." It

seemed like every breath was harder for him, like every word took more energy to get out. His brows furrowed, somewhere between pain and guilt. "Tell her I'm sorry. I didn't mean... This wasn't supposed to..." He was having trouble keeping his eyes open, and my fingers dug into his arm as if holding on tightly enough might keep him with me longer.

"You don't need to apologize. You were trying to do the right thing." Now, I could barely get words out myself, my vision blurring, my face burning. "I'm so sorry, Danny. I...if I had gotten here sooner..." I expected him to laugh at me, tell me it wasn't my fault, maybe that I would've just distracted him more. He didn't.

"Danny?" I shook him gently, but he didn't look up. I listened as hard as I could for his weak, labored breathing. Nothing. My voice pitched into a shrill cry: *"Danny?"* One of the soldatos tried to pull me away, but I pushed him away and shrieked for them to leave me alone, clinging to my brother's arm and sobbing into his shoulder.

15

MYLES

The meeting had been going so well. Better than I'd let myself hope for. Daniel actually apologized to me for Gemma's bullshit. He said not to think we were best pals or anything just yet, but that he was aware now how much of his dislike for me had come from her. He planned to testify to the Council in my defense—my family's defense—and explain the full situation to me.

"If they see that you're there with me, they'll think twice before attacking you," he said. Even smiling a little, he added, "But even once you deal with them, you'll still have to answer to Sofia. That, I can't help you with." I was still fighting with myself over whether or not to believe that Sofia wasn't working with Gemma, but I didn't bother telling him that. We needed this to go well, and I wasn't about to fuck it up by questioning his other sister's loyalties.

Then when he went to shake my hand, I just... I couldn't follow what happened, it went so fast. Someone fired a shot with no warning, and then the whole room was chaos, everyone drawing weapons and finding cover, myself included. But even though I had my gun out by reflex, I knew better than to use it.

"Hold your fire!" I shouted to my men over the quick, irregular beat of gunfire filling the room. This meeting was our last chance to get through to the Council before they signed my death warrant and effectively destroyed my family. If we took even a single shot at the Lucianos, that whole plan went down the drain.

"Myles." Nathan gripped my arm, ducking behind a mahogany pew with me. He didn't flinch once from the noise. "Daniel is down. His men aren't going to let us—" He jerked back as a bullet zipped over our heads, too close for comfort. "We need to go. Now." He was right. If Daniel was hit, if he couldn't order his men to back down, they weren't going to be interested in peace talks anymore.

"Shit." How could this have gone so completely fucking sideways? No. First things first. I had to get my men out of this position. "Everybody out! Back to the car!" I managed to shoot out the overhead light, and with the storm outside, it got dark enough to cover our retreat at least a little. That's probably the only reason I got away with a shot to my shoulder instead of my skull. It was like someone took a hammer to me, one very specific spot of solid impact, and pain shot through my arm. It was bad enough that I jerked and dropped my gun, but there was no time to go back for it. We all piled into the car, and after a quick headcount, I snapped at Jerome to get us back to the house.

"Who fucking shot at them?" I was practically foaming at the mouth with rage as we sped away from the church, refusing to let Nathan get anywhere near me to look at my wound. "Which one of you was such a goddamn moron that—"

"Myles, no one on our side fired a shot," Nathan told me calmly. "None of us. You said 'stand down,' and we listened."

"Then how the fuck did Daniel end up getting hit?" I snarled, pulling away again when he tried to reach for my jacket. "Show me your magazines." He, Gregorio, and the other two soldiers we'd brought with us stared at me in confusion. "Take the magazines out of your fucking guns and let me see them. All of you."

Although Nathan let out an impatient sigh, he did what I said, just like all the others. A quick glance was enough to tell me they were all still full. That was a relief, but not much of one. Now that I knew none of my men were the idiots who'd turned a peaceful conversation into a fucking gunfight, I relaxed a little and finally allowed Nathan to check the bullet wound in my shoulder. Up until now, I'd been grazed a couple of times but had avoided actually getting shot. First time for everything, I guess, and probably not the last. Although judging by how the situation was developing, I probably wouldn't get many more chances.

"Goddamn it," I muttered, trying to think past the growing pain in my shoulder. All the adrenaline from before was wearing off, leaving me full of cold, miserable dread. Daniel was pretty much our Hail Mary. He was the only one in the Luciano family, in any of the Council families, who knew exactly what was going on with Gemma and why we didn't deserve to be punished for it. To be executed for it. Even if Sofia knew, there was still the possibility that she was in on it. Or even worse, there was the possibility she really was concerned, and I'd ruined it by accusing her of turning on me. Marcell didn't know the truth, and it wasn't likely Gemma would explain it to him. If Daniel was seriously hurt after he'd gone off to talk to me, she was sure to use that against me too. All because one of *their* guys got trigger-happy. With terrible aim. "God*damn* it!"

"Good news and bad news," Nathan said after he'd peeled my shirt back to look over my shoulder. "Good news is it doesn't look like the shot hit anything vital. It's the wrong side for your heart and too high for your lungs. The bad news"—he snapped open the trauma kit he'd insisted on bringing just in case and tore into a package of gauze —"is that the bullet went straight through and you're bleeding like a son of a bitch."

"Call my mom a bitch again and you will be too." He rolled his eyes and shoved a wadded-up bundle of gauze against the exit wound just above my chest.

"Hold this here. As much pressure as you can." I barely had the mental capacity to argue. I held the gauze in place with my left hand, starting to notice that my right was tingling uncomfortably. I tried flexing it to work out the pins and needles. It twitched but didn't close. I tried to lift it from my side to see if there was something wrong. My arm didn't move.

"Shiiit," I groaned.

"Something wrong?" Gregorio asked from his seat across from mine. "I mean, besides the obvious."

"My arm's not working." I couldn't even gather enough energy to be pissed off or panicked. "It's just...not."

"Could be nerve damage," Nathan said, clamping his hand over the wound on my back with another gauze bundle. "If so, it's not something we can address right now."

"Couldn't we take him to the hospital?" Greg asked.

"Hospitals ask a lot of invasive questions. Considering Myles is probably being hunted by the Council's hitmen at the moment, he can't afford to be drugged for surgery anyway. The best thing to do is get somewhere secure and... try to talk to Marcell."

"I fucking hate this," I growled, staring down at the floor and trying hard to ignore the wash of vivid red staining my white shirt. "Running away. Not being able to answer an attack."

"But you're smart enough to know it's your best recourse at the moment." Nate's hand gripping my shoulder might've been encouraging if it weren't for all the blood loss. "I just hope Daniel's wound wasn't fatal. If it was, our chances of survival just went from slim to near-nonexistent."

...

The remaining handful of soldiers waiting for us at the house were already at attention by the time I got in the door. Most of them stayed expertly stone-faced, but I saw a couple wince at the state I was in. After all, they weren't expecting us back so soon, and definitely not soaked in blood.

"As I'm sure you can all tell," I said, gesturing to my still-unresponsive right arm, "things didn't go as planned. There was—I don't know what the fuck happened, frankly. But our good friend Daniel wound up getting shot somehow. Even though I know it wasn't our fault, it would take a fucking miracle to convince his family of that. So I'm going to...pray for a fucking miracle. You're all dismissed." I pushed past them to head toward my office, but no one moved. Quickly losing my patience, I snapped, "Leave! Those are your orders. All of you. If the Council wants me dead, they're *going* to kill me. No point in you all dying trying to stop it."

"You just want us to abandon you?" one of the younger soldiers asked. He was young enough to have the mindset that it was somehow better to stay and die for "honor" or "loyalty" or some shit than to be smart and minimize the body count.

"I want you to stay alive," I said plainly. "Listen, I'm grateful to all of you for sticking with me this far. But it's looking more and more like this is something I can't talk my way out of. I'm the one Gemma's bent on taking out. But I'm sure she doesn't care if any of you die, and neither will the rest of the Council. So just...take care of yourselves and let me deal with this on my own."

I left the room without giving them the chance to argue. If they all stayed and died with me, everything I'd done over the past four years looking out for them meant nothing. I would talk to Marcell myself, I would explain everything that was going on—or I would die trying. First, though, I needed a gun. I also needed an actual bandage for my shoulder, even though the bleeding had more or less stopped. And a clean shirt if I could manage it.

The first issue was easy. There was no shortage of guns in the house. My old .22, the one I brought to our last meeting with Dad, was still in the bottom drawer of my desk, for instance. But after three years of getting used to a .38, I wasn't about to downgrade. The gun I took from my safe was similar in a lot of ways, but it wasn't exactly the same, and considering I was now being forced to use my left hand, it felt a lot more foreign than I wanted it to. Nothing to do about it but deal.

When I came back from my office, planning to look for first aid supplies, I found Nathan and Gregorio sitting in the living room, apparently waiting for me. "What the hell are you two still doing here? When I said 'all of you,' that applied to you too."

Nate sighed like I was being an idiot. "We're not leaving, Myles. Surely you know that already."

"Oh my God, what is with you two?" I gestured at them with the gun still in my hand. "What do you think it's going to accomplish for you to stay? You think you're going to stop someone from getting to me?"

"I think we could stop a few, yes. Gregorio's nearly as good a shot as you are, and we do have home-field advantage."

"And then what? We'll run out of bullets way before they run out of soldiers," I pointed out. "And if you kill a bunch of their men, they'll *definitely* want you dead."

"Maybe we won't kill anyone then." Greg was reclining on the couch with one ankle crossed over his other knee, looking almost amused. "Maybe we'll just talk until they get tired of it and leave. You're good at that, boss."

"This isn't a joke, Gregorio." How was it that of the three of us, I was the one being the most rational? This day was just full of firsts. "I'm serious when I say I don't want you two to die trying to protect me."

"What, you think we do?" Again, Gregorio laughed. "I know you don't like hearing this, but you can't do everything by yourself. You don't even know the Council wants you dead. You haven't talked to Marcell. You don't know what he'll say. So quit being a fucking defeatist and let's keep working on this until we're officially out of options." Silence for a second.

"I think that's the most you've said in the past three weeks," I said.

"Yeah, well I hope you heard it." He was rubbing one side of his jaw. "Because I'm not saying it again."

"You know, I might be crazy..." I wasn't going to admit that there was any kind of comfort in not facing this completely alone. The hint of a slick smile on my lips would have to be enough. "...but I think you two are just stupid."

"With all due respect, sir, fuck you." Nathan was smirking too. "I'll see if I can find something to cover that wound. I imagine you'll want to change clothes. At least look halfway presentable for the assassins."

"Asshole," I muttered as I headed to my room.

16

SOFIA

Martín sat at my side during the ride back to the house and gave me a rundown of the meeting. I tried my hardest to pay attention, but my numb detachment from the moment made it difficult. With all this new information, I didn't know what to think anymore, so my mind had sort of shut down. And my eyes stayed tightly shut the entire time so I could pretend my brother's body wasn't in the car with us.

When we got back to the house, I stood by and watched them bring him inside, wondering vaguely where they would take him. Was there some designated place he would wait? I had no idea. Following them inside, I found Nadine standing in the hall watching the procession, and I froze. Danny's crew had wrapped him up in a length of black canvas that I suspected existed for that exact purpose. So she wouldn't have seen that it was him.

Turning toward me with worry etched into her features, she asked, "Did we lose someone? I thought the meeting was supposed to be a peaceful one. Has Daniel already gone to talk with your father?"

Seeing her, remember how he'd asked me to help her,

thinking about how much his death would affect her and Antoni, I couldn't stay detached from the situation anymore. My eyes started welling up with tears as I struggled to find my voice. What could I possibly say to her? How could I tell her gently?

But based on my expression and the blood on my clothes, she must have figured it out on her own. Her eyes went wide, her hand flying up to cover her mouth. "No."

"Nadine..." My voice broke along with my heart. "I'm so sorry."

"No...!" She shook her head hopelessly as tears spilled from her eyes, then all at once she collapsed to the floor, sobbing into her hands. I went to her side right away and wrapped my arms tightly around her. The small comfort wouldn't do much for the pain she was feeling, but it was the best I could offer: the knowledge that she wasn't alone, that someone was there to cry with her.

Gemma soon came in from the next room, and I couldn't bring myself to look at her. She had some fault in Danny's death too. If it weren't for her campaign against Myles, their meeting wouldn't have been necessary, it wouldn't have gone wrong, and he would still be with us. After several seconds, she asked quietly, "He's dead, isn't he?" Nadine sobbed harder from her words, and I shot her a glare as I nodded. Gemma's face was blank, looking sort of lost. "I didn't think... God." She covered her eyes with one hand, wrapping her other arm around herself. She didn't cry out loud the way I had, the way Nadine did, but I could hear her sniffle and gasp softly.

"Who did it?" Nadine demanded, suddenly sitting up to look me in the eye. Her face was an absolute mess, mascara streaked from her reddened eyes, but her gaze was hard. "You were there, weren't you? Who's responsible?"

"I wasn't there when it happened. I got there just before he..." I took a deep breath, trying to calm myself so that I could deliver the horrible news I had. "There was already a gunfight going on when I showed up. Myles and his people left in a hurry. And when I got there, Danny was—he'd been shot."

"Don't tell me I have to explain to you what that means," Gemma said coolly.

"I know what it sounds like," I sniped back at her. "But I don't know why he would've—"

"For God's sake, Sofia!" my sister shouted, incredulous. "What is it going to take for you to believe that he's dangerous? Are you going to keep advocating for him while he kills off our entire family one by one? Are you going to keep making excuses because you 'just can't imagine he would do that'?"

"Don't pretend you're saying all this in the name of justice. You're always looking for another reason to hate him." Despite my argument, I couldn't deny she had a point. All signs pointed to Myles being guilty, even if just by association. There was a lot I was willing to forgive when it came to him. Probably more than he deserved. But this? How could I possibly forgive him for this?

"And he keeps supplying them. Do you really plan to lie to yourself and pretend there's any way he didn't do this? When every part of the situation makes it so obvious that he did?" She spoke to me like I was a traitor, like wanting to see any good in Myles meant spitting on our family. "Or are you acknowledging that he did it but saying that doesn't *matter* to you?" Nadine had dissolved into tears again, as if she was hurt by what I'd said too.

"No! Of course, it matters. I—I know he must have done it," I admitted quietly, trying to force my heart's protests into silence. "I'm sorry. I'm sorry it took so long for me to understand." I couldn't look at my sister or my sister-in-law. The voice in my head screaming—that Gemma was wrong, that Myles would never do this, that I couldn't just abandon him—now felt disloyal and shameful. *This is my family. I have to put them first. I can't love the man who killed my brother. I can't.*

Papà arriving from down the hall came as a welcome distraction. Something else to focus on. He looked weary, exhausted, heartbroken, and a pang of guilt shot through me as I realized how little time I'd actually spent with him since I came home. I got to my feet as he came over and offered Nadine his hands to help her up. Taking a deep breath, she did, and she silently rested her head against his chest when he embraced her. "I am sorry, cara mia. I'm sure he—"

"Please," she said, taking a step back and wiping her tears away. "I can't. Antoni should know, and I'll only be able to explain if I clear my head."

"Gemma," Papà said, glancing in her direction. "You should go with your sister to support her."

"No," Nadine argued before Gemma could answer. "I'll do it alone." And she headed up the stairs, probably to Antoni's room. I wished I could offer to help since he would probably be able to deal with the news a little better if I were there—but I had to tell Papà what had happened.

As if he'd read my mind, Papà went on, "Sofina. Martín tells me Daniel asked you to explain the situation."

"He did."

"Come to my office, then, and we'll talk." He led me down the hall, and I didn't miss Gemma's glare as she was ignored. She wasn't wrong when she said he favored me over her and Danny.

Just her now.

I shook that thought out of my head as I sat on the sofa in the window of Papà's office. The usually-sunny room was dark enough at the moment from the storm and night falling that he had to switch on two lamps before coming to sit with me.

"I can't imagine this will be easy to talk about," he started. "So take your time. What happened?"

I told him what I knew about the situation: that Danny had gone to talk to Myles, hoping to bring him back to the Council to plead his case. That I got there as the Morettis were leaving and found Danny bleeding out. When Papà asked what had possessed him to go, to think Myles deserved the chance to explain himself, I explained about Gemma's vendetta against the Morettis—and Myles specifically—why he had taken revenge on Arturo and why it shouldn't have been used as evidence to get him killed.

"But that doesn't matter anymore," I said, shaking my head as more silent tears left streaks down my face. "He's responsible for Danny's death. There's no way we can excuse that." If I said it enough times, maybe I would believe it eventually.

"I am sorry it's come to this, cuore mio," my dad said, touching my shoulder gently. "I know how much you cared for him. I know you wanted to believe he was better than he is. But you're right. We can't ignore this." After planting a kiss on my forehead, he got up and tugged his cuffs down. "The others agreed that he needs to be stopped. This only shows me how urgently it has to happen. Before he can harm anyone else."

"You're going to send a crew to their house?" I didn't know why I asked; the knowledge wasn't going to make me feel any better.

"I will, and it's likely the other families will want to send a few of their own soldiers along as well. He probably has plenty of his own there ready to defend him." Walking over to his desk, he added, "Please excuse me, Sofina. I have some phone calls to make."

I nodded silently and got up to leave the room. What was I supposed to do with myself now? All I could do was wait for the news that Myles was dead. The end of the Morettis altogether. Was I supposed to be happy about that? Was I supposed to feel satisfied? That wasn't likely.

Wandering distractedly down the hall, I could hear broken sobs coming from one of the doors, the one that led to the basement stairs. It sounded like Nadine again. As I came down the stairs, I found her and Gemma on either side of a long metal table where—my heart jumped into my throat—Danny was laid out on top of the canvas they'd wrapped him in earlier. He looked horribly pale and was still covered in blood. Couldn't they have cleaned him up before Nadine saw him? Sure that Gemma wasn't the most comforting company, I came to stand at Nadine's side, not touching her but standing by in solidarity.

"It's wrong," she said softly, sounding a little breathless. "It's wrong that he went there to help, and this was his thanks." I nodded my agreement without speaking.

"He shouldn't have gone." Gemma's voice was just as low, though there was anger underscoring her pain. "He should have just listened to me. I told him it wouldn't work out. I told him it would be dangerous."

"Gemma," I said sharply. "That isn't helping. He was trying to do something good. He was trying to fix a problem *you* created. You can't fault him for that."

She acted like she didn't hear me, still staring down at him tearfully, still looking like she had no idea how to process this. "He should've done what I said. Why couldn't he just listen to me? This wasn't supposed to happen." Something about her tone and what she'd just said caught my attention.

"What do you mean 'supposed to'?"

Her hands rested on the edge of the table, and they clenched into trembling fists. "I thought he would change his mind. I thought...surely he would realize when he got there that Myles didn't deserve his help. Our help." She shook her head very slightly. "I didn't...I shouldn't have..."

"Gemma, what are you talking about?" I asked, my eyes narrowing. Nadine had started paying closer attention as well, but Gemma refused to look at either of us.

"It was his fault!" she insisted, her voice breathy and weak. "He could've stopped it! I didn't want this."

"If you don't start explaining, and *fast*—" Nadine growled.

"The Morettis didn't do this." Gemma had dropped her head, but her voice came out stronger than before. "One of our people did. I didn't think he would have to."

"Are you saying..." I swallowed hard, dry-mouthed. "*You* ordered one of his soldatos to do this?"

"As a last resort." But she didn't have much passion in defending herself. "Two of the men on his crew have been reporting to me for months. So I told them to go with him, and if Daniel didn't change his mind, if he really was going to help Myles, to put an end to it. He would've reversed everything I've worked at for years. He would've ruined us. I couldn't—I couldn't let him."

"You had my husband killed?" Nadine sounded like she could hardly get the words out, and she was visibly shaking with rage. "Because he was going to undo your *work*?" When Gemma nodded, Nadine marched around to the other side of the table and slapped her across the face with so much force the sound echoed in the open room. Gemma stumbled, and Nadine shoved her to the floor, dropping to her knees to slap her, claw at her face, and tear at her hair. As much as some part of me felt she deserved it, I couldn't stand by and watch it happen.

"Nadine!" I managed to get my arms around her and drag her away while she kicked and screamed and fought.

"No! She killed him! You killed him!" she shrieked raggedly at Gemma, still fighting viciously to get at her. I had never seen her like this before. As small as she was, it was still incredibly difficult to hold her back. "Your own brother! The father of my son! Goddamn you! God..." Her struggling slowly got weaker until she collapsed to the ground in grief, sobbing and pounding her fist into the floor.

Gemma was still on the ground, shaken, her hair mussed and fallen in her face. I felt like there was something I should be saying to her, something she needed to hear to know she was going to pay for what she'd done. But the words wouldn't come. I was still in such shock that she would go that far. Even her. As cruel as she could be, as controlling as she was...she really had lost it that afternoon. When Danny started pointing out her plans and unraveling them, when she started losing control, something snapped, and she panicked enough to give this rash, unfeeling order—an order so awful that seeing it carried out had broken her down even more. I couldn't see how I could still call her my sister after this. And I was sure Papà —

"Oh God." I scrambled up from the ground and rushed back to the stairs, back to Papà's office. When I burst in, he was looking at his phone in what seemed to be confusion, but he quickly turned to me instead.

"What's wrong?" he asked.

"Did you...have you already sent people to the Morettis' house?" God, what if I was too late? What if Myles was already about to die for Gemma's actions?

"No." Just as relief washed through me, he went on, "But I just spoke to Myles. It sounded as if another family's crew was already arriving."

17

MYLES

The sun had gone down by the time the three of us headed to the safe room in the basement. I wanted to call Rena and Whits and give them some kind of update, but I didn't really have any good news. Besides, I needed to talk to Marcell first. When I finally got him on the line, he growled into the phone, "You have a lot of nerve to call me so casually."

"Trust me, I don't think of it as casual. I need to talk to you about this situation with the Council."

"What is there to talk about, Myles? You've been digging your grave deeper for years. I thought there must be some limit, some standard to how low you would stoop. But you proved me wrong."

"What are you talking about?" Already the conversation was headed for disaster.

"I'm talking about my son," Marcell said sharply. "Who for some reason thought you were worth redeeming. He tried to help you, and you took the first opportunity to turn on him."

"Is that what he told you?"

"He didn't tell me anything. Sofia was at the church and watched him die." My blood went cold. "She's the one who informed me of what happened."

God. Sofia was *there*? In the middle of all that gunfire? Why the hell would Daniel bring her along for something like that? To use her against me? Just the thought that she'd been with Daniel when he died... He was her hero growing up. He was the good older sibling Gemma refused to be. Losing him must have hit her hard. And all I could think about was how harsh I'd been to her that morning.

"I'm..." I swallowed hard, my mouth dry, while Nathan and Gregorio looked on nervously. "I'm sorry. For what happened to Daniel. But I swear to God, Marcell, I wasn't the one who did it."

"One of your men, then. Does it make you feel less guilty to think it was indirect?"

"None of my men fired a shot. Not one. Your people were the only ones shooting. I don't know, one of their shots must've gone wide or something." I still didn't know how to explain that, and I knew how unlikely it seemed that Daniel could've been killed by someone on his own crew. "You said yourself that he was trying to help us. Why the hell would I attack him?"

"I don't claim to understand your motivations," Marcell said coldly. "For anything you do. Maybe to deprive me of my heir. Maybe to hurt Sofia after she left you. Maybe for the same reason you threatened Gemma: you were angry. I have no idea."

Wait. Gemma?

"Hang on, is Gemma there? Is she telling you all that shit?" If Daniel hadn't gotten the opportunity to explain everything, if he still believed all of Gemma's lies and didn't know about her going behind his back. "Did she tell you about how she attacked Gregorio too? Has she mentioned all the shit she's been pulling behind your back?"

"I'm aware that Gemma has been working against you, but if you think that erases what you've done—"

"I haven't done anything wrong! Ask Sofia! She knows about it too. You'll believe it if it comes from her, won't you?"

"Myles." Nathan had crossed the room to the security monitors, which showed movement outside the house. Shit. Marcell must have condemned me to the Council immediately when he found out about Daniel. Meaning my call was hours too late and there wasn't much to be done anymore. If their people were already surrounding the house—and they were, from what I saw on the cameras, multiple cars pulling up just into sight—there wasn't really time for each don to call off every one of them.

"Shit." I ended the call with Marcell and put my phone down, frantically searching my mind for some solution to this fucking nightmare. Glancing at Gregorio, I asked dryly, "Are we officially out of options yet?"

He pulled the slide back on his gun with a shrug. "Not quite."

"Don't shoot anyone just yet," Nate said, calling our attention again. "Look at this." There were plenty of soldiers moving around the house, as expected, but there was someone else too. A woman, dressed all in black—skirt, jacket, heels, gloves, and a pillbox hat with a veil over her face—walked up to the door and rang the bell.

"Who the hell is that?" The body type wasn't right for Sofia or Gemma. I thought about Louisa Maldone for a minute, but she was shorter and wider than the woman on the screen. When I looked to Nathan and Greg, they both shook their heads too. We all watched as the woman waited a minute or two, looked around, then spoke to one of the soldiers at her side. After she'd taken a step back, her men rammed the door in, and we could hear it happen above our heads.

"Maybe some specialized assassin?" Nathan asked, frowning hard at the screen. "They won't get into this room that easily. Our position is defensible, at least." I couldn't think of anything to do but watch them work their way through the house, and I kept my eyes on the unfamiliar woman for the most part. The people she had with her were obviously an assault force. She wasn't dropping in for tea. Here I'd thought I knew all my enemies, but this one was a surprise.

She moved like she already knew the house, passing up the rooms her soldiers were checking and instead, heading straight to wine cellar. It didn't take long for her to find the hidden door to the basement, and then she disappeared from the cameras. Nathan cursed under his breath and drew his gun as he went over to the door. Was he going to shoot her? We didn't know who she was or why she was there—or who might get pissed if she died.

"That's far enough," he said into the speaker system set up past the soundproof door. He was watching her through a slot in the door covered with bulletproof glass. It was too far for me to see anything, but he didn't give any follow-up warnings, so she must have stopped. What the hell was going on? Who was the fuck was this weirdly calm, polite intruder?

"Who am I speaking to?" she asked.

"You're our guest," Nathan answered coolly. "Why don't you introduce yourself first?"

"Is Myles in there?" Her tone was totally relaxed, even friendly, and I was noticing her accent sounded more New York than California.

"Who wants to know?" I called back. Nathan kept his eyes on her, his suspicion mixed with confusion.

"I..." She let out a clipped breath, like she was on the verge of tears. "I didn't think I would ever hear your voice again." Was she crazy or something? Did she have the wrong person? Another second passed, and Nathan stiffened in shock, nearly dropping his gun. He wasn't the kind of guy who was easily shaken.

"Myles." He swallowed hard. "You should come over here." Cautiously, I went to join him, and he stepped back to let me look out at her. My mouth fell open.

She had pulled back her veil, and I recognized her piece-by-piece before I understood the whole picture. Her dark brown hair curled a little like Roger's did if it got too long. Her green eyes shone and were the same color and shape as Royce's, behind cat-eye horn-rimmed glasses. Her face was sort of round. Like mine. And her nose was straight and narrow, the same as mine and all of my brothers. Well, my full brothers.

"M..." I couldn't even get the word out. I couldn't believe what I was seeing. This had to be a trick somehow. Some kind of trap to get me to lower my guard. There was no way my dead mother was actually standing outside the door, smiling at me with tears spilling down her face.

"Hello, sweetheart," she said gently. "It's been a long time."

...

She sat on the couch near the door, ankles crossed, hands folded, watching me while I paced. A couple of her people had come to check that things were okay, and she'd sent them back out to wait in the cellar. I didn't know what to say to her. I didn't know how or why she was there. I had prepared myself for one insane, unnerving night, but this was turning into a totally different one.

"How are you alive?" It was all I could think to ask.

"That's a fair question. Your father did try to have me killed, and most often, when he makes attempts on people's lives, they don't survive." She pursed her lips a little, like she had a bitter taste in her mouth. "But, I guess, I got lucky. The person he hired for the job happened to be a friend of my family. My parents' family, that is."

"D'Angelo." I remembered interrogating him with Royce and Roger years ago, looking for proof that her death was Dad's fault.

"Giuseppe, yes. A close friend of my uncle before he ever became a Moretti. And although your father was a very powerful, very dangerous man, Giuseppe defied him to save my life." I was suddenly glad Royce had persuaded me not to kill him. "Deron demanded loyalty through fear, as I'm sure you know well. Sometimes, it really is better to be loved."

"So your death was faked," Nathan concluded for her, and she nodded. He hadn't been with us long enough to actually meet her, but he'd seen the pictures of her here and there in the house, which was how he recognized her. Gregorio recognized her too, but he hadn't joined the conversation, keeping to himself by the security monitors. "Where have you been all this time?"

She smiled wryly. "That would be telling. My family kept me safe, outside Deron's realm of influence; we're very practiced at discretion. The people I brought with me are all employed by my brother. I wanted to have protection in case the Council's soldiers were already here."

"Wait, you know about everything going on with the Council?" I asked, frowning harder.

"Yes. I wasn't able to be with you and your brothers, but I did everything in my power to keep tabs on you. I made sure I was always aware of what was going on in your lives," she explained. "I've been following this mess with the Council closely since I heard that they were trying to expel you. You have no idea how much I fought with myself about whether or not I should come out of hiding."

"No, I don't. I don't have any idea what you thought about anything, because I've thought you were dead for the past twenty-three years." Maybe I was being colder than necessary, but what did she expect after throwing me for such a loop like this? How was I *supposed* to respond? She sighed but didn't seem like she was getting offended or upset.

"I know this must be hard to deal with, sweetheart—"

"Stop that. Don't call me that." I stopped pacing and shut my eyes tightly, like if I could just stop seeing and hearing her, I wouldn't have to face this along with all the other shit crowding my head. "I don't know you, okay? I was a fucking toddler when you die—when you disappeared. I don't know. Maybe this would be different for Roger or Royce. Maybe they have more memories of growing up with you, but I barely remember any of it." I stopped myself before the rest came out. *You might've given birth to me, but you're not my mom.*

She didn't raise me. Rena did. She wasn't the one who helped me deal with all the shit Dad put me through. Rena was. Sure, some rational part of my brain knew it wasn't fair to blame her, that she didn't necessarily have any control over it, but that didn't stop me.

"I understand," she said quietly. I couldn't look at her

and hoped she wouldn't start crying again. Knowing I caused that would've fucked me up even more. "I know it isn't quite the same, but I promise that being away from you hurt me too. I watched the three of you grow up from such a distance, and no matter how much I wanted to, I couldn't involve myself in your lives again; if I had, your father would've found out and made *sure* I was dead, if for no other reason than that I interfered with his plans. As long as he was around, it wasn't safe for me to come out."

"He's been dead for three years," I pointed out. "More than that. Why didn't you show up then?"

"Because I assumed this would be your reaction." She looked up at me over the rim of her glasses, and I was forcibly reminded of all the times Royce had given me the exact same look. Dad had always said the two of them were a lot alike, but the visual similarities were still freaking me out. "I thought it had been too long. I thought if I showed up after twenty years asking to be part of your lives again, it would only complicate things for you. Maybe even hurt you more, which was the last thing I wanted."

"So why are you here now? Why did you decide this was the right time?" We hadn't been interrupted by the Council's people rushing in to cut my throat just yet, but I still wasn't counting out the possibility. This was a huge distraction, one I really didn't need at the moment.

Smoothing her skirt in her lap, she explained, "My family isn't part of the Council, but we have friends who are. Friends who found out your life was in danger and brought the news to us because they thought I deserved to know. I know your relationship with the other Council families hasn't been the best lately, but I think it was only today that they actually gave the order to have you killed."

A cold shiver ran down my spine as she pretty much

confirmed what I'd been suspecting for days. My shoulder throbbed, and I forced down a pained sneer. "Great. Well, thanks for the information. Is that all you wanted?"

"Myles, I'm here to help you." For the first time since she arrived, she actually looked irritated. That was way easier to deal with than sadness.

"How? What are you going to do? I mean, correct me if I'm wrong, but you don't look like you could take on a crew of trained killers by yourself. If you think the Council's going to spare me out of respect for your 'motherly love,' you've got another thing coming." Shaking my head, I muttered, "You shouldn't have bothered. I'm the one who got myself here. If I can't fix it from the driver's seat, how in the hell are you going to do something from the outside?"

She took a deep, slow breath, then let it out just as slowly and looked at Nathan and Greg. "Could we have a moment alone, please?" Oh great, I was in trouble now. The two of them looked at me for an answer, and I waved my still-working hand to let them know it was fine. They stepped out into the hall and pulled the door shut behind them while my mother (what the hell else was I supposed to call her?) got to her feet. She was so composed it made *me* want to scream, to shake her. How could she be so calm while our world—the family's world—was completely falling apart? "I know you have a hard time accepting help, Myles. You've always been that way. And before you say I don't know you, keep in mind I've been keeping track of your life all these years, even if I wasn't here."

"Whatever."

With a sympathetic smile, she went on, "And I know you don't like admitting to needing it in the first place. Deron raised you and your brothers to think that needing other people in any way is a weakness. Yes, value your family, but only insofar as they're useful to you. Your interests have to come first. Et cetera."

"What's your point?" Like she needed to tell me all that about him. Like I didn't know it just as well as she did.

"My point is that it's been a long time since this family has had leadership that wasn't entirely self-centered. Deron was the way he was because it's how he was taught. It's how his father was taught, how his grandfather was taught, and so on."

"So what, it's how I was taught too?" I asked defensively. "You're saying I'm just like him, right? Royce says that shit too. And y'know what's funny: no one ever says it unless they mean it as an insult. I didn't get any of his positive qualities, apparently. Just the terrible ones."

"Myles, your father had no positive qualities." Her voice had turned a lot colder than I expected.

"He knew how to run a business."

"He knew how to run a *dictatorship*," she snapped. "His 'business' was built on the lives of people who were too afraid to question him, and he knew very well he was taking advantage of them. It's the reason he was so quick to silence anyone who publicly disagreed with him: he wanted to keep the 'lesser' members of the family in line. Your father was not a leader. He wasn't a patriarch. He was a monster."

"But you think I'm different somehow?"

"I know you are. Being raised by your father without anyone opposing his twisted mandates and morals, it would've been so easy for you to turn out just like him. Selfish. Cold. Pitiless." She took a few steps closer, clasping her hands tightly like she was desperate for me to hear her. "But you didn't. Do you know how many members of this family have been killed within the past three years?"

I looked away. Goddamnit, my shoulder hurt. "Not off the top of my head."

"None. Not one. You've kept it from happening. You've certainly never intentionally sent one of your loyal soldiers to his death because it was convenient. If you have difficulties, if the business isn't as profitable, it's because of the way you treat people."

"I know, all right? I'm a prick sometimes, but—"

"I'm talking about your people," she said, shaking her head firmly. "You treat them with respect. You value their lives. Maybe that costs money sometimes. But you do it regardless. And if anyone in the family is willing to complain, it means they know you care about improving things for them. I don't know if you realize how remarkable that is in this business."

"What else am I gonna do? They're my family." I was starting to see the point she was making, but after so many years of being told that I was terrible at the job and would never get any better, it was tough to accept. "If not getting them killed left and right is impressive, then the bar is pretty damn low."

"And you're modest too," she said with a teasing smile. I had to force myself not to return it, not to let myself have fun with this moment. "This job isn't easy. Not for anyone. But you've risen to the challenge so spectacularly. Every piece of intelligence I received when you first started said that you wouldn't be able to handle it. They said you were too young and you would crack under the pressure. You didn't."

"I had help. Royce basically taught me everything I know. He's the one who was supposed to be doing this."

She looked sort of reserved, her eyes wandering somewhere to her right. "I'm sure Royce would have made an exceptional replacement for your father," she agreed evenly.

"But the family didn't need someone who operated just like Deron. If Royce had stayed and taken the job, I'm sure nothing would've changed. You're something else. You don't do things the way either of them would—and I think that's an attribute, not a flaw."

That statement hit me a lot harder than I wanted to admit. Royce had always been the golden child of the family, the one with all the confidence and authority, the one everybody else relied on, and of course, the absolute *ideal* Moretti heir. So for her to say I was a better fit for the job than him? That I was doing our family more good than he would've? I'd literally never been told I was better than Royce at anything.

Sofia's words, about the way I acted around her, came back to me. When I couldn't bring myself not to care about her feelings. When I couldn't be entirely self-centered. *I think you're more like yourself. And less like whatever it is you think you're supposed to be.*

Without meaning to, I let out a kind of nervous laugh and cleared my throat to hide it, pushing my fingers through my hair, not sure how to respond. Mom came closer and lifted my chin up with both hands to smile at me. "This family needs you, Myles. And I think if I go with you, the Council will be more receptive to what you have to say. I know all of them personally, and my family's influence might be helpful too."

"I don't...actually know anything about your family," I admitted. Technically they were my family too, but I'd never had any contact with them.

"They can be hard to pin down. I'll explain on the way. For now, you should call Marcell."

18

SOFIA

I didn't know what was going on anymore. I'd relayed to Papà what Gemma confessed, and after locking himself in his office for two hours, he came out and calmly told her to leave. That she wasn't welcome at the house anymore. That she wasn't his child anymore. The composed, calculating older sister I'd grown up with had disappeared, leaving a frightened, panicked mess in her place.

"Where am I supposed to go?" she asked.

"You're a smart girl, Gemma," he told her without a hint of remorse. "I'm certain you'll do fine for yourself."

She disappeared, and I didn't see her again. She was lucky not to have been put in jail—or killed because of what she did to Danny. And he was right: she probably would find a way to be stable again. Financially, at least. I wasn't sure she'd ever be stable mentally.

Only a few hours later, around midnight, all the Council dons convened at the villa again. They were already in town from the meeting earlier, so it didn't take long for them to arrive. Apparently, this conversation couldn't wait until morning, and knowing it was about clearing Myles's name, I was glad they were addressing it right away. Papà asked me to join them in the conference room, something I'd never done before, but I went along anyway, sitting nervously at his side. In Danny's seat. As I realized that, it finally hit me that I was his only remaining child, and I had to blink back tears to keep from breaking down in front of the Council.

When Myles finally arrived—they had a long drive, to be fair—Nathan and Gregorio were with him, but so was a woman I didn't know. Most of the men in the room stood when she entered, and she smiled at them graciously. Dominic Capelli was the first one to speak.

"I half-expected that this was a ploy just to get our attention," he said softly. "But it really is you."

"It's nice to see you too, Dominic. Luisa, Vincent." She nodded at each of them in turn before turning her eyes on Papà. "And you, Marcell." Something about her was strangely familiar. If Papà knew her, could we have met before? She must have noticed me staring, as she met my eyes and gave me an appraising look, then leaned in to mutter something in Myles's ear. He cleared his throat and turned away without answering her, then shot me a glance and a crooked smile.

"Gentlemen," the woman said, taking her seat so they all did the same. "And ladies. I want to thank you all for agreeing to meet with us. I'm sure you're all interested in how I can be here when my late husband tried to have me killed, but that's a story for another time." Suddenly, I realized who this woman was, though I could hardly believe it. "I didn't come here to speak for my son, but I will say on behalf of my brother Francisco that the Morettis—and their don—have the Romeos' full support."

The Romeos? I almost thought that family was a myth, they were so discreet. Even the people who were part of cosa nostra hardly knew anything about them. From what I'd heard, they were somehow involved in a little bit of everything, with connections and informants everywhere. People used to say the Romeos heard everything since you could never tell when you were speaking to one. Meaning Myles basically had a legend at his back.

"Well, personally," Vincent said, leaning back in his chair and nodding to Myles, "I'm awfully interested in how you're gonna explain this all as a big misunderstanding."

"Not a misunderstanding," Nathan said, shaking his head. "A deliberate smear campaign."

He and Myles then went into explaining all the ways Gemma had been turning people against them over the years, some blatant, some shockingly subtle. I listened with rapt attention; half of this, I'd never even heard. Danny never got the chance to explain it to me. When Myles got to the part about the attack on Gregorio, Dominic interrupted.

"And do you have any proof that this attack was orchestrated by the Lucianos?"

"Not all of them. Gemma told me herself that she was the one who ordered it," Myles explained. "One of the many, many unauthorized actions she took behind her dad's back."

"And where is Gemma herself? Could she not answer these accusations?"

"Gemma is no longer a member of my family," Papà announced clearly, shocking pretty much everyone in the room. "In addition to going against my wishes on many occasions, she confessed earlier this evening to arranging the death of my son."

The words sucked the air out of the room, leaving us sitting in tense silence. Papà glanced at me, and I realized he must expect me to support that claim. So I stood and recounted the whole day, how Gemma had been rattled that afternoon, then how she fell apart even more after Danny was brought home. Keeping my voice level despite the tears in my eyes, I explained being with him when he died. And then the shock of her confession.

"The men who attended the meeting this afternoon were interrogated," I finished, "and the two who confessed to being on her payroll were dismissed. We'll be investigating who else has been working for her and dealing with them accordingly."

"It seems to me that we were misinformed about you, Don Moretti," Luisa said, eyeing Myles thoughtfully.

"There is still the matter of your father's death," Dominic pointed out.

"That part, I won't argue with." Shifting his weight, Myles spoke as calmly and confidently as I'd ever seen him, and I only just noticed that his right arm was tucked inside his jacket, still against his side. "And I won't apologize for it either. You all knew my father, and while we can agree he ran an incredibly profitable business, it was just that to him: a business. Nothing else. My brothers and I got the closest to 'respect' that he gave anyone, and even that ended with him threatening our lives. He didn't know what the word 'family' actually means. I do. And it's more about protection than it is about control. I don't regret teaching him that lesson, and I don't regret the way I've been running things. So if that's your reason for not associating with me, fine. Once again: I'm not changing shit for you." He said that last bit with a playful smile and took his seat again to wait for an answer.

God, I wanted to kiss him! Not only because I loved his attitude, not only because watching him run his fingers through his hair—swept to the side again, not straight back like his dad's—gave me shivers. But the things he said! *I think 'admirable' is exactly the right word.*

"I say fair enough," Vincent said with a shrug, sweeping his gaze around the table. "Cards on the table, I never much liked Deron to begin with. Don't act like the man wasn't a mean old cuss. Stingy, too, and that ain't good for business however you look at it." He talked like these were things he'd been meaning to say for a while, and Myles's little speech had given him the opportunity to do so.

"You're suggesting we bring the Morettis back into the Council?" Luisa asked.

He seemed a little cowed by her severe stare but cleared his throat and agreed, "Yes, ma'am. We could take a vote on it at least?"

Luisa folded her hands on the table and tilted her head to one side. "I'm certainly in favor. Particularly since it means a connection to the Romeos." She inclined her head to Myles's mom, who returned the gesture with a smile.

"Well, when you phrase it that way," Dominic muttered. After another few seconds of reluctant consideration, he sighed and threw his hands up. "Fine. Aye."

All eyes turned to Papà, who smiled. "It's unanimous, then. You and your family are welcome to rejoin the Council, Don Moretti. And entirely of your own merit. That's not something your father ever accomplished, I can promise you."

"Okay, Marcell, don't butter me up too much," Myles said with a roll of his eyes, but he was still grinning ear to ear. When I managed to catch his eye, his smile softened a little, and all I could think about was getting him alone.

"Now that that's all resolved," Dominic said, pushing away from the table. "Can we all get back to bed?" It *was* around two in the morning by then. So the meeting disbanded, sending everyone to their respective rooms and hotels, and I hurried to catch up to Myles after wishing Papà goodnight.

"Ahem. Excuse me. Don Moretti?" I called while he and his family were talking at the door. When I reached him, I had to force myself not to pounce on him immediately and instead settled for holding onto his arm. "Could I have a word?"

"Uh, yeah, I was hoping for that actually." As I took a step back toward the staircase, Myles hesitated and looked to his companions. Nathan rolled his eyes.

"We'll pick you up tomorrow, sir."

"And I do hope you and I will get a chance to talk," his mom told me pleasantly as they were leaving. Once the door shut behind them, I grabbed Myles's hand—but he winced and pulled away.

"What's wrong?"

"Sorry. My arm is fucked up from earlier," he said, gesturing to his right side. "It should get better, but—"

"Noted." Grabbing his left hand instead, I dragged him up the stairs, and he laughed at my impatience.

Once we were in my bedroom, I closed the door behind him, and he started, "So, I—mm!" I cut him off with my lips against his, gripping his shirt to pull him down to meet me. After a split-second of hesitation, he wrapped his arm around me and kissed me back, delving into my mouth as longingly as ever. Pressing my back against the door, I yanked him closer and worked at the buttons on his shirt. "Uh, Sofia. Shouldn't we talk first?"

"I can't yet," I told him plainly. I was too overwhelmed with relief after we'd finally resolved the feud between our families. He was safe. Our families were at peace, doing better than ever. We were together. And I needed to spend all this nervous, excited energy before I could focus on a conversation. "After. Okay?"

I paused to give him what I hoped was a meaningful look. Most of the time, I didn't think of sex as a "need," but at this moment? I needed him. He must have seen it all over my face, since he smiled and leaned down to kiss me again, already pushing his hand underneath my shirt, up my stomach, to tease along the edge of my bra. It was a little strange to not have both of his hands exploring as much of my skin as possible, but I figured it was more frustrating for him.

"Oh." I tilted my head back while he placed slow, open-mouthed kisses over my neck, his tongue gliding across my skin and making me shiver with desire. "I guess you can't... hold me up against the door at the moment."

"Ugh, don't remind me," he groaned, stealing a contemptuous glance at his right shoulder.

"Don't think that means you're off the hook." I made sure the door was locked before dragging him over to my bed to push him down on his back. After slipping my shoes off, I crawled up to straddle his hips, resting mine against him and grinding down roughly.

"Fuck," he muttered, digging his fingers into my thigh to keep me moving. Without stopping in my rhythm, I leaned down to kiss him again and pressed my chest into his. His breath faltered a little as he tangled his hand into my hair to hold me closer and kiss me deeper. I could already feel him getting harder under me, which sent heat rushing between my legs too. When his hips bucked up against mine for more, I let slip a little giggle.

"Did you miss me, baby?" I asked as I reached down to unfasten his pants.

"The whole time." His dark eyes wandered down to watch my hands work. I didn't bother actually taking his pants off; I just pulled them down enough so I could get to his cock. My fingertips teased over the head, and he let out a short huff. "Come on, kitten..."

"So impatient." Still, I liked that needy, desperate look on his face. I crawled off the bed to edge up my skirt and slip my panties off, then bent over him to run my tongue up and down his cock, making sure it was dripping wet. And since that felt so nice, I went ahead and took him in my mouth, dropping my head until my lips were flush with the base of him. Another wave of heat rushed through me, and I moaned deeply around him. He let out a groan, and I felt him grab a handful of my hair. Turning my eyes up toward him, I expected him to hold me still and fuck my mouth.

But instead, he lifted me back up, pulling my mouth away from him. Despite smirking deviously as saliva dripped from my lips and I quickly wiped it away, he told me, "That's not what I want, princess. Come here and do it right." Since it was phrased as an order, I didn't bother arguing with him, seating myself over his hips again to rub my soaked pussy over his cock. Again, he grabbed at my leg and growled, "Hurry up."

"Maybe you should say please," I purred sweetly, leaning forward and lifting my hips a little to lead him to my entrance, then pressing teasingly against him without letting him inside.

His eyes narrowed, and he instead said, "*Now.*" It wasn't like I could hold it against him when the hard tone of his voice was getting me so hot. So I stopped teasing and pushed my hips back to let him slide halfway in, stealing the breath from both of us. I rocked my hips a little, giving him just enough friction to make him impatient. When he looked up and met my eyes, I gave him a mischievous smirk so he knew I was doing it on purpose. Rather than giving me another command, he thrust his hips up to meet mine, burying himself inside me and forcing a deep moan from my lips. I quickly pressed them together to keep myself quiet, but that was hard to do with Myles already building up a rhythm of fucking me, using a surprisingly tight grip on my hip to keep me from going too far.

"God. Myles!" My hands braced against the bed over his shoulders, and I arched my back to let him go as deep as possible. My eyes were quickly getting hazy, my breath coming in high-pitched gasps and sighs. Maybe it was just because I'd missed him so much, but everything felt especially good.

"Damn, you're beautiful," he muttered, surprising me. When I chanced a look down at him, he was watching me so closely I had to look away, biting my lip, feeling my cheeks start to flush.

"Mm, Myles. You really did...miss me, didn't you?"

"I told you." The way he fucked me—hard and fast and purposeful—could've said the same thing. When he started getting close, I could see it on his face and hear it in his voice. His pace picked up even more, forcing me to cover my mouth with one hand so I didn't scream, then he let out a deep, distinctive moan, and my insides flooded with warmth. Since he was distracted, I sat my hips back down against him and went back to grinding, leaning forward on his chest so my clit rubbed against him with every move. He let out another shocked, appreciative moan and slid his hand down my thigh. "Oh, *fuck* yeah... Mm, work those hips for me, kitten. I wanna see you cum."

I nodded fervently and kept moving, losing my breath a little more every second, until I shuddered and came around him with a low moan. "God...so good...!" Myles sighed like he appreciated it too, and he led me close for another kiss while I was coming down. But I had to break away from him to catch my breath, and I carefully moved to let him slide out, trying my hardest not to think about getting cum stains on my bed. Being close to him was a lot more important. This time, he didn't seem surprised when I cuddled up against him, and he easily wrapped his arm around me.

Once we'd both calmed down some, I forced myself to address the less fun part of this little tryst. "So. We probably should talk."

"Yeah." But he didn't let me go. "I didn't really want to think you were working with Gemma at any point. There was just...a lot that didn't make sense otherwise. And she's a good fucking liar."

"I know. Besides, you were already dealing with a lot at the time. Everything she was putting you through, and that...weirdness that happened between us. That was, at least, partially my fault."

"Maybe. Do we have to actually do 'I'm sorry's', or can we just agree we both made some mistakes and we're not holding it against each other?"

Sitting up a little, I raised an eyebrow at him. "That was almost shockingly mature, Mister Moretti."

"Yeah, that's me." He dragged me back down against his side, but I couldn't say it bothered me. "I could be wrong, but it almost seemed like your dad and I were getting along okay in there."

"Mm-hm. I wonder if that means he's any less opposed to us being together." There was a long moment of silence, longer than it should've been, while I tried to work up the nerve to say what I needed to. There was still the chance it would be too much, that it would scare him off, but I got the feeling that it wouldn't be the case. Besides, after the week I'd had, all the thinking about it I'd done, I was sure that keeping it quiet much longer would drive me insane. Resting my head against his shoulder, running my fingertips across his chest, I said softly, "I do love you, you know."

Myles's hand gripped my shoulder. "Yeah," he said after a few seconds. "I think I do. Know that. Not sure I deserve it, all things considered, but I guess I can't talk you out of it."

"Nope." Surely he knew I wanted a better answer than that. Did he not feel the same way? Did he just not want to say it? Was he really going to make me ask? "What about you?"

"Oh, I figured you knew already," he said with a slight laugh. "I've been into you for...what, thirteen years now?"

"I know you're 'into' me." Why was he making this so difficult? "Anything *else*?"

"I mean I feel like it's obvious that I'm attracted to you."

"Myles."

"Will you relax?" he laughed. "I'm just fucking with you." Considering that was what he'd said that last time we'd had this conversation, I didn't really see the humor. With a frustrated huff, I got up and started to leave the bed, to get dressed—but Myles grabbed my hand and pulled me back into his lap. "I love you. Okay? I'll say it again if you need me to. I'll say it as many times as you want. But you really should know it already."

"Once is enough," I said, all irritation disappearing from my attitude as I stole another quick kiss. "For now."

...

The next day, as promised, Nathan, Gregorio, and Myles's mom (Latasha, he'd said) showed up to take him back to San Diego. Reluctant to watch him leave after we'd been separated so long and finally gotten back together, finally taken another step forward in our relationship, I held tight to his hand as we stood outside the door.

"I can always come back, you know," he reminded me when I yanked him back so he couldn't leave. "It's not that far. Or you could just come with us right now. Don't pack or anything, just run off with me. I'll buy you a whole new wardrobe. I'll buy you whatever you want." Even though it was presented as a joke, there was a note of pleading in his voice that said he really meant it.

"I want to," I told him honestly. "But I already told you. I can't." Antoni had yet to come out of his room for even a minute after Nadine gave him the news about Danny. It was going to be difficult enough for him trying to adjust to life without his father; if me being there might help, how could I run off and be selfish instead?

"I know. What about tomorrow? I know my mom is—" He cut himself off with a brief laugh. "It's so fucking weird saying 'my mom is' anything. My point is, I know she wants to meet you. I bet you'll like her. She's smart. And a little prissy. You'll get along fine."

"That sounds nice." God, it really did. It was probably going to be a difficult thing, getting used to her being back in his life, but I hoped it went well for him. And I wanted so badly to be a part of this new period of his life. We would make it work. Whatever we had to do, we would make it work.

"Sooo, are you coming or what?" Gregorio called from the car. "Uh, with us, I mean." Myles flipped him off over his shoulder.

"I really should go."

"*Fine.*" I stepped in close to him and stood up on my toes for one more deep, perfect kiss.

"I love you," he muttered when he let me go, refusing to meet my eyes as he said it.

Despite the urge to tease him, I kissed his cheek and answered, "I love you too. And I'll see you tomorrow."

"You're damn right you will."

19

MYLES

We wound up taking Whits home earlier than intended. And we brought a certain surprise guest along with us. Maybe I should've warned Roger and Royce that Mom was going to be with me, but I didn't know any better way to say it than to just show up with her. In the week before we headed to London, she stayed in the house, and it was...I'll admit, it was weird. Rena seemed terrified of her, like she was an actual ghost, but Mom was apparently good at settling pretty much anyone's nerves; she quickly made it clear that she didn't hold anything against Rena and had no plans to chase her or her boys out of the house.

Whitney was beside herself when they met, and she had what seemed to be a never-ending supply of questions, which Mom answered with a lot more patience than I could've managed. Maybe she had missed having kids in her life. In return for her own answers, she started asking Whitney questions about Royce, Roger, and me. They would trade back and forth for hours, enough that by the time we were headed to London, I felt like Whitney knew her better than I did.

About ten hours into our flight, Mom started getting antsy, probably realizing just how soon she was going to see her other kids again. It was probably easier with me since I was alone, but having us all there at once? That was bound to be a lot for her. "You okay?" I asked, watching her bite her lip and pick at one of her cuffs.

"I am...fantastic," she said with a smile. "Just nervous. I don't know how Royce or Roger will react to seeing me. What if it's traumatic for them? What if it dredges up some horrible memories about your father?"

"I don't think that'll happen. It sounds like you're assuming they've just blocked you out of their heads for the past twenty-three years. As far as I know, they think about you all the time."

She took a deep breath, holding her eyes closed for a few seconds, probably to keep from tearing up. "Is it too cliché to say I thought of you three every day? Every. Single. Day. I spent so long waiting, and..."

"Hey, relax," I said, leaning back in my seat to lead by example. "You're here now. They're going to be insanely glad you're here. I'm glad you're here. And not just because you saved my ass." She rolled her eyes.

"You did that yourself, sweetheart."

"I dunno, that Romeo endorsement was pretty persuasive." I still barely knew anything about the Romeos, but Mom had said she would introduce us to some of them at some point, and maybe we could work together more closely. She liked the idea of the Morettis being able to claim an alliance with the Romeos; it was a surprisingly big statement when talking to people who knew what was what about the mafia, or *cosa nostra* as Sofia and her family insisted on calling it.

At the moment, she was sitting with Whitney across the

cabin, sharing a pair of earbuds and rocking along with the beat of whatever they were listening to. Probably Tar & Sugar. Sofia had decided that when it wasn't loud enough to burst her eardrums, the music itself actually wasn't so bad. I'd persuaded her to come along for this trip, just a few days away from home, partially because I wanted her there, partially because she obviously needed a break from being a half-parent to a grieving seven-year-old. After spending so much of her life being the one others took care of, it must've been difficult figuring out how to take care of someone else.

When we landed, Whitney didn't bother waiting for any of us before rushing out of the gate to go find her parents. But that made finding them easier on us since we could just look for the streak of black and hot pink dashing through the crowds. When we caught up, she was already wrapped in an embrace between her dad, her mom, and Deanna, and she actually looked happy there. Mom hesitated, stopping behind a pillar by the escalators before anyone could see her.

"Ahem." I waved to my brothers and sisters-in-law, hoping they weren't pissed at me for letting anything dangerous happen in Whitney's vicinity. They were about to have a whole new reason to be pissed at me, anyway. Roger had cut his hair shorter than usual, and Jill's was dyed kind of blonde. Royce looked the same as ever—not that I expected him to change—including the appraising, slightly judgmental way he looked at me. "Uh, hey. Long time no see."

"No kidding," Roger agreed, eyeing Sofia where she stood at my side, holding onto my hand with both of hers. With a nod at her, he said, "You're a surprise."

"Am I? I feel like we've been headed in this direction for years," she said, shooting me a little smirk.

"Good," Jill said plainly. "I hope you make him a little less reckless."

"I am standing right here."

"Um, is your arm all right?" Deanna asked, finally noticing that my right arm hadn't moved.

"Y'know what? There's actually a lot of shit you guys need to get caught up on. First things first, though." I stepped back until I was in Mom's line of sight, and she looked at me with wide, nervous eyes. Again, I told her, "Relax." And I nodded toward the others. After a deep breath in and out, she followed me back to meet them—and the looks on Royce and Roger's faces were *priceless*. Roger's mouth fell open, and I thought for a second he might collapse. Royce went stone-still, not even breathing. Both of them stared, wide-eyed.

"Hello, boys." Mom's voice shook a little, and so did her smile. "I suppose I have some explaining to do. But I was hoping that..." She paused as Royce strode over to her and immediately pulled her into a tight hug. After a split-second of frozen shock, she wrapped her arms around him too, and Roger came over to hug her as well.

"And you were worried," I said with a smirk.

...

We all gathered up at Royce's apartment, all ten of us—including Jonathan and Whitney—so Mom, Sofia, and I could explain everything that had been going on at home. It took hours, but we finally managed to get through the whole thing, from Mom's faked death to Gregorio's attack to the big Council meeting and their decision to reinstate us.

"Holy shit," Roger said once we'd finished the story, and pretty much everyone nodded in agreement.

"The way I see it," Mom continued, "the family is much better off now. Better off than we have been in years."

"We?" Royce repeated. "You mean you're staying?" She almost looked like he had insulted her.

"Of course, I am. You think after all this time away, I would come back just to say hello and then disappear again?" Folding her hands in her lap and sitting up fully straight (she really was a little prissy), she said firmly, "Absolutely not. In fact, I'm going to be taking a much more active role in operations this time around."

"We're gonna give the whole underboss thing a try," I explained. "I've never had one, but I doubt anyone else in our family is as qualified for the position as her."

Jill hesitantly started, "I don't mean to sound rude or anything, but...exactly how are you qualified?"

If the question bothered her, Mom didn't show it. "Keep in mind, I grew up in the same sort of environment as these four did," she said, gesturing to me, my brothers, and Sofia. "And I've been studying the entire business for the past twenty-three years or so. I would say I'm more than qualified."

"Wait, so you're actually handing over some power to someone who isn't you?" Roger asked, looking me over warily. "Who are you and what have you done with my little brother?"

"Ha, ha." I rolled my eyes.

"I think the two of you don't know your younger brother as well as you might assume," Mom said pleasantly. I had to admit it was nice having someone else to back me up when my brothers made cracks like that. "He's done a lot of growing over the past few years. Maybe you should spend some more time together and reacquaint yourselves."

"That's a little hard to do when we're halfway across the world," Royce said.

"Well. Maybe you shouldn't be so far away, then," she continued innocently. The room was silent for a few seconds.

"You want us to move back to San Diego?" Deanna asked, and Mom nodded.

"Deron isn't there anymore to hurt you. And the business is very different these days than it was under his rule."

"Hold on." Margot was finally speaking up, like I knew she would when this idea was presented. "You can't be serious. I may not be part of your Moretti dynasty, but I'm most certainly part of *this* family"—she gestured to Royce, Deanna, and Whitney—"and you're trying to take them from me again?"

"That's not what I want at all," Mom said, shaking her head.

"But you don't mind if it happens. If that's what it takes for you to have all your little goslings back in the nest." Margot crossed her arms tightly, setting her jaw, stubborn as ever. "For so long, I wished I could've met you, and now that you're here, now that we've *just* gotten comfortable, you're disrupting us again."

"Maggie, calm down," Royce muttered, reaching for her shoulder, but she pulled away.

"Margot, the last thing I want is to take your family from you," Mom said in earnest. "Believe me, I know what that feels like, and I would never wish it on anyone." She hesitated for a second before going on, "Could we talk for a minute? Just the two of us?" That was her secret weapon, apparently: the one-on-one talk. She was insanely good at reading people and telling them what they wanted to hear. Maybe I did get some things from her after all.

Despite looking suspicious, Margot sighed, "Fine." The two of them went into Whitney's room to talk, leaving the rest of us alone. Jill immediately started in on Sofia, trying to learn everything there was to know about her, and she was ecstatic to have other women to talk to. Since some other conversations were forming, I figured now was as good a time as any to talk to Royce.

"Hey," I said with a nod. "Do you have a minute?"

"Sure." He looked suspicious too, but he led me into the dining room, away from everyone else, and leaned against the edge of the table to look at me. "What's up?"

"I just—I wanted to apologize for the way I acted when you were worried about Whits," I said, hands in my pockets. "I mean, obviously being there is more dangerous than being here. So it makes sense you would worry. And I acted like an ass instead of just telling you I was going to keep her safe. And *then*, this whole fucking war thing happened with Gemma, and if she'd been in the house with me, she *could* have gotten hurt, so I pretty much put my foot in my mouth there..."

"Well." He seemed surprised that I was saying all this. "She *is* okay, right? Not missing any parts I don't know about or anything?" I thought about the deal at the concert, the way she still flinched just a little whenever a man tried to touch her. She'd been getting better, and we'd been talking about it pretty much every day for the past week. She still reacted pretty badly to being grabbed or pushed, but most of the time, she was okay. So that wasn't worth mentioning, right?

"No. All in one piece."

"Then it's fine. Once you realized she might be in danger, you sent her away. And you got her back to me. So we're okay." He offered his hand to shake mine, then suppressed a snort of laughter at the glare I gave him. "Oh, right. That's not happening."

"You're lucky I only have one arm right now, or I'd kick your ass," I muttered, which only made him laugh again.

"I think Mom might be right," he said after a few seconds. "Maybe we should be around more. Assuming Margot's not going to tie us to the couch. Deanna would like to be near her grandpa again, and I'm sure Jill would be happy to see her mom and sister more."

"I mean, I'd be happy to have you—all of you—around," I admitted, going for casual but not sure if it was coming across.

"Yeah. I guess I'll talk to them about it then."

The way I understood it, Margot did take some convincing. Even after Mom talked to her, she and Royce and Deanna spent another few days talking it over after we'd left. But with Whitney so strongly for it and Royce being the great debater he is, they eventually managed to convince her. Within two months, the house was chock full of Morettis again, so full that we started planning some expansions to the place. Including a mini-dojo along with the gym, where Whitney assured me she would drop me as soon as my arm healed.

It took a couple of surgeries and more than a few different painkillers, but I eventually got back most of the use of my arm. It still hurt like a bitch sometimes and got numb at others, but it was functional at least. Meaning I could hold Sofia up against the wall any time she wanted with only minimal complaining.

So fuck what I said about love before, because having a house full of it (and then some) was so much better than the past three years of quiet rooms and brief, awkward interactions. Holidays that used to be somber became huge celebrations. Successes for the business were something everyone shared in enjoying, and even the low points were easier to deal with. And color me fucking shocked that my brothers were actually relaxed and happy working under me. Even Royce, who had wanted nothing more than to get out of the house and away from the family for *years*, was a hell of a lot more laid back than I'd ever seen him before.

For the first time in who knows how long, maybe ever, we felt like an actual family.

The only thing I could find that wasn't perfect was the fact that Sofia still lived at her dad's place. Sure, I saw her four or five times a week, but it wasn't the same as what Roger and Jill had, what Royce and Deanna had. A part of my family was missing. And eventually, I had to fix that.

A little after my 28th birthday was my six-month "anniversary" with Sofia. It shouldn't have been a big deal, but she took any excuse to get dressed up and go out to dinner. I made a point of showing up a little early to chat with Marcell. Someone must have told Sofia I was there because she eventually came into his office all dolled up with a frustrated pout on her face.

"I'm sorry, was this a business call for you?" she asked, her red lips all pursed. I'd be lucky to get her out the door before the urge to kiss her overpowered me.

"Sorry, we can go." I paused to shake Marcell's hand, and he smiled.

"Thank you for coming by. Let me know how it turns out. Have fun, Sofina."

"What were you two talking about?" Sofia asked as we got outside, and I had to take a moment to kiss her hard before I could answer.

"Business," I said simply, leading her to the car. Damn, she looked good in red. Throughout the drive and the whole time we were at dinner, I was only 75% there. I paid attention to her, obviously (as if I had a choice), but in the back of my mind, there was always this anxiety about the end of the night.

"But I'm really proud of his progress," she was saying, sitting in the booth beside me, talking about Antoni like she did pretty often. "He studies so hard, and he's such a quick learner! I really would like him and Whitney to meet sometime. She's so outgoing, she might be able to—What?"

"Huh?" I blinked out of a kind of daze, and she made a face at me.

"You keep staring at me like that. *Cosa stai pensando?*"

What are you thinking? She'd been teaching me bits of Italian over time, mostly just because she liked hearing me saying it. She also said it reminded her of her family, which was doubly encouraging.

"Nothing. I mean. Just about you." Smooth.

"You've been acting weird all night," she said, raising an eyebrow at me. "I mean, it's cute seeing you trip over yourself now and then, but is something wrong? It's this dress, isn't it? I knew it would be too much for you." She smirked and brushed her hair back over her shoulder so I had a better view of the low-cut neckline. As if this wasn't hard enough already.

"No, it's not that. Don't get me wrong, the dress is amazing; I can't wait to get you out of it. But there is something I wanted to talk to you about." I tried to make it sound casual, like a business proposition. "I feel like our families have been working really well together lately. Professionally."

"Of course," she said with a mock-serious look on her face.

"So, since that's working so well and since the Morettis and the Lucianos are probably the biggest Council families,

I was thinking it might be...advantageous," I said, well aware that this was nowhere near casual anymore, "to formally connect the two. Legally, you know. So, you're available. And I'm the oldest Moretti son who isn't already spoken for. Maybe—"

"This sounds an awful lot like a proposal, Myles." Sofia sounded a little breathless, and she was watching me even more intently now. "Is that what I'm hearing?"

"I mean, sheesh, if you *want* to make it into a big, official thing." I reached into the pocket inside my suit jacket and took out the ring box I'd been discreetly checking on all night. Sofia's eyes went wide, and when I opened it and set it in front of her, both her hands flew up to cover her mouth. Mafia princess or not, even she probably hadn't seen many rocks that big. When she didn't answer me right away, I started worrying that casual wasn't the way to go about this. "I can do the whole thing if you really need me to. Get on one knee. Say the actual words. I already went to the trouble of getting your dad's blessing. Maybe I should've done something more—"

"Shut the hell up and put that ring on my hand," she demanded, thrusting her left hand at me. I did what she said with a grin, and her next command was, "Now *kiss me* until I tell you to stop."

I took that order to heart, pushing my fingers into her thick hair to lead her closer for a firm kiss. And she wasn't shy about kissing me back. The way she leaned into me and slid her hands over my shoulders, I found myself hoping that she wouldn't tell me to stop. That she'd never tell me to stop. Because I could really get used to doing this for the rest of my life.

Printed in Dunstable, United Kingdom